DARK COMPANY

NATALE GHENT

DOUBLEDAY CANADA

Doubleday Canada and colophon are registered trademarks of Random House of Canada Limited

Library and Archives Canada Cataloguing in Publication is available upon request

ISBN: 978-0-385-66733-3
eBook ISBN: 978-0-307-36819-5

Cover image: (sky) Jozsef Bagota / Shutterstock; (businessmen) LANTERIA / Shutterstock; (blood) siam sompunya/ Shutterstock; (girl) commodore / Shutterstock; (skull) © Hery Siswanto /Dreamstime.com
Cover design: Kelly Hill
Printed and bound in the USA

Published in Canada by Doubleday Canada,
a division of Random House of Canada Limited,
a Penguin Random House Company
www.randomhouse.ca

10 9 8 7 6 5 4 3 2 1

For Darcy

"The connection must be severed completely," Francis said. He had his thumbs hooked through the belt loops of his faded blue jeans, acting casual.

Skylark stared at the demonic entity across the dingy hotel room. Francis called him the Speaker, but she could think of a few other choice names for him given the way he was dressed. He was lethally out of place with his flawless grey suit and carefully sculpted white hair. His face was emotionless and smooth as polished marble. But it was his eyes that disturbed her the most. They were the colour of ice chips and twice as cold. Just looking at him made her bad arm start to ache. She leaned toward Francis, whispering, "Are you sure he can't see us?"

Francis shook his head. "We're on a different frequency. He can't see us until we engage him. Then there's no turning back."

"My scar hurts," Skylark said. She rubbed her right arm, easing the pain in the scar that ran in a lightning bolt from her shoulder to her index finger. She could feel the binding strands of the healing cord beneath her sleeve and prayed it would keep her arm strong until she had a chance to shoot.

"Just stay focused and be ready when I give you the signal," Francis said. "It's gonna happen soon, I can feel it." He began worrying the fringe of beard along his lower lip.

This was not a good sign. Skylark looked at the other man in the room, the one sitting on the edge of the bed sweating in his undershirt. He was human. Not so dangerous, she thought—at least, not to anyone but himself, it seemed. In one hand, he held a revolver. In the other, a half-drunk bottle of whiskey. What would the Speaker want with this train-wrecked guy? More important, what was she doing engaging a demonic entity of the Speaker's calibre? She was just a recruit. She barely had any training other than a bit of target practice. But Francis had insisted, going on about the element of surprise, despite the directive from head office. He was supposed to bring Kenji, not her. Kenji had been on the case since the beginning. They were going to catch hell back at headquarters when Timon found out about their cowboy antics, that was for sure. If she had any brains, she would jump out now, before things got critical.

"Do you really think this is a good idea?" she asked.

Francis ignored her, pushing his white Stetson High Point down firmly on his head. Skylark reached up to stroke Sebastian, the mouse sitting on her shoulder. He'd been tickling the hairs on the back of her neck the whole time with his little paws, trying to calm her. He didn't agree with this half-baked escapade either, though there was little he could do to prevent it. The role of animal totems was to guide but not interfere. Any recruit knew that. "Don't look him in the eyes," Francis said. "And whatever you do, don't listen to his voice."

She nodded, tugging the cuffs of her shirt over her knuckles.

The Speaker moved toward the bed and there was the faintest sound of tinkling glass. Skylark shot Francis a look.

"I hear it too," he said. "Those are the soul vials of the ones he's gathered."

She opened her mouth to speak but he waved her quiet. The mouse reared up and grabbed two fistfuls of her black hair, preparing for whatever was coming.

The Speaker raised a small metal funnel to his lips. He sighed into the mouth of it, and to Skylark's horror, a dark tendril wriggled from the end. It squirmed, reaching across the bed and working its way into the man's ear. The man's shoulders slumped and his head tilted to one side as the tendril wormed deeper. His eyes fluttered and his hand relaxed, dropping the bottle of whiskey to the floor.

The Speaker's voice was an opiate lulling the man into submission. Skylark cleared her mind, protecting herself from his words.

"There's nothing left to live for," the demon said. *"Everyone will be happier when you're gone."*

The man sobbed and cocked the gun. He pressed the tip of the barrel to his temple, the sweat trickling in rivulets down his face. Skylark glanced at Francis. He held up his finger.

"Wait for it . . ."

"It's so easy," the Speaker crooned.

The man exhaled, slowly squeezing the trigger.

"Now!" Francis said.

In a blinding flash, Skylark transformed, her gold breastplate gleaming, her raven hair now white and flowing. She winced as she drew her bow and arrow, the scar on her arm flaring with pain. But she held steady.

Beside her, Francis had also changed. His cowboy boots, hat and jeans had transformed into white sandals and a long robe that shimmered like river-washed opals. His hair and beard had turned from grey to silver, but his eyes remained the deepest shade of blue. A beam of light blasted from his palms and he trained it full strength on the gun. The muscles in Skylark's hands jumped, preparing to fire, but she skipped a beat when the holographic face of a girl appeared in front of her. It was

Caddy—that pretty loner with the hazel eyes who'd stolen her boyfriend's heart. What was *she* doing here?

"Shoot!" Francis shouted.

Skylark gritted her teeth and fired. A streak of light seared from her bow and her soul leapt because she knew the shot was good. There was an electric snap and a crescendo of breaking glass as the arrow sliced the tendril in half, its severed tail a live wire whipping back into the funnel. The Speaker didn't falter. He snatched the arrow from the air and hurled it in her direction. This she had not anticipated. The arrow had blackened at his touch and it flew with unimaginable speed, piercing the small gap between her breastplate and shoulder armour.

"Francis!" she cried, and collapsed, her bow clattering to the floor. From the corner of her eye she could see the mouse lying next to her, unmoving, his grey fur blue with frost. "Sebbie . . ."

There was a gunshot and moments later Francis was kneeling beside her, his concerned face fading in and out of focus. She wanted to tell him something, but the shivering had started and she couldn't make her mouth move properly. In fact, she couldn't move at all. Her whole body was cold as ice.

Francis gathered her in his arms. "Hold on, sweetheart."

"The g-girl . . ." Skylark tried to tell him through the cold. "I—I saw the girl . . ."

—«««« 1 »»»»—

CADENCE

Caddy lay on the bed, her long auburn hair a tangled halo around her stricken face. It was coming, the bad feeling. She could tell by the warning smell of burnt toast in her nostrils and the way her hands were shaking. She didn't want to go—not now, not again. Clenching her fists, she dug her nails into her palms, nearly breaking the skin. But the pain couldn't stop the swell from taking her under. It rose in her stomach, rushed through her chest and spilled into her head.

"No . . ."

The wave hit, dragging her to the place she called the Emptiness. She'd called it that since she was a child. And it was always the same. Bitter cold. Wind clawing at her hair. Her bare feet half buried in the ash that flew through the frozen air and collected in long, lifeless drifts across an endless expanse of grey. It wasn't the icy wind or ash that she feared most. It was the faces of the dispossessed pushing through the ether. An eye. A nose. An open mouth. And then the moaning would begin.

Caddy shivered uncontrollably, her lips turning blue, her eyelashes gathering frost from the moisture in the plumes of breath that curled from her mouth. She covered her ears and hummed her shining song, the one her mother used to sing to her when the bad feeling would come. *"There is a light that shines in the night ... there is a light ..."* The voices were only whispers then. Now they were angry and loud, demanding that she listen.

"Please, stop," she begged.

The mouths twisted and gaped. Gnarled fingers punctured the grey. They reached for her, grasping her arms and legs and clothes until she doubled in half and screamed.

The sound zippered shut and Caddy fell back into the now. She lay on the bed, rocking back and forth, hazel eyes open, glassy, waiting for the shivering to stop. When she was sure it was over, Caddy rose, slowly, steadying herself on one elbow before sitting up on the edge of the bed. Hands stiff with cold, she took the brush from her night table and moved it in deliberate strokes through her hair. Such a simple act. It grounded her. Kept her from disappearing altogether. At seventeen, she was more frightened than ever by the Emptiness.

"It's a gift," her mother used to tell her when she was small. "One day you will understand its purpose."

To Caddy, the visions were a curse, bleeding seamlessly through the ages along her father's ancestral lines, haunting generation after generation, to rest here, in the nightmares of a frightened and reluctant girl. This was her legacy. And no matter how her mother tried to convince her otherwise, Caddy knew the visions were the furthest thing from a gift. She was marked, not chosen. Born to suffer in confusion and fear, like her father and the dozens of equally cursed relatives that came before him. Whatever purpose the visions served, she wasn't ready to know, nor did she think she'd ever be. She'd grown up hearing her father crying out in the night, and her mother's voice, soothing him through the agony of his helplessness. There were too many souls in the Emptiness, too much pain. He couldn't help any of them—no one could. Why did her mother and father expect anything different from her?

The visions made her an outcast, a freak. She kept to herself, didn't make friends because she never knew where or when the bad feeling would come on or how much it would take from her when it happened. The threat of it followed her relentlessly, a malevolent spectre.

And after her mother died, it got harder and harder to take. The car accident had killed her instantly. It had robbed Caddy of her father, too, but slowly, one drink at a time. He'd always taught her to be self-reliant and strong. In the end, he was the one who gave up. Now she had to deal with things on her own. There was no one to put her back together once the bad feeling came on.

Caddy stopped brushing her hair and listened to the silence. Her father hadn't come home last night. Or somehow she'd missed the familiar sound of him stumbling to his room and his usual loud argument with the dark. Cleaning the hair from her brush, she tucked the little nest of auburn strands into the small linen bag she kept in her night table drawer. She would burn the hair outside, later, along with her nail clippings, the way her mother had shown her. It was meant to protect her from "bad intentions." This had stuck with her as a child because she wasn't really sure what "bad intentions" meant, or who was behind them. Her mother never explained that part. Whether the hair-burning ritual worked or not, Caddy had no way of knowing. She instinctively feared things would be worse without her mother's superstitious practices, so she performed them without question.

Caddy changed out of her nightgown into a pair of old jeans and a blue T-shirt. She checked the clasp on her necklace. It was a simple gold chain with a small oblong stone of polished green fluorite her father had given her for her fifth birthday. A talisman to ward off negative energy. She called it her "safe stone." She never left home without it.

Grabbing her phone off the dresser, Caddy quickly pinched her cheeks to bring the colour up. She didn't need a mirror to know how thin and pale she looked, especially lately. The bad feeling was coming so often these days it left her drained. "I'm still here," she said to no one.

Her father's door was half open. His bed was unmade and empty. It was always unmade, unless she made it. But empty? Never. Not this time of day. She checked her phone. He hadn't called. She surveyed the mess in his room for clues, her eyes skipping over the endless bits of nature he'd collected over the years—bird eggs, dead bugs, leaves, stones. And seeds. Always the seeds. Gathered from every plant he found and kept in little bowls and cups and envelopes scattered throughout the house. He insisted on teaching her the names, including the Latin. He'd even taught her how to germinate them, their pale green shoots pushing up through the soil, searching for light.

Caddy closed his door. There was nothing out of the ordinary in his room as far as she could tell.

In the kitchen a chair lay on its back like the victim of a bar fight. Dirty dishes crowded the sink. She tested the taps for water. The pipes whined and sputtered, coughing out rust. No surprise. It was water-rationing season. Sometimes it got so bad the dishes would sit in the sink for days.

Abandoning the taps, Caddy righted the chair and checked the living room. An empty whiskey bottle and a newspaper lay where they'd been dropped by the couch, next to a yellowed glass ashtray mounded with spent cigarettes. The room stank of stale smoke. She shook her head at the sight of the newspaper. It was another one of his eccentricities. No one read the paper anymore. He wore an old watch, too, the wind-up kind, one his father had given him as a boy. And he read books—real ones. So few people did. She used to poke fun at him for that, calling him a relic. But she never chided him for leaving the TV on. It helped drown out the loneliness, she knew that.

The TV flickered, soldiers marching soundlessly across the screen. "A simple show of force." That's what the government had said it would be. Then one country pushed another too far. Now there was talk of bloodshed and bombs.

Caddy stared at the screen. It was too horrible to fathom. Was the world really heading for war? She looked for the remote. When she couldn't find it, she turned up the volume manually. The marching soldiers were interrupted by a blare of music, and the bright face of a young girl appeared. She smiled hopefully into the camera, holding a small sheaf of wheat in her perfect little hands. *"Real solutions for a better world,"* the voice-over proclaimed. *"Brought to you by the Company."*

Caddy scoffed. The Company never did anything for anyone unless there was money to be made. It squeezed oil from sand to keep the cars running, bottled and sold water to the highest bidder, mined uranium and dammed rivers to keep lights burning. It even developed seeds guaranteed to solve world hunger—for those who could afford it. Yeah. She knew all about the Company. It thrived when everything else failed. It shuffled employees like playing cards and tossed them just as easily. And somehow, its hands were always clean. Her own father had been thrown on the discard pile along with so many others. He'd worked in the company research department doing . . . something. She didn't know what exactly because she'd never asked. When he got fired she just assumed he'd locked horns with someone he shouldn't have over something he cared about. That was his problem. He cared too much. At one point in his life he actually thought he could change things. It didn't take a genius to see that the Company was self-serving and corrupt. And someone like her father, no matter how brilliant, would inevitably become a problem.

"God bless the Company," Caddy muttered. She searched for the remote again, stumbling over the whiskey bottle and upsetting the ashtray on the carpet in the process. Yanking pillows from the couch, she found the remote wedged between two cushions. She aimed it at the TV and pressed the power button several times. Nothing. She checked the batteries. Missing. Typical. She tossed the remote back on the couch, shut the TV off, and retrieved the newspaper to scan the headlines, even though there was no point. They were always the same. War, drought, epidemic, jobless rates. Then this: *One-Armed Bandit Strikes in South Town.*

Good old Scum Town. It amused her that they called it South Town because it wasn't a town at all. It was an industrial wasteland on the margins where the city fell away to decay. Another casualty of the crumbling economy. No one went there unless they absolutely had to. And even then, only in daylight. Caddy skimmed the article. It was the third murder in less than two weeks, it said. So why wasn't it all over the news? Not that murder was extraordinary in South Town. Lots of bodies showed up there. But this was different. This was weird. The victims were all found with their left arms missing—and no other obvious connection. Even stranger was the fact that the arms had apparently been removed with a knife.

Caddy flapped the paper on to the couch and picked the cigarette butts from the floor, dropping them back in the ashtray. She balanced the tray to the kitchen and dumped the contents into the trash, coating the discarded Styrofoam takeout containers and dirty tissues with a thin grey film. It was a sticky mess and she was considering changing out the bag when she noticed something: a tiny square of white paper, singed at the edges and folded several times. She plucked the paper from the garbage and shook it open, careful not to tear it. There were light pencil marks, barely visible. Holding the paper up to the bulb over the sink she could see it was an address written in her father's choppy hand. 80 Knox—a South Town address. What were the chances of that? Why would her father want to go there?

For a while after losing his job he went around the city scavenging scrap—copper pipe torn from abandoned buildings, sheets of metal roofing. He was never comfortable going to South Town. If that's where he'd spent the night, she had reason to be worried. Was he in trouble? Maybe she should go to 80 Knox, to make sure he was all right. No, she was getting worked up for nothing. It was just a piece of paper with an address. Who knew what it meant? Her father would be back before she got home from school, she told herself. He'd probably stepped out for more booze and cigarettes. Besides, she had a Physics quiz today. She'd already missed two this month when the bad feeling came on before class. She'd missed so much school because of it—sometimes hiding in the girls' washroom, sometimes crouching in an alleyway. Or not even getting out of bed. Refolding the square of paper, she slid it into a crack between the cupboard and the wall for safekeeping.

Caddy checked the time. She was going to be late for school—again. Stuffing her feet in her sneakers, she shrugged on her jean jacket and swung her small leather duffle bag over her shoulder. She stepped into the hall, quickly closed the apartment door and then stopped before turning the key in the lock. Maybe she should stay home and wait for her father after all . . . She thought about this for a moment, decided against it and locked the door.

Navigating the minefield of garbage on the stairs, Caddy cursed under her breath the entire five flights to the landing, the sound of people arguing and babies crying filtering through closed doors. How she hated this dump of a building. It wouldn't be bad living on the top floor if only the landlord would fix the elevator. There was no hope of that. It'd been broken for as long as she could remember. Caddy averted her eyes when she passed another tenant in the foyer. She had no interest in knowing anyone else who lived here.

Outside, the air was sour and the sky heavy with smog. It made it difficult to breathe. Caddy flipped up the collar on her jacket, put on her scowling face and walked beneath the shadow of the tenement buildings. Picking up the pace, she nearly stumbled over a rat as it scurried past her feet. She jumped back with a shout. More than anything, she hated rats. Their twitching noses and sharp yellow teeth. Their ceaseless digging and squeaking and fighting in the walls of her bedroom at night. They were a plague in the city, crawling up through the plumbing, biting babies in their cribs. "Get out of here!" she yelled, kicking a stone. The rat dodged it and vanished down a sewer grate.

One minute to the bell. Breaking into a trot, Caddy crossed the street and had just reached the curb when she heard the screech of tires against asphalt. There was a sickening thud, followed by the cymbal crash of a bicycle hitting the pavement. Instinctively, Caddy grabbed for her safe stone, clutching it through her shirt as she spun around to see a girl flop helplessly beneath the wheels of an old car. Blood pooled on the ground around her head. There was a heartbeat of perfect silence as Caddy froze, unable to move. She knew the girl pinned under the car. It was Meg Walters, Poe's girlfriend. Beautiful, grey-eyed Meg, the most popular girl in the school.

A man in a tin-coloured suit stepped calmly from the car, straightened his tie and walked away as though nothing had happened. And then a boy began shouting.

"Someone's been hit!"

In an instant, hundreds of students poured into the street. Caddy pushed against the crush, panic taking over. She couldn't stand witness to another car accident, ever—not after her mother. She was only ten years old when it happened, strapped in the back seat of the car. Her mother never wore a seatbelt. It made her feel claustrophobic, she said.

Searching for a way through the crowd, Caddy caught a glimpse of Poe reading a book at the top of the school stairs, as absorbed and earnest as ever. Even now, with students rushing and shouting everywhere, he didn't look up from the page. He was another one like her father. Always chasing some arcane bit of knowledge. He had no idea Meg Walters was lying beneath the wheels of a car. *His* Meg Walters.

Should she call out to him? Let him know what had happened? She didn't want to be the one to deliver such awful news. Not to him. It wasn't as if they were friends. They'd never really talked much, despite sharing three classes. Yet there had always been something between them, something unspoken. She was intrigued by him—maybe because he reminded her of her father, or because he was more handsome than she was willing to admit, she didn't know. She would catch him looking at her in class sometimes, and she would look back, like they shared some kind of secret, though neither of them had done anything about it. He was Meg's, and Caddy would never get in the way of that, even if she had the chance.

Poe raised his head and their eyes locked. They held each other's gaze for what felt like an eternity before sirens pierced the fabric of city noise and a cry rose above the crowd.

"It's Meg!" someone shouted. "Meg's been hit!"

Poe dropped his book and flew down the stairs, his normally cool face lit with disbelief. Was it Meg? he seemed to be asking her. Caddy tried to speak but the crowd surged, forcing them apart.

She couldn't go to school now. It was all so unbelievably awful. Freeing herself from the mob of students, Caddy escaped down an alley and joined the morning rush on Main Street. People shoved past. Some wore face masks, protecting themselves from germs. Others hunkered against walls, holding signs begging for food, money, work. The usual crowd of noodle vendors and tables of sun-faded junk cluttered the sidewalk. On the sides and tops of buildings, billboards loomed, advertising the giant *C* logo of the Company and all its benefits. Someone had defaced one with red spray paint—*The Company Giveth and the Company Taketh Away.* The sign was already being replaced with a new one.

Caddy shouldered her way through the stream of people for several blocks, stopping to catch her breath in the shelter of a storefront. She leaned against the window, hands shaking. "Please, not now," she said, praying the bad feeling wouldn't come.

After several minutes, her heartbeat softened, but her mind whirled around Poe. His girlfriend was trapped under the wheels of a car, probably dead. She wouldn't wish that pain on anyone. She checked her hands. They were fluttering around like injured birds. She thought to hide in the doorway for a while longer, wait for her hands to settle down, but then the store owner rushed out.

"Junkie! Get out of here!"

The guy came flapping at her, waving a small wooden bat. Caddy sidestepped him and pushed back into the fray.

Morning traffic had slowed to an angry crawl. Cyclists whizzed past, exchanging heated shouts with drivers. She moved through the crowd, ignoring the cries of barkers hawking everything from defunct gas masks to ineffective water purifiers. On one corner, a small group of protesters chanted slogans demanding change. Good luck, Caddy thought. Stuffing her hands in her jacket pockets, she willed her mind to go blank. It was no use. Seeing Meg like that had hit her, hard. She couldn't stop the images rolling through her brain—of Meg, of her mother. She should have stayed to help Meg. That's what a better person would have done. But she couldn't face it. She wasn't strong enough. She needed to find her father, to make sure he was okay. What was his connection to South Town?

Caddy walked to where the crowds thinned and the streets emptied, past buildings with boarded-up windows and lonely alleys strewn with litter. After a long while she found herself standing in front of the South Town tunnel, its dark throat wavering in the heat. Its walls were tagged with graffiti. She peered inside, covering her nose with her hand against the stink of urine and diesel fuel. Between the piers were the tattered blankets and flattened boxes of a hobo squat. This place had bad intentions written all over it, she thought. It was the perfect place for someone like the One-Armed Bandit to hide. Pulling her necklace from beneath her collar, Caddy rubbed the green stone between her thumb and fingers as she considered the tunnel. Was her father somewhere on the other side? It frightened her to think about it. At least her hands had stopped shaking. She should turn around and go back, wait for her father at home. That was the sensible thing to do. That's what he would want.

Caddy held her breath and stepped into the tunnel. A flock of pigeons burst from the shadows, winging over her head. She ducked and began walking, singing her shining song in her head, the sound of her footsteps chasing her as she went. There were whispers and muffled moans around her. The high-pitched wails of a woman echoed off the walls. Or was it a baby? Halfway through the tunnel, Caddy was sure another set of footsteps joined hers. Too scared to look, she ran the last twenty feet and burst into the safety of the sunlight, whipping around to face whatever was following her.

The tunnel's black mouth yawned back at her. There was no one there—no one she could see. Caddy stared into the darkness, taking several steps away from the tunnel before feeling brave enough to turn around. When she did, she saw a crosshatch of train tracks running in every direction. There were no signposts or indicators of any kind. There was nothing to see except thin tornados of dust whirling over sequins of broken glass, and a small forest of cold smokestacks standing among the abandoned warehouses. What did she really expect to find here? Her father was probably home, safe in bed. But she'd come this far . . .

Choosing a random direction, Caddy wandered toward the warehouses and discovered that there were hundreds of them. And they all looked the same. Alley after alley. Where was 80 Knox in all of this? She stopped to look around. What could her father possibly be doing in such a desolate place? "This is stupid," she said aloud.

Caddy continued to explore and eventually found a name scrawled in faded blue paint on the broken concrete at her feet. *Wilson.* This was hopeful. She kept going and discovered the names Brydon, Cherry and Stanfield. And then, finally, Knox.

The alley was dotted with Dumpsters and windblown trash. There was an unnerving silence. Caddy looked over her shoulder to be sure she hadn't been followed. She didn't want to be the next one-armed body in the news. Pulling her keys from her pocket, she laced them between her fingers and made a fist. If nothing else I'll put up a good fight, she thought.

Keys poised, Caddy skulked along Knox searching for numbers. After several hundred feet, it was clear there were none. Now what? Start again from the beginning? Count the doors until she got to 80? She realized she had no way of knowing the increments, or which side of the alley was even and which odd. So she kept going, her sneakers crunching over gravel, until she saw something that made her stop. Beside a Dumpster at the end of the alley, two men looked back at her. They were dressed alike, in tin-grey suits, white shirts and black shoes—just like the man who'd hit Meg.

The hair stood on the back of her neck. The men blocked the alley. Caddy clenched the keys in her hand. Turning slowly, she walked in the other direction. The men followed. She could hear their dress shoes stepping in unison over the gravel. Her first impulse was to run. She forced herself to remain calm and casually pick up the pace. The men matched her speed. Caddy broke into a trot and the men trotted too. The second this happened, she bolted, arms pumping, sneakers flying over the ground. She was nearly to the street when two more men in identical grey suits appeared, cutting off the exit.

Caddy skidded and tripped, falling back on her hands, bits of broken glass stabbing her skin. She struggled to get up and someone grabbed her collar, yanking her to one side and pulling her back down. She screamed, kicking wildly as she was dragged like a rag doll across the alley and into the shadows, her hips and sneakers thumping over the metal lip of a threshold into a room. The door slammed shut, taking the light.

"Let me go!" she screamed.

A sweaty hand that smelled of woodsmoke clamped over her mouth. Caddy bit down, hard. The man grunted, shaking her by the collar. She yelled, more frantic than before.

"Shut up," he growled in her ear.

Hoisting her onto his hip, the man carried her through the dark. Caddy stabbed at him with her keys. He slapped them from her hand. She clawed and punched, the man taking her deeper and deeper along a tunnel toward a glimmer of light. When they got closer, she saw that the light framed a door. The man heaved against it and they entered a room lit by a single candle. He dropped her, pounding and hollering, to the ground and locked the door.

---(((((**2**)))))---

MEG

M eg didn't see the car that hit her, or hear the crash of metal on concrete as her Schwinn disappeared beneath the tires of the old Buick. She didn't feel the snap of bone as her arm broke, or the shatter of skull against the street as the Buick bucked to a stop over her lifeless form. The man driving the vehicle put the car in park and left it in the street. He didn't acknowledge her but simply brushed himself off and vanished down an alley. Within minutes a crowd of students had gathered and the wail of sirens could be heard.

Meg loitered on the sidewalk, watching the scene unfold. A carefully manicured man stood beside her. His hair was white and styled to perfection. His skin was pale and smooth as porcelain, offset by the silvery grey of his impeccable suit. And his eyes—they were strange. As cold and colourless as ice chips. There was a faint sound around him, like tinkling glass.

"What happened?" Meg asked.

The man said nothing, absorbed with the accident. Meg stared at the mangled bicycle and wondered at the absurdity of the girl's foot sticking out from under the car, bare, exposed, like the dislocated leg of a mannequin. And her arm—it was bent at an impossible angle. There was a shoe in the middle of the road. A blue suede sneaker. Just like mine, Meg thought. Looking down she was surprised to see one of her feet was bare. How had she lost her shoe? She was about to retrieve it, when someone picked it up and carried it off. "Hey!" Meg shouted, but the guy disappeared into the crowd. The police showed up, cordoning off the street to prevent people from getting too close. To one side, an ambulance waited, lights flashing mutely. The attendants crouched near the wreckage as the car was backed away. The girl's arm flopped, her body rolled to one side, and for a heart-beat Meg thought she was still alive. Then she saw the streak of blood curling in a crimson smile from the girl's lips.

"Is she dead?" Meg asked.

The man in the suit nodded, showing neither sympathy nor concern.

"Can't they do anything for her?"

"It was her time." His voice was soothing and hypnotic.

Meg sighed. "She's so young."

A dark-haired boy came rushing onto the scene, wild-eyed and yelling her name. It was her boyfriend, Poe!

"I'm here, Poe!" Meg called, waving her arms. But he kept throwing himself at the barrier to reach the girl on the road, the police restraining him and pulling him away.

"I don't understand," Meg said. "Who is she?"

The man remained silent. She would have to find out for herself.

No one stopped her as she walked past the police and dipped under the caution tape. One hand on the car, Meg bent down and peered at the body. Beneath the tangled mass of bloodied blond hair was the ashen face of someone she knew. She moved closer, leaning in to get a better look. The girl's grey eyes stared lifelessly back. And then it struck her. *She* was the girl beneath the car! Meg reeled to her feet in horror.

"But why?" she asked the man.

He smiled, the light flickering across his frozen eyes. "It was your time."

There was a brilliant flash and an otherworldly being appeared, a dove held in its hands. It was tall with slanted gold eyes and radiant skin the same yellow colour as the light that surrounded it. It was neither male nor female, its robe furling in an unseen wind.

"Please come with me," it said.

Meg turned to gauge the reaction of the man in the suit but was surprised to discover him gone.

The yellow being gently placed the dove in her hands. "Come," it said again.

Meg held the bird, its heart beating against her fingers for several moments before it flew into the air, a staccato flurry of sunshine and shadow. There was a rush of wind and Meg felt herself rising with the dove toward a blinding light.

Meg woke in an empty white room. Her stomach was knotted tight and a fever gripped her. Pain tore through her body causing her to cry out. Her voice fell flat, dampened by the ethereal acoustics in the room. Too frightened to move, she investigated her surroundings as best she could. She had no idea what had happened to her or where she was. The room was unusual. There was no door and no real walls to speak of, just a cottony-white mist defining the space. But it was a room, of sorts. This she was sure of. It was also clear that she was alone.

"Hello!" she said, testing the sound. There wasn't the slightest trace of echo. Her voice dropped off, the same as before. What was this place, and how did she get here? She strained to look at her feet. She was wearing only one shoe. What had happened to the other one? All at once it came tumbling back to her—the bicycle, the car, the girl beneath its wheels.

With great effort, Meg attempted to get up and was shocked to see her right arm flop uselessly to one side. "Oh," she said, her forearm dangling heavily at the elbow. She tried to raise herself with her other arm but gave up when the pain spiked through her. She lay back. The table was a giant feather pillow, spongy and light. She was too sick to move again, so she just lay there for the longest time, fighting the nausea and the pain.

"Poe," she murmured, reaching for something familiar to hold on to. "I was on my way to school to see Poe." She wondered where he was and if he was worried about her. They had planned to listen to music and do homework together after class. She had an assignment due! When she thought of him, her soul filled with a loneliness so deep she felt she would drown. She wanted to feel his arms around her, feel the firmness of his lips against her mouth.

The pain surged, sweeping her down into a fathomless liquid black. She seemed to stay there for an eternity, her anguish and the darkness vanquishing even the smallest chance of hope. She would never see Poe again. Or her mother and father or any of her friends. She wanted to go home. She wanted to be with them all again. She fought to hold onto the images of their faces. Hard as she tried they were beginning to gutter and fade. Yet the other face, the face of the man with the ice-chip eyes, it haunted her and would not leave. Who was he?

After a great span of time, a being emerged from the vapour. It didn't maintain a constant shape, but moved in and out of form like a brilliant cloud, its face dissipating as quickly as it formed. It stood beside her, emitting a delicate and diffuse white light. Meg was so relieved to see someone that she didn't mind at all how they looked. She even managed to smile through her misery.

"Hi," she said, waving the fingers on her good hand.

The being gazed at her benignly. Meg was encouraged.

"Um, can I ask you something? Can you tell me where I am and what I'm doing here?"

The being spoke, its voice polyphonic as though many voices spoke as one. It was modulated and distant, like the voice from a half-remembered dream. "You are on the other side."

"Oh." Meg looked around the room. It was the same cottony mist as before. "The other side of what?"

"Manifest life."

Meg thought about this for a minute. "You mean, this is heaven?"

"Some call it that. We simply call it the Light." The being disappeared and reappeared on the other side of the bed.

"That's a neat trick," Meg said. She was going to ask about her missing shoe when a bolt of pain shot through her arm. She winced and cried out. "I don't know what's wrong with me."

"You are transforming."

Meg looked at her floppy arm. "Transforming . . . ?"

The being split in two and merged back into one. "You are transforming," it said again. "When you are ready, you will be reassigned."

"I see," Meg said. But she didn't understand at all. "What am I transforming into?"

"Whatever fulfills your soul's purpose."

"Does everyone transform?" she asked.

"No. Many are reincarnated as human and return to the earth plane."

This gave Meg hope. "That's what I would like."

"Not possible."

The being shifted again. She squinted her eyes to catch it, but it wouldn't stay still. She frowned, frustration and sadness welling up in her. "I liked my human life. I just want to go home."

The being responded by undulating like a jellyfish, igniting hundreds of tiny lights that twinkled throughout its form. Meg found it so relaxing to look at, so fascinating and beautiful. Her frustration ebbed. "I hope I'm not being rude," she said, "but, what are you?"

"I am your Incubator."

"You don't look like anything I've ever seen before."

"My shape is necessary to ensure your transformation is as clean as possible."

"You don't have any shape at all."

"We can't allow you to assume the configuration of another," the being said. "We don't want you to be contaminated."

"We? How many of you are there here?"

"Our numbers are ever-changing."

"Are all of you formless?" Meg asked.

"We take shape according to our purpose."

"So . . . what's my purpose?"

"As yet to be determined."

It was all so vague. Meg felt frustrated again. She wanted to sit up but the effort still proved to be too much. She wilted back down onto the bed. "I feel so sick."

"It is a very important time," the being said. It shimmered and began to fade.

"Please, don't go," she begged, the pain arcing in her body and drawing her back into the dark.

When Meg resurfaced, she felt as though she'd been gone a thousand years. She couldn't remember anything coherent. She wondered who she was and what she was doing. Her thoughts were slippery and ephemeral, as shapeless as the atmosphere in the room. There were images, like snapshots, and attendant emotions, but their significance and connection were lost to her. There was the boy. His face struck her with a longing so profound she thought she would cry, though his name she'd long since forgotten. She fought with all her strength to hold onto him, focusing on his face and the memory of his lips against hers. She would never let him go, ever—she promised herself that. She would fight her transformation to the very end. And then she would find the boy, no matter what it took, and uncover the mystery of her past and her life with him.

"I will not forget," she vowed.

Meg blinked at the white atmosphere around her, listening. She was feverish and sick, but the pain had mercifully subsided, leaving a throbbing ache in its place.

"It's not what I imagined," she said.

"What did you imagine?"

It was the Incubator. It had returned.

"How long have I been here?" Meg asked.

The being drifted in and out of focus. "We don't measure time here. Everything that ever was and everything that ever will be exists simultaneously."

Meg thought about this. "If everything exists simultaneously, then why can't I just snap my fingers and transform instead of going through all this suffering?" She attempted to make her point by snapping the fingers on her bad arm. It flopped insolently around, the same drunk fish as before.

"Process is necessary," the being said.

Meg tried to follow it as it swirled around the bed. "So, there is an order of operations."

"If you want to think of it that way, yes."

Meg bit her lip. There were so many questions to ask. Only she was finding it difficult to grasp the words. Something important had happened to her. She just couldn't put her finger on it. Her mind was a shoebox of old photos, a jumble of untethered images. She couldn't make sense of any of it. One thing she did know, she hadn't always existed in this weird cloud world. Her memory of the boy was proof of that. She missed him so much.

"Why do I have to be alone?" she asked. "I don't like to be alone."

"You must be quarantined until you are fully formed."

Her longing for the boy made her bold. Meg raised herself awkwardly. "What if I don't want to be . . ."—she searched for the right word but came up empty-handed—"whatever it is I'm becoming? What if I just want to go back to the way I was . . . before all this?" She made a gesture across the room with her good arm.

"Not possible."

"But, why?"

Her question hung in the air unanswered. The being had already left.

In the ensuing void, Meg remained alone. It was impossible to trace how long she had been in the white room. Mysteriously, she was no longer bored but was fixated on the slow and deliberate changes that were taking place in her body. Something was definitely happening. Her floppy arm was still floppy, but the pain that had overwhelmed her for so long had nearly vanished. She floated directionless in the ether, her mind releasing memories that fluttered beyond the understanding of words. She knew that she was forgetting great chunks of things, that her memories were slowly eroding as surely as her body was changing. But it wasn't a clean process. Some memories were stubborn, clinging to her subconscious like burrs, eventually leaving only the barbs behind—just enough to remember the idea of the burr that created the hooks in the first place. The ice-chip eyes never left her, though, nor did the boy's face, much to her relief. His image rose and fell in her mind's eye, an anchorless ship, its appearance inspiring longing, but with nothing to tie it to.

After a vast empty span, a new being arrived—a silver being. This one seemed to have a set form, though it fluctuated as well, as if its body continually experienced a kind of mild tremor. Its eyes were the colour of burnished steel and slanted upward. It had high cheekbones and a pointed chin, giving it the sylvan quality of a woodland faerie.

The being stared at her. Meg stared back at him—if it even was a "him." It was hard to tell. There was an androgynous aspect about it. It didn't seem to be wearing any clothes, either, just a gossamer fabric with a life of its own, a flowing extension of its form. Meg turned away. She felt funny looking at the being, like it could see right through her.

"Rise," it ordered.

It didn't move its mouth when it talked, but she could understand it perfectly, as if it was somehow speaking inside her head. Meg sat up and hung her legs over the side of the cottony bed. To her amazement she was able to stand.

The being looked at her with visible concern. "There's something wrong," it immediately deduced. With a swift motion of its hand it produced a full-length mirror so she could see her reflection.

Meg was shocked by her image. Although she couldn't remember how she'd once looked, she knew that it was nothing like the way she appeared now. Her skin and hair were so white they were nearly blue, and her eyes were a fantastic shade of violet. There was a soft magenta glow around her—not nearly as brilliant as the being's silver halo yet a glow nonetheless. Her features were slanted upward and as smooth as the silver being's. But she had somehow retained characteristics from her former life. Her nose and chin were rounder. And she had a distinct shape. She was decidedly female. This made her smile. It was a small victory but it meant so much to her. The transformation hadn't erased her entirely.

The being pursed its lips. "It shouldn't have any colour at all," it said to the ether. "Recruits are white until their Frequency is determined. And look at its form—and its appendages . . .

It's so . . . stunty. It should have grown much more during the transformation."

Meg lifted her floppy arm. It dangled uselessly from her elbow. It had a deep, jagged scar that ran like a lightning bolt from her shoulder to the tip of her index finger. She could have done without that. But it was a small price to pay to retain elements of her human life, so she was willing to put up with it.

The silver being studied her as though evaluating a toxic dump site. "I've never seen anything like it."

"What's my name?" Meg asked.

The silver being looked at her as though her head had just dropped off. "Why does it move its mouth?"

"I don't know," Meg said.

"What a mess," the being groaned. "The Council will not be happy about this. In my entire existence I have never seen anything like it. It's an absolute aberration."

The heat rose in Meg's cheeks. She didn't want to stand there being insulted by this being. "Please stop calling me 'it,'" she blurted out. "I'm not a thing. And how do you tell us apart if we're all supposed to look the same?"

The being gaped, incredulous. This made her more upset.

"If I'm so awful, why don't you transform me back and go work with someone else? I never wanted any of this in the first place."

The being sighed with exasperation and righted itself. "I have no choice, unfortunately. And to answer your question, we have no trouble telling recruits apart. Each being has its own energetic print—like a thumbprint. We don't need distinguishing features to set us apart from one another. And we have no need for names here either."

"But I like having a name," Meg said, her anger subsiding. "I don't feel comfortable without one."

"Comfortable?" The being waved her quiet. "You should have relinquished all of that long ago in the Place of Forgetting."

Meg looked around at the white walls. "Is that what you call this cottony room . . . the Place of Forgetting?"

"Yes," the being said. "Your mind should be clear as a child's, except for the information we provided during your transformation."

"It isn't clear," Meg said. "It's all tangled up. I feel things." The boy's face flashed in her mind, and in the mirror she saw tears of liquid light welling in her eyes. "I'm confused and lonely. I want to go home."

The silver being grew impatient. "You'll just have to learn to control yourself." It looked at her floppy arm in dismay. "We have to fix this before the Council sees you."

The being produced something it called a healing cord and began binding her arm from her shoulder all the way to her wrist. The cord was shimmery and it hardly weighed anything. It seemed to instantly strengthen and straighten her arm, but did nothing to hide the scar. Meg didn't mind. She was happy her arm worked at all. She flexed her fingers.

"It feels strong."

"It's not a cure but your appendage should be functional now," the being said. "We still need to dress you."

With a flick of its fingers it produced a gleaming white robe and draped it over her body. The fabric was light and glimmered like moonstone. It fused to her skin, flowing as though alive. The being fussed with the robe in a futile attempt to cover her arm. The robe waved tauntingly, accentuating both her scar and her female form. The being picked at the fabric like a disgruntled monkey.

"I don't know what else to do," it finally conceded. "It's time for you to leave the Place of Forgetting and stand before the Council." With a finger snap, it dismissed the mirror back to the ether and glided away from her across the room. It glanced over its shoulder, expecting her to follow.

Meg struggled where she stood. Her feet were heavy and clumsy as stones. She couldn't move them.

"Think," the being instructed her. "Use your thoughts to project yourself."

"What do you mean?"

"Think about where you want to go and you will go there."

Meg concentrated on the wall. Nothing happened.

"Think harder," the being said. "Imagine yourself moving toward the wall."

Meg focused as hard as she could. All at once there was the sound of air rushing through a tunnel, and her body lurched forward several feet as if she were sliding on ice. The feeling was so exhilarating, she shouted, "Hey! This is amazing!"

"Please, control yourself," the being admonished. "Such outbursts will not be tolerated before the Council."

"Oh." She lowered her eyes in embarrassment. "I just can't believe it actually worked."

"Of course it worked. Now try again."

Meg furrowed her brow, concentrating her intention. The whooshing sound grew to a roar, and in a stream of glittering stars she slid wildly across the ice again. "Holy smokes!" she exclaimed, forgetting what she'd just been told.

The silver being folded its arms with strained forbearance. "There is no need for such an emotional response. In fact, you should have left your emotions behind eons ago. Something isn't right. You're supposed to be pure—a blank canvas. But you're the furthest thing from it. I can't imagine what went wrong."

"It's not my fault," Meg said, even though she was sure that it was. She'd done everything in her power to prevent her transformation from happening.

"Whose fault would it be?"

She shrugged. "I don't know. The guy in the white room said he was in charge of my transformation . . ."

"Your Incubator? Don't be ridiculous."

"Maybe I was contaminated," she said. "He seemed to be so worried about that."

"Nonsense," the silver being clipped. "You're just going to have to control your thoughts and movements and not let whatever it is that's affecting you interfere. An essential degree of subtlety is required here. You don't need so much power just to get about."

Meg frowned to keep from smiling. She liked having power.

When the being saw the look on her face it misunderstood and reconsidered its approach. It assumed a gentler stance, softening its tone.

"Think of yourself as . . . a leaf upon the water."

Meg concentrated again, imagining a lovely green leaf bobbling along on a sparkling blue river. To her delight, she began to glide forward with the most pleasant swishing sound.

"Good," the being congratulated her. "Now follow me—and try not to talk with your mouth open."

ABDUCTION

Caddy crouched on the ground, a cornered animal. The man glared at her, his face shifting in the flickering candlelight. She wanted to memorize everything about him, to take what she could before he killed her. He was tall, dark-skinned—Native, maybe—dressed in jeans and a worn black suit jacket with a battered top hat pushed down over his dark mane of hair. Over his shoulder he wore a fringed tan leather satchel. His hands were the size of dinner plates. It was clear she couldn't fight him off, though she would try. She didn't want to die like this. She clutched her safe stone, gathering her courage.

"Are you the One-Armed Bandit?"

The man looked at her as though she was an idiot. "What did you come here for?" he asked.

His question confused her. What did he plan to do? She needed to act quickly, to find something—anything she could use to defend herself. The room was empty except for the candle guttering on the floor. The only way out was the door behind him. She was trapped. And then she remembered her phone. Pulling it from her jacket, Caddy pressed the key for emergency speed-dial.

The man reached her in one step, knocked the phone from her hand and shattered it with the heel of his boot.

"No phones."

"Please, let me go," Caddy begged.

"Why did you come here?"

She thought to lie but found herself telling the truth. "I was looking for my father."

"Your father isn't here."

Caddy felt a sharp pain in her hands. She held them up in the candlelight, saw blood and started to cry. "I'm sorry. I don't know what you want from me."

The man was unmoved. "We have to go."

Caddy broke down. "Please . . . I haven't done anything. I just want to go home."

A scuffling sound outside the door set the man in action. He pushed her aside and brushed some dirt from the ground, uncovering a hatch. Grabbing the handle, he tugged it open. "Come on."

Caddy made a break for the door, fumbling with the hasp as she tried to unlock it. "Help!" she shouted, pounding on the door with her fists. "Someone help me, please!"

The man picked her up and stuffed her through the hatch into a tunnel. He jumped in after her, pulling the lid shut.

"Get away from me!" Caddy yelled, hitting his face and chest until he snatched her up and carried her on his hip again.

She fought him the entire length of the passageway, the man cursing and muttering under his breath. At a bend in the tunnel, he dropped her to her feet. There was another hole. This one had a ladder leading down. The man pointed at the ladder.

"Climb," he said.

Caddy started to object but he looked at her with such malice that she lowered herself onto the rungs. She clung to the ladder, peering between her feet at the water running along a massive concrete culvert below. Was he going to kill her down there? She glanced at him and he scowled, forcing her to move. The rungs were damp. Her sneakers slipped and squeaked as she went.

The man descended after her, a menacing bear. At the bottom of the ladder, Caddy stopped. The culvert smelled of worms and muck and rotting tree roots. And it was dark. Her stomach tightened. No one would ever find her body there.

"Move," the man said.

The water gushed cold over her shoes. There was no time to care because the man nearly landed on top of her when he splashed down. Opening his satchel, he retrieved a thin, tightly bound bundle of sticks wrapped at the top with a piece of cloth. A torch, Caddy thought. Whoever he was, he'd come prepared. The man lit a match and the torch jumped to life, the flame snapping like a sheet on a windy clothesline. Black smoke rolled up the ladder. The man motioned with his head.

"Go."

They sloshed through the water, the torch casting eerie shadows on the walls. Caddy walked in front, clutching her necklace and wondering if she could outrun him. The man was practically on her heels. She squinted through the dark. The torchlight caught something in the distance. It flashed and disappeared, then flashed again. The water solidified, spreading in a wave up the walls and growing in speed and size, rolling toward her.

"Rats!" Caddy yelled.

The wave crashed over her feet and surged up her legs in a frenzy of teeth and nails and glinting eyes. The man caught her as she fell back. One arm around her, he stabbed wildly with the torch, the rats squealing and leaping away from the flame. The wave broke, streaming past in two grey torrents. Caddy didn't resist when he lifted her off her feet, clinging to him like a frightened child until the rats were gone.

By the time he set her down, her whole body was shaking. She looked at him with a mixture of gratitude and disbelief. He'd protected her. Why would he do that if he wanted to kill her? Maybe she could appeal to him—even convince him to let her go. "Thank you," she said.

He glowered. "Go."

Caddy's heart pounded. "You're very brave."

He shoved her shoulder. "Go," he repeated, this time more forcefully.

She walked, looking back periodically to discern the man's intention. His face was hard as a shovel blade. She had to think of a way to change his mind before her chances ran out.

At the end of the tunnel was another ladder, this one leading up. The man threw the torch down, extinguishing it in the water. Caddy thought to sprint up the ladder to get ahead of him and slam the door shut at the top. If there was a door. Or maybe kick him in the face from the top of the ladder and run. Anything was better than going quietly. Did she have the guts to actually do it? She would never find out. As soon as she gripped the rungs the man flopped a cloth bag over her head, cinching it around her neck.

"Hey! You don't have to do this!" she cried, clawing at the hood. He jerked her hands away and placed them on the ladder.

"Climb," he ordered.

Caddy probed for the ladder with her feet, her breath heavy and moist inside the bag, her mind flattened with fear. "I can't breathe . . ."

He nudged her harder. She moved in stops and starts, mouthing the words of her shining song. At the top, she felt around and pulled herself up. Squatting on her heels, she frantically worked the cord on the bag. It was tied tight. She could hear the muffled sounds of the city over her breathing as her fingers deciphered the knot. The smell of gas filtered through the hood. Were they in a garage? Her heart leapt when the cord began to loosen, but the man got to her first. He yanked her to her feet by one arm and dragged her behind him. She heard a car door open and he forced her in, pushing her head down so she wouldn't hit it getting into the vehicle. She realized now that he would never let her go. He was going to drive her to the middle of nowhere to kill her, and no one would ever know or care.

The second her legs touched the seat, Caddy exploded, kicking and yelling and swinging her fists. The man swore when she struck his face. He grabbed her arms. She threw her body to one side, feet flailing. Wrenching her upright, he pulled her hands behind her back and wrapped her wrists together with a piece of rope, pulling it taut. She lurched forward. He held her against the seat and fastened the belt.

"Let me go!" she screamed.

The car door slammed. Another opened and the vehicle rocked as the man got in. Keys jangled. The engine turned over. Caddy screamed louder, thrashing and bucking against the seatbelt. A damp rag covered her nose and mouth, the cold rush of solvent filling her lungs. It numbed her lips and made her neck loose. The car rolled forward, her head lolling from side to side, the movement of the vehicle sloshing her brain back and forth. Back and forth. Sounds blared and receded around her. The dark rose up and she surrendered, drifting into the void.

—⟨⟨⟨⟨⟨ 4 ⟩⟩⟩⟩⟩—

THE FREQUENCIES

Meg glided alongside the silver being. The cloudy walls of the white room dissolved, revealing a great and magical city that stretched uninterrupted as far as the eye could see.

"The City of Light," the being announced.

Meg had never seen or dreamed of anything like it. Had the city been here the whole time she'd felt so alone? She hardly knew what to explore first. Every building gleamed with the brilliance of white marble, crystal and glass. The skyline was studded with domes of gold. There were rivers that gushed with no traceable source into ornate fountains, and pools of water so still it was nearly impossible to determine where the water stopped and the sky began. Meg wanted to see everything. She trailed her fingers in the spray of a huge fountain, and marvelled at the majestic trees lining the streets, and wondered at the impossible flower baskets that hung by magic, their blossoms tumbling in a riot of colour to the ground. Everywhere there were other beings—countless numbers—moving through the streets, their collective voices a roar in her ears. It was all so blindingly beautiful and strange and . . . completely overwhelming.

"Where's everyone going?" she asked.

"To the Great Hall for the initiation ceremony," the silver being said. "It is a very important day. These events don't happen often."

Meg gawked at the crowd. "These are all recruits?"

"Yes."

Now she understood why the being had been so confused by her appearance. The recruits were entirely white and genderless, as the being had said they should be. And they were tall. She was suddenly self-conscious. All the other recruits were gliding purposefully along, chatting telepathically with their silver beings. They all seemed to know who they were and what they were doing and where they were going. She thought about her bad arm and her female form. She'd fought so hard to retain her past, to prevent her transformation from happening. Now she felt horribly out of place. She couldn't fit in if she tried. The city and all its glittering wonders—they weren't meant for her. They were meant for everyone else. Her soul sank. This wasn't home. She couldn't say exactly what home was like, but she was confident it was nothing like this. She tried to catch bits of conversation, to feel like part of the action. The voices rushed in a garbled stream through her head. She held her hands over her ears.

"It's too much. I can't hear myself think."

"Tune it out," the being said. "Adjust the dials in your mind."

Meg winced. "It's like standing under a waterfall."

"Concentrate. Diminish the sound."

Meg focused on the noise. It was a fluid rainbow of colour. She imagined two strong hands pushing the rainbow of sound into a narrow band of white light. The voices crackled and receded like a distant radio transmission.

"Good," the being encouraged her. "Now, see if you can control the input."

The voices flared and withdrew. Meg found herself looking at a tapestry of light, a multidimensional fabric of colourful threads, all woven and intermingling. She reached to touch a single sparkling strand and discovered that she could hear the owner speaking quite distinctly. What's more, if she concentrated harder, the face of the being talking emerged from the ether of her mind as though it were standing right in front of her. "This is incredible," she said, and despite how low she felt, she began plucking strings, as lively as a harp player, skipping from one conversation to another. Until the silver being intercepted.

"It is forbidden to eavesdrop. There are strict communication protocols."

Meg dropped the string she was holding and the conversation slipped away.

"Shall we continue?" the being said.

They glided through the city, the being playing tour guide. Meg wanted to pay attention, but she just felt more and more sorry for herself the farther they went. She couldn't appreciate the gilded domes of the Hall of Records where *The Book of Events* was kept, or feel excited by the soaring pillars of the Tower of Knowledge where the Pools of Knowing held the vast expanse of intelligence in the universe. She smiled politely at the river that bubbled and snaked through the streets, and the green pastures that strolled for miles beyond the city to rest comfortably at the feet of snow-capped mountains. And she only pretended to care when the silver being stopped in front of the crystal-walled conservatory of the Auditorium to listen to "the most exquisite music" rising above the murmurings of the crowd.

"It's nice," Meg said, feigning interest. The closer they got to the Great Hall where the initiation ceremony was to take place, the worse she felt. What was waiting for her there?

On the stairs of the Hall, she paused and stood beneath its marble archway. It was carved with an elaborate series of mysterious symbols. Was she supposed to know what they meant?

She panicked, thinking she'd missed something important she was supposed to have learned during her transformation. She was tempted to turn around and leave, go anywhere but here. And then she was struck by the most unsettling feeling. She was being watched.

Lowering her gaze, Meg met the questioning eyes of hundreds of recruits and their silver beings. They were staring at her bound arm and the impossibility of her shape. The heat rose in her face for the second time that day. She pressed her arm against her body to conceal it. Now she really wanted to run and hide.

The silver being placed a hand on her shoulder. "You must learn to rise above such things," it said. But then it gave the spectators a look so scathing they quickly retreated into the Hall.

Meg shadowed her silver being up the stairs, practically gliding over its robe in the process.

"There's no need to travel so closely," it admonished her.

She apologized, and kept tailing it all the same, she felt so exposed.

Inside the building, a fountain flowed. Meg hardly glanced at it, or the armoured sentries that stood on either side of the Hall. She was so nervous about the initiation ceremony she didn't acknowledge the ethereal singing floating through the corridor, ushering the seemingly endless number of recruits inside. The silver being led her into a cavernous room, blithering on about the wonders of the city. It pointed out the massive marble pillars and alabaster walls, and the ceiling, all gilded and glistening. It noted the brilliant warm light illuminating the space, "like the composite flame of a million candles," even though there were no candles to be seen—as if the room were generating light on its own. "And look how the walls seem to breathe and expand to accommodate the multitudes," the silver being went on.

"Yeah," Meg said, distracted by a large stage behind a heavy marble table at the back of the hall. There were sixteen golden beings sitting there. They looked very important—even more important than the silver ones. "Who are they?" she asked.

"The Council," the being said. "Two for each Frequency represented."

The Council members sat side by side, their golden energy radiating around them. Meg counted eight additional silver beings at the foot of the stage, each carrying a tall pole bearing a coloured flag. There were eight flags in all: violet, indigo, blue, green, yellow, orange, red and white. Meg didn't like the look of this. What were they expecting her to do?

The silver being happily explained. "When you feel the call, you must go to the flag-bearer who carries the colour of your vibration. Then you will know for certain what Frequency you belong to." It held its hand up, anticipating her next question. "Each colour has a unique vibratory Frequency. The colours you see here belong to the order of Spectrals—or single wavelength beings. They are the core Frequencies that make up the spectrum of Light."

"Are you a Spectral?" Meg asked.

"Of course not," the being said. "I am a Metallic—something entirely different."

"But how can all these recruits fit into so few categories? And how will I know when I'm called?"

"They fit," the being assured her. "And you will know. You will feel the call inside you and join your rightful Frequency among the Spectrals."

A trumpet sounded, and a profound hush fell over the crowd. From the wings of the great room, a magnificent being appeared. It looked similar to the silver and gold beings in features, but was taller and possessed an iridescence unlike any other. It was every colour, and none, like mother-of-pearl, or some kind of lustrous fabric.

"The Prism," the silver being said. "This being has the ability to vibrate at every frequency. It is unique in its purpose. There is only one."

"Is he the guy in charge?" Meg asked.

The being gave her a look. "In charge? No one being is in charge here. We are a collective."

"Oh," Meg said. She didn't really care anyway. She was just being polite.

The Prism glided to the stage. Drafting behind it were two silver beings carrying an instrument that looked like a series of tuning forks stuck together, eight in all. They positioned the instrument on the podium. Without further ado, the Prism raised a delicate silver mallet and tapped the smallest fork. A clear, high note, like the song of a bird, filled the room. Meg felt nothing. The Prism's colour changed to a deep shade of violet. The corresponding flag began to flap and within the crowd, thousands of recruits responded to the sound. They glided toward the stage and changed colour, glowing with a violet light. Meg watched with nervous fascination as a shower of glittering stars appeared from nowhere and twinkled over the recruits. "What's that?" she asked.

"The Light of Corometh," the silver being said. It joins the members of a Frequency together. This group of recruits is now bound to one another, as the members of other frequencies are bound to their own kind. It helps them in their work."

"What do the purple ones do?"

"They are Chroniclers, Keepers of the Charts."

"What charts?"

"Blueprints—maps of every individual life that ever lived and ever will live."

This caught Meg's attention. Could she search the charts for memories of her life before this time? Would she be able to find the boy? She promised herself, the first chance she got, she would search the charts for him. If only she could do it right now and forget this initiation stuff altogether. The silver being sensed her agitation, though it mistook the source.

"Rest your mind," it said. "In time you will not have to think. You will simply know."

The tuning fork finished sounding and the Prism returned to its original colour. The room fell silent and the next fork was struck. A ringing filled the air, lower than the first, yet no less pure. The Prism turned indigo and the corresponding flag waved. Thousands more recruits vibrated to this sound and moved toward the stage. Their robes turned indigo and the Light of Corometh sparkled over them.

"Messengers," the silver being said. "They help shape collective consciousness by delivering ideas and inspiration through the universal energy field."

"Ah," Meg said. Whatever that meant. "Whose consciousness?" she asked.

"The consciousness of those on earth."

"So, the Messengers are controlling what people think."

"Not controlling," the silver being answered. "Assisting people toward a common goal."

"Is that what people want—a common goal?"

"We hope so."

"And the Messengers achieve this by delivering ideas and inspiration through the universal energy field?"

"Yes."

"Okay," Meg said. "And what's the universal energy field?"

The being grew impatient. "It's the field of energy that connects everything together—like a giant net. It's in and around us. It's everywhere. You should know this already."

Meg shrugged. She knew now.

The next note the Prism struck was even lower than the first two. It caused the Prism to turn a brilliant colour of blue.

"Musicians," the being explained as the recruits approached the stage. "Their song helps build and maintain the universal energy field."

"Got it," Meg said. "So, they work with the Messengers?"

The being sighed. "No. Pay attention."

"But they both work with the universal energy field, right?"

"Yes. But not together."

She looked blankly back at the being.

"They both work with the universal energy field in different capacities. The Musicians help create the field through sound, while the Messengers use it to transfer information to beings on earth. Every one of us uses the field to transfer information—images, thoughts, feelings . . . it's the matrix that connects all things."

That makes sense, Meg thought. Kind of. Which was good enough. She would leave it at that. She didn't want to risk sounding stupid again. Besides, did she really need to completely understand everything right away?

The next fork sounded and the Prism turned a deep shade of green.

"Healers," the silver being said.

Oh, good, Meg thought. Those ones didn't need explaining. "These guys heal people," she said, just to prove she knew something.

"Not people," the silver being said dismissively. "Other beings in the Light."

"Ah, yeah, right," Meg said. "That's what I meant."

The Light of Corometh twinkled over the green recruits, binding them for eternity. The Prism tapped the next fork and the yellow flag began to wave.

The silver being spoke in a reverent tone. "These are Carriers. They assist in crossing over—both in life and in death."

"Hey," Meg said, suddenly interested. "I know these guys. I think one of them brought me here."

"Of course," the silver being agreed. "They bring everyone here, for the most part."

Meg was thrilled to finally have the opportunity to prove she wasn't completely out of it.

The next note caused the Prism to change to orange and thousands of recruits moved toward the flag of the same colour.

"Advisors," the silver being said. "They document the evolution of each soul and make decisions to help the individual achieve its goal. They work exclusively with the Keepers of the Charts and the Messengers."

Meg nodded. "That's great." She'd stopped listening again. There were only two orders left. When would she feel the call? The silver being didn't appear concerned, though she was sure she could sense its anticipation.

The Prism raised the silver mallet. It paused, as though wondering which fork to sound next. With a sharp blow, it struck the last and largest fork. A deep moan vibrated through the room. The Prism shuddered and the light bled from its form. It stood before the assembly, black as death. A telepathic gasp rose from the crowd. Meg was terrified.

"What is it?"

"Nightshades," the silver being whispered. "Never in my existence have I heard this note struck. They are the transporters of dark entities—ones that cannot be transformed. They work alone, and do not fraternize with other Frequencies."

The crowd fell back to either side of the hall. A small group of beings, only three hundred or so, stood in the middle of the floor. They shook and convulsed, the moaning growing louder and louder. Meg covered her ears, afraid she was going to fly apart.

With great effort, the Nightshades lurched toward the stage. The white flag hung limply from its pole. There was a sound, like water sucking through a gigantic drain, and the flag turned black.

The Nightshades writhed, falling to their knees, their screams mingling with the moans of the vibrating fork. Meg cried out as several recruits burst and vaporized, a horrible sulphurous smell filling the room. The other Nightshades struggled through the transformation until they were completely and utterly black. They no longer radiated light like the other beings, but absorbed it. When the last recruit was transformed, the moaning stopped and the Prism grew bright again.

Meg lowered her hands from her ears and waited for the Light of Corometh to bind the dark ones. It didn't appear.

"Are they bad?" she asked.

"No," the silver being said. "There are no bad beings in the Light. Nightshades work with profound evil and must move undetected through it. Should they be captured, the Light of Corometh would only reveal the location of their brethren and endanger them all."

"Why were some destroyed during the transformation?"

"They resisted the frequency."

"But, what if they didn't want to be Nightshades?"

"They are what they are," the silver being said. "Their role is essential."

"Why does evil exist at all?" Meg persisted. "Why don't you just prevent it—or destroy it altogether?"

"There has always been free will. That is the gift of the Light. Darkness is a choice."

"But . . . the Nightshades had no choice," Meg said, becoming emotional. Hadn't she experienced the same thing? Wasn't she forced to transform whether she liked it or not? "Where was their free will?"

The silver being was getting irritated. "The frequencies are innate. They exist from the beginning."

"But—"

"Enough," the being silenced her.

Obviously there was a double standard here, Meg thought. Free will wasn't for everyone. Some were apparently freer than others.

The Prism raised the silver mallet. The entire crowd shrank with trepidation. Everyone, including Meg, stared at the red flag. The second-last fork was hit, and a clear, low sound rang across the hall.

"Warriors," the silver being said.

Something flared inside her. But it fizzled out quickly, leaving a hollowness in its wake. Meg watched, bewildered, as the remaining recruits glided toward the stage. The red flag waved and the recruits glistened with a corresponding glow as the Light of Corometh bound them. The silver being looked expectantly at her.

"Did you not feel the call? It is a great honour to be a Warrior."

Meg didn't answer. Something was stirring in her body, though it wasn't in response to the call. She stood alone with the silver being before the Council and the questioning eyes of the multitudes. The voices of the other recruits rose, their confused chatter a roaring hurricane in her head. If she'd felt different from everyone else before, it was nothing compared to the way she felt now. I'm a freak, she thought. I don't belong anywhere.

The gold beings huddled, throwing glances at her. They debated for the longest time before breaking and sitting back in their seats.

"Approach," one of the Council members ordered.

The silver being glided obediently toward the stage. Meg was bolted in place. "You must do as the Council says," it told her.

Meg felt a pulse, throbbing in her chest, growing stronger. Was she going to explode like the Nightshades? If she could just move. She centered her thoughts, willing herself to glide. *I'm a leaf on the water,* she told herself. *I am a leaf* . . . Her body started to shake. Then she dropped to the floor as though pushed, twitching and jerking, her colour spiralling through the different shades of the frequencies. The recruits recoiled in horror. The Councillors stood from their seats, gripping the edge of the table. There was a scorching muzzle flash and Meg shot through the ether like a bullet through water. Lights swirled around her in incandescent webs. She was moving too fast. She was going to break into pieces with the speed. She suddenly hit something, hard, and fell to the ground in a heap.

Meg was no longer cowering beneath the scrutiny of the Council in the Great Hall. She was on her hands and knees, freezing, fingers buried in a fine grey powder. The wind howled, whipping her hair in wild tendrils around her face. She rose to her feet, shielding her eyes against the icy gale. The sky fell down to meet her in an endless stretch of grey. Frozen twigs poked like beard stubble throughout the landscape. She looked at her hands. The tin-coloured powder fell away from her fingers in a disintegrating shadow. Ash. Everything had been reduced to ash. Where was she?

A deep moan climbed over the wail of the wind. It was if the land were weeping. The wind took form and faces birthed from the ether, mouths and eyes gaping. The moaning grew and a profound sadness overwhelmed her. It was her fault—all of it— the sea of ash, the frozen remains of trees, the wailing souls, damned for all eternity. Somehow, she was responsible. "Please, stop," she sobbed. The tortured faces surrounded her. Teeth flashed, fingers groped through the grey. They clawed at her arms and legs, tore at her robe. She pushed them away but the tormented spirits kept coming.

"I can't help you!" she cried.

Drawing herself in, Meg conjured an image of the Great Hall and imagined herself there. The hungry souls plundered her consciousness, ripping the image from her mind. She fought back, reaching for the narrow band of light. With a loud whip crack, Meg hurtled forward, tearing away from the grasping hands. Streaking back through the ether, she landed in a wind-blown mess before the shocked faces of the recruits. The room exploded in telepathic turmoil. A gavel hammered on the table.

"Order!" one of the Councillors demanded.

"What happened?" the silver being practically shouted in her head. When it saw the haunted look in her eyes it collected itself. Searching her face, its own eyes grew wide as it understood. "You . . . you fell between the frequencies."

Meg swooned, listing to one side.

"No one has ever returned from between the frequencies in the same form," the silver being said. "It's not possible."

The gavel hammered again. "Order, please!"

"You mustn't tell a soul," the silver being instructed her, then prostrated itself before the Council, its face nearly touching the hem of its robe.

Meg did the same, bowing as dramatically as she could given her troubled state.

"Rise," one of the golden beings ordered. It fastened its unwavering eyes on her. "Did you not feel the call of the Warriors?"

Meg shook her head. This caused a new wave of confusion in the Hall. The Council huddled together, speaking as though she were no longer there. She couldn't help eavesdropping.

"Is it mute?" one asked.

"Look at its appendage," one muttered. "It's the oddest thing."

"And its shape," another spoke. "It's so strange."

"Is it female?" another asked.

"What about its colour? We've never seen a magenta recruit before. Has it been contaminated?"

"It's so small."

"What could have caused such an aberration?"

"Why did it leave the room, and where did it go?"

"Who can say?"

"Then what shall we do with it?" one asked.

There was a long pause as the Council members pondered this conundrum.

"It seemed to respond to the frequency of the Warriors," one said. "Why not place it there?"

"What if we are wrong? Should we not seek higher counsel?"

"We are the Great Council," another asserted. "We are supposed to know what to do, not go running for help like senseless recruits."

"But this is most unusual."

"Most unusual indeed."

"Perhaps we should ask it," one member suggested.

"Good idea."

The whole time the golden beings were discussing the matter, the silver being was bowing lower and lower, until Meg thought it would disappear through the floor. She was about to throw herself at the mercy of the Council when one of them addressed her directly.

"Did you feel anything at all during any point in the Ceremony of Spectral Frequencies?"

There was a heavy silence as every being in the Great Hall held its thoughts, waiting for her to answer. Meg shifted on her feet, hiding her scarred arm in the folds of her robe.

"Does it understand us?" a frustrated Council member asked.

"Yes, I understand," Meg finally spoke.

The room erupted again.

"It speaks with its mouth," one of the Councillors gasped.

"I did feel something," Meg continued, the Council members staring at her lips as she talked. "The Warriors—I felt some kind of resonance with them."

"Did I not tell you!" a Council member said. "It belongs to the Warrior Frequency."

"Do you think it will be all right?" another asked.

"We'll try it there and see what happens."

This satisfied the Councillors who unanimously agreed that putting Meg somewhere was better than nowhere at all. They turned to the Prism. The being raised its silver mallet and hit all eight forks at once. A dissonant chord filled the air. It twined to the ceiling, growing in volume and sweeping through the Hall in a freight train of sound. It tore at the coloured banners, bending the recruits in half with its force. Meg leaned into it, using all her power to hold fast. Whatever changes she would undergo she would accept, no matter what.

When the wind stopped, she looked at herself. Her magenta glow was gone, and the scar on her defective arm was more visible than before. The Light of Corometh hadn't appeared for her either. She turned to the silver being in dismay.

It blinked back at her. "Your eyes are a deeper shade of violet."

Meg shrugged. "I guess that's something."

The Prism left the stage, followed by its two silver beings. The Council members exchanged looks.

"Now what?" one said.

The Councillor with the gavel hammered it down on the table. "Take your place among the Warriors," it ordered.

The silver being nodded at Meg. She joined the Warriors, reluctantly, the recruits eyeing her warily.

The gavel struck the table one last time. "All right," the Council member said with some relief. "Let us begin the next phase."

5

HEX

C addy woke in a darkened room. An antique glass oil lamp glowed beside her on a small wooden table. Her hands had been cleaned and wrapped in cloth bandages. She touched her forehead. Her brain throbbed. Her tongue felt like tinfoil and the acrid taste of solvent lingered in her mouth. She was slumped in a worn green upholstered chair that looked as though it had been dragged from the garbage. Her whole body ached. How long had she been sitting here? She pushed herself upright, causing small grenades of light to burst across her field of vision. Raising her head, she caught her breath when she saw a woman staring back at her from a chair across the room.

Eyes scanning, Caddy searched for a way out and found the man who'd abducted her standing in front of the door. There was nowhere to go.

The woman spoke, her voice heavy with a Russian accent. "Please, don't be alarmed."

Caddy squinted through the subdued light. She could see now that the woman was really just a girl—twenty-two at most—not much older than herself. Her skin was smooth and pale. Her blond hair was pulled back in a severe ponytail and covered with a blue cotton kerchief, accentuating her prominent cheekbones and lips. The oil lamp offered little light, yet the girl wore sunglasses. She had the beauty and poise of a debutante, though her clothes were plain.

"What do you want from me?" Caddy said, her tongue clumsy in her mouth.

"I should ask you the same thing."

"I want to go home."

"I'm afraid that's impossible."

"Please, I don't understand . . . I just want to go home. I haven't done anything—" Her voice broke, betraying her fear.

"Are you thirsty?" the girl asked. She made a small movement with her hand. The man filled a glass with water from a tarnished metal pitcher and placed it on the table next to Caddy's chair.

"Please, take it," the girl said.

Caddy looked at the glass with suspicion.

"It is safe, I assure you," the girl said. "It will help remove the taste of solvent from your mouth."

"Why should I trust you?"

"We don't wish to harm you."

This made Caddy angry. She pointed at the man. "He put a bag over my head. He nearly suffocated me. And he broke my phone."

"Necessary precautions," the girl said.

"Against what?"

The girl's face was stoic, the light from the oil lamp reflecting in her glasses. It was clear she wouldn't be easily intimidated. Caddy tried a different tack.

"Please, just tell me what's going on."

The girl relaxed into her chair. Her voice softened. "What brought you to the warehouses?"

Caddy didn't answer. She wasn't sure it was a good idea to tell this girl anything.

"We only want to help you," the girl said.

Caddy stole a look at the man. So he hadn't intended to kill her as she'd feared. At least, not yet. They wanted something from her. If there was any hope for escape, she'd have to play along. "I found an address, written on a slip of paper."

"Where?"

"At home."

"What made you want to pursue it? It was just a slip of paper with a meaningless address. Why would you seek it out?"

Caddy crossed her arms.

"Please," the girl said. "We're concerned for your safety. We think you're in danger."

Danger? Who's the one being played? Caddy wondered. Maybe the girl knew more than she was letting on. Maybe she knew something about her father. She would tell her enough to get her to tip her hand.

"I don't know, really . . . except that it seemed weird—mysterious, somehow, to find an address like that. I was . . . curious. I just wanted to see what was there."

"And what did you discover?"

"Nothing. I couldn't find the place. There were no numbers or anything. I was going to leave and then some men showed up."

"The men in grey suits."

Caddy's heart jumped. So the girl did know. "Yes. They started chasing me. I panicked. I ran." She gestured at the man. "And then he grabbed me."

"Red Cloud," the girl said, naming the man. "But he just goes by Red. He likely saved your life. Do you know who those men are?"

"The ones in grey suits?" Caddy asked.

The girl nodded. "Did they speak to you?"

"No." Caddy looked at her hands. They'd started to shake. She felt nauseous, the taste of the solvent coming back to her. She reached for the glass of water and took a small sip. It was cold and clean on her parched tongue. She took another sip and placed the glass back on the table. What if it was laced with something? At this point, did it really matter? She couldn't escape if she tried.

"Did your father ever tell you anything?" the girl asked.

I knew it, Caddy thought. It was her father they were interested in. She tried to appear calm, steadying her voice. "About what?"

The girl leaned forward, her face glowing in the lamplight. Slowly raising her hand, she removed her sunglasses. Where her left eye should have been was a dark, sunken knot. "They did this to me." She fixed on Caddy with her good eye. It was as blue as a summer sky, its beauty in violent contrast to the obscenity of the empty socket. Replacing her sunglasses, she sat back in the shadows. "The men in grey suits are a cabalistic society, dedicated to the dark forces. They follow an entity they call The One. It is an ancient society, older than the Rosicrucians, though not as old as the entity itself, which is older than time."

Caddy touched her safe stone with her bandaged hand. "What does this have to do with my father?"

The girl motioned to Red again. He gave Caddy a thick, leather-bound tome. It was deadweight heavy and seemed to whisper in a near-audible voice, like it was trying to speak to her, like it had a life of its own. The pages were thick—made of some kind of skin—and smelled of must and antiquity.

"Open it," the girl said.

Caddy opened the book with one hand, the other still holding her safe stone. The pages were illustrated with ancient block prints of the most disturbing scenes. People bound and hanging by ropes. People impaled on stakes. It made her feel sick to look at them. The girl studied Caddy's reaction as she flipped through the pages, the whispers growing louder with every turn. At the image of a decapitation, Caddy slammed the book shut. The thing should be burned. The girl motioned for Red to take it and Caddy practically threw it at him. She felt lighter the second it left her hands.

"Satanists?" she asked.

"Not exactly," the girl said. "But their goal is similar—to assist the dark energies on the earth plane. They desire total annihilation."

She's talking about the Emptiness, Caddy thought. Hadn't her visions warned her of something like that all along? Was this the connection to her father? It was clear the girl was deranged, though, some kind of radical who'd gone off the deep end. The last thing Caddy wanted was to trigger her or add fuel to the fire of her delusions. Who knew what she was capable of?

"Why would anyone want that?"

The girl folded her hands together. "To create a world where the forces of evil enjoy complete control. Power is their prime directive. Power over the Light and those who serve it."

"People do all kinds of crazy things," Caddy said. "Evil has always existed. So far, the earth is still here—as messed up as it is."

"Look around you. It doesn't take a genius to see that things are unravelling faster than ever before. We've reached critical mass." The girl tilted her head slightly. "Are you aware of who's responsible for the current state of affairs?"

"The men in grey suits?" Caddy answered innocently.

The girl gave a small smile. She paused, no doubt assessing Caddy's sincerity. "The Company."

"The Company . . ." Caddy repeated.

"Yes. The men in grey suits work for the Company. They dress in the image of The One. The Company is in league with dark forces. It's funding the war—a perfect cover for its activities. The war is simply a sleight of hand, a distraction on the world stage from the real trick, the systematic divestment of governmental power, the systematic control of global wealth. When that is achieved, they will usher in The One and his dark armies, and their dream of annihilation will be closer to reality."

Caddy slowly righted herself in her seat. God knows she'd heard her father say enough bad things about the Company. But the idea that it was in league with dark forces hell-bent on total annihilation was insane. Not even her father had pushed it that far. She judged the distance to the oil lantern. She could throw it at the girl if she had to.

"So, the Company men are killing people, and this is allowing dark forces to take over on earth."

"In a nutshell, yes."

"There have always been wars and destruction," Caddy said.

"And the planet can no longer sustain the abuses," the girl continued. "The Dreamers have been struggling for centuries to push back the Dark. But we're losing ground. The Dark is too powerful. So many people in the world have given up hope. We're on the brink of defeat. The entire planet and all we hold sacred will be destroyed."

"The Dreamers?" Caddy said.

"The ones who work for the Light."

Right. Caddy had had enough. She positioned her bandaged hands casually on her legs in case she needed to move quickly. "Obviously this is important to you . . . but I don't see what it has to do with me."

"Those men would have killed you," the girl said.

"Then I have you to thank for my life. But I'm sick, and I'm tired, and I want to go home to see my father."

"I told you, that isn't possible."

"Why not?"

"Because your father is already dead."

Caddy lunged for the lamp but Red was too fast for her. He pushed her back into the chair and held her down.

"Let me out of here!" Caddy screamed. "I want to go home— now!"

Red restrained her until her anger broke into tears. The girl let her cry for a while before she spoke again.

"There was nothing we could do. They traced your address

through your phone. Your father was already targeted. It's amazing he lasted as long as he did."

Caddy wiped her face with the sleeve of her jacket. "What did he ever do to them? Why would they kill him?"

The girl leaned into the lamplight again. "Because he was one of us," she said. "He was a Dreamer."

6

THE MOUSE

The recruits filed from the Great Hall into the streets, parading with their flag-bearers to a large green field. Meg hung back when the Warriors began to move, looking to the silver being for guidance.

"You must go," it said. "And remember to keep your mouth closed."

"But who will help me?" she asked. "Who will tell me what to do?"

"You will know in your soul."

Meg didn't have a clue what was in her soul. It was a twisted knot. She'd made such a mess of things—refusing to transform like the others, clinging to her past so fiercely. And now, after falling between the frequencies and failing the initiation ceremony, she was more upset and confused than ever.

"I'm afraid," she said.

The silver being touched her forehead and a sense of tranquility washed over her.

"I will check on you when I can," it said. "Go now. You are no longer my charge. You are bound to the Warriors and must answer the call."

Meg turned, obedient, though she didn't want to face the scrutiny of the other recruits. Gliding from the building, she glanced back and saw the silver being watching her. It raised its hand in farewell. She raised hers in return, feeling lonelier than ever. She had no choice but to follow the other Warriors to the meadow.

After the recruits had assembled in the field, a trumpet sounded and a new being appeared. It looked similar to the silver one, only fiercer and bigger. And it was the colour of pewter. It skimmed up and down the ranks, communicating telepathically.

"You will now receive your totem. This is your animal aid. It will assist you and offer guidance and friendship. It will be your eyes and ears. It will resonate with your thoughts and feelings. But it will not make decisions for you. Any action you take, any decision you make, is ultimately your own." The being slowed as it passed Meg, taking note of her arm. She thought it would say something disparaging, but it simply continued its address. "You do not choose your totem. Your totem chooses you. Stay in position until your totem has made positive contact."

The being signalled to start the selection and the trumpet blared. Clouds gathered, and the ground tore open with the sound of ripping fabric, the animals bursting forth. The first to come were the elephants, lions and wolves. The sky darkened with flocks of saw-whet owls, ravens, falcons, doves and canaries. To the Keepers of the Charts came the elephants. To the Messengers flew the saw-whet owls. The canaries found the Musicians; the wolves chose the Advisors; the doves fluttered to the Carriers. The falcons soared to meet the Healers, who received them with outstretched hands. To the Nightshades, the ravens flew, their dark forms merging seamlessly with the lightless beings. And to the Warriors, the lions came, with flowing manes and fathomless gold eyes.

Within minutes, each recruit had a totem and was ready for the next challenge. Except Meg. She looked around despondently

The cavernous opening in the ground rumbled closed, disappearing without a trace.

The pewter being hovered nearby, radiating disapproval. "Each recruit must have a totem." It skimmed through the ranks, searching for a totem that may have lost its way. There were none. "You will have to make do," it told Meg.

She wanted to cry. She wanted to fly from the meadow. Then the grass wiggled at her feet. It tickled her toes and she laughed when a small grey mouse appeared, scurried up her robe and sat on her shoulder next to her ear.

"Excuse my tardiness," it said. "Darned elephants nearly flattened me."

"Are you my totem?" Meg asked.

"Yes." The mouse began grooming itself.

"You're not a lion."

The mouse chuckled. "Not since the last time I checked."

The recruits turned as one to stare at the small creature on Meg's shoulder. She forced a smile and tried to look casual. Before the gossip could start, seven additional pewter beings appeared and signalled for the trumpet to sound the beginning of the next challenge. At the blast of the horn, the recruits and their totems fell into line behind their flag bearers, following their pewter beings to their respective training grounds. Only the Nightshades didn't go with the rest. They were spirited away to an undisclosed location to train in secret.

The Warriors glided in formation, their lions trotting beside them. The mouse busily groomed itself on Meg's shoulder, unaware of their odd pairing.

"There is value in all things, no matter the size," it finally said.

Meg felt guilty. "I'm sorry. I didn't mean to insult you with my thoughts."

"I was referring to you."

"Oh."

The mouse rubbed its small pink hands over its whiskers. "In time our purpose will be revealed."

"Do you know our purpose?"

"No."

Meg drooped. She'd hoped it could shed some light on the matter. "Does everyone get a totem?" she asked.

"No. Just those that need them."

"So . . . those with a Frequency need them . . ."

"Every being possesses a Frequency," the mouse said. "Only the Spectral frequencies—the single wavelengths—have totems. It helps to unify you in your purpose."

Once again Meg felt confused. Did everything have to be a riddle?

The mouse fussed with the hairs on the back of her neck. "It's best if you stop questioning and simply accept," it advised.

Meg didn't care, really, who had a totem and who didn't. She was just happy to have someone to talk to, even if the mouse was kind of stuffy. "Do you have a name?" she asked.

"We have no use for names here."

Meg sighed. "That's what everyone keeps telling me. I had a name once . . . I just can't remember it."

"Attachments are unnecessary and cumbersome," the mouse said. "Your name is a relic of your former life. It's time to let it go."

"But I want a name. It would make me happy. What am I supposed to call you? And what will you call me?"

The mouse clucked. "There's no need for calling. We'll evolve together, becoming telepathically linked as the bond between us grows. I will feel what you feel. I will see what you see. And vice versa. Names are restrictive."

"Names are comforting," Meg said. She thought about this for a moment. "I'm not sure why, but they are. I really want a name. And you should have one too. How about . . . Sebastian. That sounds nice. It's a boy's name, I think. And you can call me . . .

Skylark." It was the first thing that popped into her head but she liked it already. "From now on, my name is Skylark. I won't answer unless you call me this."

"If you insist. It makes no difference to me."

Skylark fell silent, rolling the sound of her new name around in her head as she glided with the other Warriors. At last the flag bearer planted its banner in the ground. The pewter being stood at the head of the ranks.

"This is one of the most important ceremonies a Warrior will experience," it said. "The Weapons Ceremony represents the final stage in the galvanization of your frequency. Warriors are known for their dedication, bravery and capability. While there are no favourites in the Light, your role in the Unfolding is of utmost importance."

The recruits listened intently, lions at their feet. The mouse was tickling the hairs on Skylark's neck again. It was distracting.

"What's the Unfolding?" she asked.

The mouse twitched his nose. "Well . . . the Unfolding is the evolution of the universe . . . which is only possible through the Light. The purpose of the Light is to create, and to allow everything within it to create, thereby allowing the universe to evolve and expand, and everything within it evolves and expands accordingly."

He sounded just like the silver being. "Is something trying to prevent the universe from evolving?"

The mouse scratched behind his ear with one foot. "Yes. The Dark. It hates the Light and everything in it. It wants to destroy the Light."

"Why?"

"To gain power."

"So, how are things supposed to evolve without the Light?"

"They don't," the mouse said. "That's the point. The Dark desires stasis, not growth. It wants to keep things frozen for all eternity."

"Oh, of course." She thought she had it. "So, Warriors fight the Dark to prevent it from gaining power?"

"Yes!" the mouse said. "But the Warriors only fight the Dark in this dimension ... though any victory we experience here helps secure the Light on the earth plane."

Skylark sighed. It was getting complicated again. "You mean, if we lose the battle here, the Dark can take control of the earth?"

"Kind of. It is up to us to control the Dark here, and for people on earth to control the Dark there. What happens here affects them there. What happens there affects us here."

"What if they don't control the Dark on earth?" Skylark asked. "What if people just give up?"

The mouse pondered her question. "Then it makes our job much more difficult. We really need to work together to help each other."

The pewter being glided by, glowering at Skylark. She straightened herself and pretended to pay attention. As soon as it passed, she picked up where she left off with the mouse. "Why is everything so confusing here?"

"Don't let it bother you," the mouse said. "All you need to know is that the Dark is bad. The Light is good. You fight the Dark. Get it?"

Skylark made a face. "Yeah, thanks."

The pewter being gave her another biting look before continuing its address. "The weapon of the Warrior is the sword and shield. Today, as you received your totem, so shall you receive your weapon. It will become an extension of you. It will bond with you as you bond with your totems and each other. It is a manifestation of your intention and an expression of the Light's will."

The being moved to one side to reveal endless rows of swords, scabbards, belts and shields, all bearing the lion insignia. "Recruits with weapons stand to the left and wait until the others are finished the ceremony."

The recruits lined up to receive their weapons, one after the other. They moved quickly, and once outfitted, gathered in a group to the left of the field.

"I don't think there's a shield with a mouse on it," Skylark joked as she waited for her turn. She tried to peek over the shoulder of the recruit in front of her but it was too tall. When she reached the head of the line, there was a row of swords hovering in the air. She raised her hand to take the closest one and the sword flew away, clattering to the ground as if pulled by a wire. What was wrong with it? The pewter being stared at the errant sword, then pointed to the next. Skylark reached for it, and this sword flew away too, as did the next and the next, until a dozen swords littered the ground. The recruits watched with detached fascination as sword after sword flew away. Eventually, the pewter being grabbed a sword from the row and attempted to hand it to her. The sword sprang from her grip as though polarized. The being reached for a shield and tried to force it into her hands. It shot into the air and dropped, spinning on its edge before rattling to the ground. The recruits gaped in amazement.

"That will be enough," the being finally said when it became apparent no weapon was willing to be hers. It held its hand up to silence the troops. "Please step aside and allow the others to complete the ceremony," it told her.

Skylark moved to one side. The Warriors retreated, keeping their distance. She tried not to let it bother her, but she couldn't control her thoughts.

"They're afraid," the mouse said. "They sense the confusion of the pewter one."

"Is it confused?" she asked.

"Very."

"So am I. What does it mean?"

"It means that this is not for you."

When each recruit had a weapon, the pewter being called for order again. "Everything until now has been relatively easy," it said. "From this point forward, you will face some very difficult challenges. We will test your mettle to the fullest. We will train you to be swift and bold so you can fight the Dark in all its forms. The Dark is your enemy. The Dark hates the Light. You are of the Light, therefore the Dark hates you and everything you stand for. It will not hesitate to cut you down so you must not hesitate to strike first. Your initial challenge is sparring. Fall into pairs."

The Warriors quickly chose partners to avoid sparring with Skylark. She stood self-consciously to one side of the field, wishing she had blown up like the Nightshades during the initiation ceremony. The pewter being gave the signal and a riot of clanging swords and roaring lions ensued. By instinct, everyone knew what to do. Skylark watched with envy. What was her purpose if not to fight alongside the Warriors? Where did she belong? And what was the point of pretending to be a Warrior if she really wasn't one? She let her thoughts stray to the boy. If only she could go back and be with him. The mouse pulled her hair the second she thought this.

"Ow!"

"Stay focused on the task at hand," he scolded.

Skylark folded her arms and begrudgingly watched the recruits, trying to keep her mind from wandering. But whenever she got bored and let herself drift, the mouse would tug on her hair, until she wanted to knock him from her shoulder.

At last the pewter being gave the signal to cease fighting.

"Very good!" it said. "You have transitioned well. Your skills will improve greatly with training and experience, but for now you understand the principals of combat." It glided along the ranks. "The next challenge is flight training. We call it jumping.

It's a form of teleportation from one location to the next—without gliding. You will make ten lines and jump together in groups."

Skylark loitered near the back as the Warriors formed ranks. Once the lines were established, she slipped into a space on the end.

"Being able to move quickly and undetected is a Warrior's greatest asset," the pewter being explained. "The Dark is fast and ruthless. We must therefore be faster and braver still. Your first jump will be a short one—to the other side of the field. Once you have mastered that, we will increase the distance. And don't forget to include your totem in your flight equation. Expand your energy appropriately."

The trumpet sounded and the first ten recruits jumped. They vanished for a second, only to reappear across the field.

"Well done," the pewter being praised.

The next line of recruits performed equally well, as did the next and the next. A few unfortunates got misdirected, reappearing in the canopies of trees, or nearly landing on top of other recruits, but most were able to perform the task admirably.

When it came time for Skylark to jump, every eye was on her. She fought the urge to run, focusing all her intention on the point across the field.

"You can do it," the mouse said. "Clear your thoughts."

Her mind was in turmoil. To fail at such a simple task in front of thousands of her peers, especially after her disgrace during the Weapons Ceremony, would be humiliating.

"*I'm a leaf on the water,*" she told herself, repeating the silver being's words. "*A leaf on the water . . .*" The roaring filled her ears. The stream of stars in her head accelerated. There was a cannon blast, creating a light so bright the recruits cowered, covering their eyes. The light collapsed, and Skylark found herself standing on a city street in another dimension and time completely. A group of people gathered soberly around an old car. To one side of the scene stood a beautiful man, dressed in an expensive grey suit, a slight smile pasted on his porcelain face. Skylark's scarred arm flared with pain.

"Where are we, Sebastian?"

The mouse shook its head and looked around. "This isn't right. We shouldn't be here."

Skylark glided cautiously into the street. It was an accident scene. Someone was crushed beneath the wheels of a car. There was a mass of bloodied hair. A bare foot stuck out from under the vehicle. And there was a shoe. A blue sneaker. Lying in the middle of the road. The pain in her arm was bone-splitting.

"I know this," she moaned. "For some reason, I know this."

The man in the suit turned, the sound of tinkling glass accompanying him as his frozen eyes met hers, shattering a hole in her consciousness.

Skylark staggered back, her mind spinning with images—the car, the lifeless girl beneath its wheels, the perfect man in his perfect suit—those horrible eyes! She'd seen them before, during her transformation. What torments had they witnessed? Who was this man and what did he want from her?

"We must go," the mouse insisted. "Put it out of your mind and hold your thoughts on the practice field."

Sebastian tightened his grip on her hair as Skylark forced her mind back to the training field and the hordes of recruits standing there. The roaring grew louder and the stars began to run. At the last moment, her mind tripped, and they hurtled wildly through the ether, landing with an undignified thud in the middle of a field. They looked around, dazed. Something was wrong again. The Warriors and their lions were nowhere in sight. Bullets and cannonballs flew through the air. Bodies of the dead and wounded lay everywhere. Men in uniforms—some beige, some blue—were strewn over the ground. Soldiers ran past, shouting and firing. The sky was black with discharged gunpowder. Among the men, Carriers glided through the chaos, doves on their shoulders.

The mouse blinked against the musket fire. "This isn't the right field," he said. "This isn't even the right dimension. We're on the earth plane—in the Civil War. How did we end up here?"

Skylark floated over the trampled ground, the pain and terror of the men cutting through her. A wounded soldier lifted his hand to touch her robe. His gun lay next to him like an amputated limb. Blood dribbled from his mouth. "Please . . ."

Skylark knelt beside him. He was so young. Just a boy, really. No older than the boy she loved. His eyes settled on hers. "He can see me . . ."

"The dying can," the mouse said. "It's their soul's quickening pace, vibrating in frequency with your own in preparation for the Crossing. You will come to understand this and control your response to it."

Skylark could see the man's spirit flickering at the edge of his physical form.

"My darling," he murmured.

A shiver ran through her body. It thrilled and saddened her to hear such words from this dying man's lips. Hadn't she lost something similar? Hadn't she once been held and loved? She groped for something to say, something to express the feelings she had for him in his pain. All she could say was, "I'm here."

The man coughed and clutched his chest. Skylark opened his coat. The lapels flapped back, revealing a tattered, bloody wound, blossoming like a red flower across his shirt. He convulsed, once, and death stole the light from his eyes.

"No . . . please, don't go." Skylark cradled his head in her arms, grief and loneliness pouring over her. It was too much. Too much to bear.

Someone squeezed her shoulder. Skylark looked up and saw a yellow being standing over her.

"I am this man's Carrier," it said, placing the dove in the man's hand. His spirit rose in a swirl of mist, entering the bird. The dove took to the air with its Carrier, its wings a blur of expanding light.

"We can't stay any longer," the mouse said.

Skylark clenched her fists, anger mounting. How could she reconcile such pain and loss?

"It is but a shadow," the mouse explained. "A fragment of another time. You must let it go."

"No!" she cried. "It isn't fair!" She rocketed into the sky, a wall of light shooting from her hands. It hit the advancing armies, blowing men to the ground like leaves. The soldiers dropped their weapons, their faces lit with dread as they looked upon the terrifying face of divine retribution. Skylark soared higher and higher, corkscrewing through the air, the mouse clinging to her hair.

"Stop!" it shouted. "It is not your place to interfere. These scenes are already written!"

A group of Carriers swept in, forcing Skylark back with beams of light. She dropped to the ground, scrambled to her feet and jumped. Burning through the ether, she landed in the centre of the practice field, and just in time to dodge the crushing blow of another recruit's sword. She was in the right place but at the wrong time—back in the sparring exercise. Swords rained down around her. Lions roared. Grabbing the arm of another recruit, Skylark wielded its shield to avoid several vicious blows then jumped from the fray and landed clumsily at the feet of another recruit. This one halted mid-strike.

"You have no weapon."

Skylark stood and brushed herself off. The recruit looked at her scarred arm.

"Beings are talking," it said. "The Council doesn't know what to do with you. Some of the recruits think you're a demon."

She frowned. "And what do you think?"

The recruit looked at her dispassionately. "I think you've lost your totem."

Skylark's hand flew to her shoulder. It was true! In her rage, she must have lost the mouse on the battlefield! She had to go back. But how? And when?

The pewter being glided over, visibly perturbed. Skylark turned her back on it, hoping it wouldn't notice that her totem was AWOL.

"Recruits without weapons cannot participate in the sparring exercise." It pointed to a neutral zone outside the melee, indicating that she should go there. Then it raised its hand in the air, stopping the battle and silencing the Warriors.

She knew what was coming next: the jumping exercise. This time she would get it right. No reckless rides through time and space. Just a simple trip across the field with the rest of the recruits . . .

The Warriors filed to one side of the field in orderly ranks, creating ten lines. When it came time for Skylark to jump, she eased her mind and compressed her thoughts. She wouldn't think of the mouse, trapped on some battlefield in another time. She wouldn't think of the dead soldier, or the boy she once knew, or the man with the frozen eyes. No. She imagined herself a leaf on the water . . . a leaf on the water . . . and she jumped, neatly, cleanly, appearing on the opposite side of the field without incident.

It was clear she wouldn't be able to go back for the mouse just yet. The pewter being was watching her with a hawk's eyes after her impromptu and weaponless battle with the recruit on the sparring field. Whatever leniency it had shown the troops earlier had dried up completely, despite their success in the jumping exercise. They were forced to glide in formation, around and around the field, the lions moving in perfect step alongside their Warriors. Back and forth, high and low, swords raised, swords lowered, again and again, until it seemed like the drill would never end.

When at last the being was satisfied that the recruits had had enough, it dismissed them to their quarters. By this time, Skylark was nearly delirious with worry about the mouse. If the pewter being had noticed Sebastian's absence, it didn't indicate as much. And she wasn't going to wait until it did. She hurried along, past Advisors with their wolves, past Messengers with their owls, past the glistening river where the willow trees trailed trembling fingers in the water. She didn't stop to look at anything. She had to get to the Hall of Records to discover exactly where and when in time she'd left the mouse behind.

7

THE DREAMERS

Caddy stared hatefully at the Russian girl sitting in front of her. "How could my father have been one of you?"

The girl adjusted her dark sunglasses, choosing her words carefully. "We are a collective of like-minded people. We've been gathering for generations, dreaming together to shape the new world."

More vagaries, Caddy thought. If the girl had information about her father she'd better get to the point. "What does that even mean?"

The girl was unruffled by Caddy's anger. "We work together to keep the Light strong and hold the Dark at bay," she said. "We do this by changing the energy on the planet. Everything that exists—every rock and tree and animal—your very thoughts—has its own unique vibration or frequency. The Light reflects all frequencies. The Dark absorbs all frequencies. The Dark is the absence of Light. When we gather, when we work together, we focus on the frequency of light energy and amplify it with our intention to push back the Dark. We call this Dreaming. Our ultimate goal is to vanquish the Dark altogether, to create a world where evil does not exist. Your father joined us as a young man. He possessed . . . an unusual talent for the work."

The idea of her father doing anything but drinking was ridiculous. "My father is an alcoholic. His only talent is hitting the bottle, which he does—a lot."

"It wasn't always that way. He came to us with many ideas. He was so hopeful."

"How could you possibly know anything about my father as a young man?" Caddy said. "You're not much older than me."

The girl dismissed the question with another. "Do you know how your mother died?"

This was too much. How dare this girl mention her mother? She may as well have slapped Caddy in the face. Caddy's voice was a knife. "Of course. A car accident."

The girl seemed amused. "Are you sure?"

"What are you getting at?"

"The truth," the girl said. "Your mother was murdered."

Now Caddy had her. "No, she wasn't. It was an accident. I saw it with my own eyes."

"That's what they want you to believe. It was a clever ruse."

"My father believed it was an accident too."

"He was protecting you from the truth." The girl reclined in her chair. "Your mother was killed by Company men—"

She sounded even crazier than before. "And now you're going to try to convince me that my mother was a Dreamer too. That's an absolute lie."

"The Company men didn't kill her because she was a Dreamer. They knew that she wasn't. They did it to . . ."—the girl searched for the right words—". . . upset your father, to create a rift in the dream. And it did. That's when he started drinking. Without him, our progress has been slow. And the Dreamers were suitably frightened."

"That's a great story," Caddy said. "And then the Company men killed him too. So, where's the body? How did they do it?" The girl stared back at her. Caddy wanted to laugh. "You don't even know."

The girl's mouth twitched, and Caddy thought she had her. She quickly regained her composure. "There's a small possibility that he's hiding. Though we are almost certain he's dead."

Her words cut Caddy to the bone, but she refused to believe her. "Why?"

"Because he hasn't contacted us."

And you were hoping he'd contacted me, Caddy thought. "What makes you so sure the Company men killed him?"

"They were there when you arrived at the address you found. Why do you think that is?"

"And now you think they're after me?"

The girl didn't answer. Was she weighing the value of telling the truth? Caddy wondered. Or simply formulating another lie?

"We believe they wanted to eliminate the possibility of substitution," she finally said.

"Substitution? What's that?"

"Dreams have a unique signature, like a fingerprint. For years the collective worked together, weaving the dreams of many people into a whole, into a stronger frequency, as the colours of the spectrum entwine to create white light. This is not easy. It's difficult to work the individual strands of the dream into a unified vision. Each Dreamer carries one thread. If we lose a Dreamer, it sets us back. The thread is broken and the dream cannot hold. It cannot manifest. Working someone else into the fabric takes time. The Company men know this and have been systematically cutting the threads. At first, we simply replaced them. We can no longer afford the luxury. We're too close to the brink. The Company men are more organized than ever, more aggressive. But we've discovered that the sons and daughters of Dreamers have the ability to . . . step in for their parents. They bring a similar thread, a similar signature. It's much faster and efficient to work this way, although some are better at it than others."

"Are you someone's daughter?" Caddy asked.

The girl rested her elbows on her knees. "Yes. And *you* are someone's daughter."

At last Caddy understood. They were recruiting her—whether she liked it or not. "No! I can't do this! I don't want to."

"You are the child of a Dreamer," the girl said. "A most important one. We know you've had visions before—just like your father. This is a very rare skill. A gift. You simply need to learn how to control your ability. We can teach you how."

Caddy buried her face in her hands. How could any of this be happening? "No."

"You are frightened. I understand. It's not easy to hear these things—to comprehend the magnitude—but hear it you must. We can no longer afford to be polite. We cannot wait for people to come searching for us the way we used to. The Dark is baying at our heels. I cannot emphasize enough that we've almost run out of time."

Caddy's voice shrivelled to a whisper. "I can't."

"We'll take you there, so you can see for yourself," the girl offered. "You're not alone. None of us are. We need each other—now more than ever."

"Take me where?"

"To a gathering of the Dreamers."

Red stepped from the shadows, the black bag dangling from his hand.

Caddy jumped to her feet. "Don't put that thing on me!"

"Please," the girl soothed. "It's for your own safety. If the Company men catch you, it's best you know as little as possible."

"How can I tell them anything?" Caddy said. "I don't even know your name. What good could I possibly be to them?"

The girl stood, as graceful as a swan. "I'm Alexandra. But people call me Hex. And you are Cadence. But people call you Caddy—except for your father. Cadence was his favourite name." She offered her hand.

Caddy refused the girl's overture. "It isn't fair that you know so much about me and I know nothing about you."

Hex lowered her hand and smiled. "I understand. I hope you will come to trust me in time."

Caddy could see the faint edge of Hex's empty eye socket through the dark lenses of her glasses. Surely she had suffered. Perhaps it made her uncompromising. All the same she couldn't be trusted. This play at intimacy was just another trick, Caddy thought. Hex had her trapped.

She didn't struggle when Red placed the sack over her head, leaving the cord loose. She would bide her time and wait for an opportunity to escape—the first chance possible. He led her from the room and down some kind of corridor, Caddy taking small, cautious steps. A door opened and she could smell gasoline again. Red guided her into the back of a vehicle and buckled her in. He pushed her down on the seat and covered her with a blanket.

"I can't breathe," she said. "It's hot. I don't like it."

"It's only for a short while," the girl promised. "It's for your own safety. Please, remain calm."

The engine started. Caddy clutched her safe stone. There was the mechanical whirr of a garage door opening. The sunlight was warm against the blanket. The car left the garage and wove through the streets. No one spoke. Caddy's head bounced lightly against the seat as she mouthed the words of her song, her stomach churning. She never did well riding in cars. She reached inside the hood to scratch her nose and held the sack open so she could get some air. Her mind raced. Would they kill her after all? And what of her father? Was he really dead? She started to panic, her breath coming shallow and fast. To control her thoughts, she counted traffic stops. After thirteen, the car pulled over and her door was opened. They removed the blanket, but to her dismay they kept the hood on and escorted her into another vehicle.

More stops and turns, and then a long, unbroken stretch. She was about to mutiny when the girl spoke.

"You can sit up now."

Caddy ripped the hood from her head. Cranking the window open, she gulped mouthfuls of fresh air, the wind tossing her hair around her face. They were on a back road, moving away from the city. Red was driving. Hex sat next to him in the passenger seat. A fence raced the car along a grassy field, the cedar posts a blur. Caddy checked the door. It was locked. Childproof. No chance to jump out.

"Where are we?" she asked.

No answer.

They made a right turn onto a gravel road, the tires kicking up a storm of dust. After several minutes, the grey hump of a barn appeared against the sky. Red slowed the car and turned into the laneway. The place seemed abandoned. The lane was grown over with tall grass that brushed past the windows as they drove. There was no house, just the gap-toothed hulk of the barn and nothing else for miles.

Red stopped the car at the end of the lane and released the lock on the doors. "You get out here."

Caddy didn't move. Was this it? Was this where her life would end?

"Let's go," Hex said. She left the car and walked toward the barn.

Caddy got out, eyes searching the field. The wind hissed through the grass in billowing waves. What if she were to run? Would she have a chance? Without a second thought she shot down the lane, arms pumping, feet flying over the ground. Red was on her like a dog. He tackled her, Caddy's bandaged hands grating through the gravel. He seized her by the arms and shook her.

"Stupid girl."

Blind fists swinging, teeth clenched, she grappled and fought. He shook her harder.

"I'm trying to protect you," he growled.

Exhausted, Caddy surrendered, her arms dropping helplessly to her sides, her face crumpling as she sobbed.

Red yanked her to her feet, and for the first time since he'd dragged her through the tunnels she looked him in the face. There was a ferocity in his eyes that made her heart pound in her throat. But there was more. A glint of earnestness she hadn't seen before, as if he were trying to convey something to her, something he didn't want Hex to see. She began to speak and he shook his head, just enough to silence her. What was he offering? An unspoken pact? A secret alliance? She needed to believe it. She had no choice. Wiping the tears from her face, she allowed him to escort her to the barn.

Hex waited at the door, her face wooden. "You are only making things more difficult for yourself," she said.

Red pushed Caddy into the barn and left her at Hex's mercy. Whatever connection they'd had moments ago was gone. She started to doubt herself immediately. Maybe she'd just imagined it.

"Come," Hex said. "The Dreamers are inside."

The barn was dark and smelled of dust and hay. Through the gloom, Caddy could make out the phantom shapes of wooden stalls. They were empty, but there was a rustling sound coming from somewhere. Hex brushed past, glasses still on, and beckoned Caddy to follow. She stopped at the foot of a small ladder that led to the hayloft, stepping to one side.

"Please," she said, indicating that Caddy should climb.

A shadowy form stood at the top of the ladder then disappeared. "Who's that?" Caddy asked.

Hex said nothing, gesturing again that Caddy was to climb, which she did, whispering her song under her breath as she went.

When Caddy reached the top of the ladder, she was astonished to see dozens of people squatting like refugees on the hay-covered floor. They looked at her with curiosity, though no one spoke. She pulled herself up. Hex followed close behind.

A middle-aged man approached and clasped Hex's hand. He nodded toward Caddy.

"Is this her?"

"Yes." Hex guided Caddy to an open space on the floor. "Sit here. You'll know what to do. Trust yourself."

Hex took a place next to the man who'd greeted her. Caddy sat down. The group lay back and she did the same, clasping her necklace in her bandaged hand. Across the loft, someone hummed a single deep note. It hovered in the air like a giant bee. The others joined in, matching the frequency, the entire barn pulsing with the vibration. The note was a narcotic in Caddy's veins. Its draw was irresistible. Her eyelids fluttered and her hand flopped to her side. In spite of her fears, in spite of everything that had happened, her mind relaxed, and her consciousness loosened. She'd pulled away from her body as easily as shedding an old coat when a hand slipped into hers. Turning her head, Caddy found Poe's deep brown eyes looking back at her.

8

MISSING IN ACTION

S kylark raced through the glistening streets of the city, impervious to the sweet song of the Musicians and their canaries. How could she appreciate anything when the mouse was lost somewhere? How could she have been so stupid? She skimmed along the sidewalk. Everywhere, there were beings and totems moving purposefully, some carrying books, some huddled in scholarly groups talking, some ascending stairs with their totems into buildings that were so shiny and tall and imposing she could never imagine having a reason to go there. What a mess she'd made of things! Overtaking a group of recruits, she caught her reflection in the window of some administrative-looking place and stopped dead. Her feminine shape and violet eyes shimmered mockingly back at her. There was no hiding her shame. She'd really screwed up this time. Sebastian was lost and it was her fault.

A group of silver beings scrutinized her as they glided by. She turned away from her reflection in disgust and continued cruising through the bustling streets. No one else seemed stressed at having lost their totem, or about interfering with the written text of the Unfolding, that was certain.

But where was she going? Skylark stopped again and nearly caused a collision with a group of Messengers gliding behind her. She apologized, thought to ask one of them for directions to the Hall of Records, then realized she need only think of the place and she would be there. Closing her eyes, she envisioned the Hall's gilded domes and ornately carved pillars. Were the stairs marble? She couldn't remember so she left that part out. She could only hope that her partial memory of the building was enough to take her there.

"I'm a leaf . . ." she whispered, "I'm a leaf on the water . . ."

In an instant she was standing at the base of the stairs, staring up at the grand entrance to the Hall. It was far more elaborate than she'd remembered. She took a tentative step onto the first stair. No alarms rang. No guards hustled out to escort her off the premises. Emboldened by the lack of response, Skylark floated as casually as possible up the stairs, swerving around a group of Chroniclers who were leaving the building. They were lost in discussion and barely noticed her as she slipped through the tall brass doors.

Skylark entered an immense room flanked by rows of arched doorways. The floors were yellow granite and glowed with the subtle lustre of a ripe pear. There was a hushed atmosphere, and she understood immediately that this was a place of great importance and learning. In the rooms beyond the doorways, beings of every Frequency hunched over tables, studying.

At the end of the main hall was another arched doorway. Adopting a serious face, Skylark conveyed herself to the room as though she had every right to be there and peeked inside. It was like looking through a porthole into a small ocean. From the domed ceiling, long spines of honey-coloured light stretched all the way to the floor. In the centre was a simple grey marble podium supporting a large, leather-bound book. Was this *The Book of Events* the silver being had spoken of? There were no

signs, no indicators of any kind. She waited, expecting someone—or something—to show up and tell her to leave. When
nothing happened, she drew closer.

The book was thick with a plain brown cover and not a single
identifying mark. Skylark ran her finger along the edge to open
it. The book was fused shut. She used a measure of force and still
it wouldn't open. She picked the thing up. It wouldn't budge. The
book had a mind of its own. How was she supposed to find the
mouse if it wouldn't cooperate? Gritting her teeth, Skylark set
upon it, yanking on the cover until the curator materialized—a
silver being with a seriously frosty attitude.

"We don't do it manually," it said disparagingly.

Skylark hid her hands in the folds of her robe and waited
for further instruction. The curator just faded out, leaving her
alone again.

"Excuse me," she said. "How do we do it?"

The being's disdainful face reappeared. "With your thoughts,
of course."

Skylark concentrated on the scene in her mind, conjuring
the soldiers in their uniforms and all the guns and smoke. She
focused on the face of the dying soldier. Sadness and anger welled
up in her, and she had to struggle not to cry. The book began to
shake. The more she thought of the scene, the angrier she grew
and the more the book shook, revving like an engine. All at once
it blew open, the pages rattling past in a blur, turning faster and
faster, the book threatening to launch off the podium and fly
across the room.

"Stop!" she shouted, and the book slammed shut.

She cringed when the curator returned.

"The book is not to be abused with negative emotions. Please
control yourself."

"Yes, sorry." Skylark smiled politely and tried to think of the
scene without feeling the pain. As soon as she thought about the

soldier, the book cracked open and began flapping faster than before. She ordered it to stop again and was just about to give up when she got an idea. She would remove herself from the scene.

Closing her eyes, she imagined the battlefield and the soldiers lying there. She contained her thoughts, avoiding the images that evoked the strongest emotions. To her delight, the book opened as if brushed by the gentlest of breezes. It serenely furled its pages and came to rest. Skylark peeked at the page. There it was before her, the entire battle scene in miniature, playing out in words and pictures like a movie. A learned voice began to narrate:

"The Seven Days Battles. American Civil War, June 25 to July 1st, 1862. Confederate leader Robert E. Lee attacks Union general McLellan near Richmond, Virginia. The battle resulted in heavy losses for both armies—"

"Thank you," Skylark said, cutting the narration short. It seemed rude, but she didn't have time to listen to some long-winded explanation right now. She had to find the mouse.

And then she had an idea—the kind that would likely get her into trouble. What if she were to ask about the boy? She convinced herself that her situation couldn't possibly get any worse, and decided to summon the face of the boy in her mind. The book's pages slowly flipped and there he was, sitting on the steps of a school, reading! Her soul nearly leapt from her body. It had actually worked!

"Go to a time when we were together," she said.

Pages turned and stopped. The boy was holding a girl—a beautiful blond girl with soft grey eyes. Skylark's particles ignited at the sight of her. She had the loveliest face. Who was this magnificent human?

It came to her in a burst of light. *She* was the grey-eyed girl! This exquisite creature in front of her was her human self. Joy surged through her. She could actually feel the weight of the boy's embrace, as though he were holding her, right here, right now. She watched him kiss the girl and her own lips sparked as if electrified.

"What are their names?" she whispered.

"Walters, Megan," the book recited in its neutral voice. "Edgar, Allan. Also known as Poe."

At the sound of his name, Skylark swooned. The dam broke in her mind and the lake of human memories flooded over her. Her knees shook as she gripped the podium, barely able to keep herself from flying apart, the images tumbling over her in roiling waves of emotion. Her entire life in blistering seconds. From the moment she came bawling into the world, through every childhood loss and victory. Her parents' faces flashing in and out. Her friends, her frustrations, her bliss. Her home! With its red-brick walls and hollyhocks in the garden. And then the haunting strains of the loveliest song she'd ever heard. She was a young girl, standing on her father's feet, dancing in slow circles across the living room, her mother looking on with so much love.

"Skylark," her father called her. "My little Skylark." It was his favourite song.

Glistening tears of liquid light streamed down her face and dropped onto her robe. The memories collided and swirled past—until they reached her life with him. Here they began to slow, every image of Poe causing a deep tremor of longing in her soul. How fine he was to her! How much fun they used to have together! Just looking at him made her dizzy with happiness. Every kiss, every caress made her burn ever brighter for him. She was Meg and he was Poe. Together. Forever. And look! There she was, riding her bike to school to meet him. She could feel the breeze in her hair, feel the thrill of anticipation, her feet pushing against the pedals—

The reel of images abruptly broke, flickering like old film before disappearing altogether. Skylark cried out in anguish. "No! Bring him back!"

The sound of her voice echoed off the alabaster walls. The book had closed. Skylark paced around the room in desperation. She had to see him again. What was stopping her from going to him, right now . . . ?

The mouse. She felt a stab of conscience when she thought of him. She was duty-bound to retrieve Sebastian before she did anything else. She had no choice. He was a part of her now. Biting her tongue, she suppressed a scream of resentment. She would return for Poe, she promised herself. The second she got a chance. No matter what. Now that she knew he was real, now that she knew how to find him, she would never rest until she held him in her arms again.

Skylark streaked from the Hall, immune to the inquisitive looks from passersby. She searched the streets for a quiet place to make the jump. She wanted to be alone when she transported herself, in case something went wrong.

Several blocks from the Hall she found a peaceful little garden with a small stream trickling from a limestone boulder. There was a stone bench beside a cluster of pink lilies. Perching on the bench, Skylark slowed her mind, reluctantly pushing Poe from her thoughts as she focused her intention on the place in time where the Seven Days Battle had happened. The rumbling began and the stars blurred. With a vigorous cork pop, she appeared in the middle of the field. She looked around. The air was clear and silent, the battlefield empty. Was she too late?

A solitary bluebird called. Skylark drifted, a lonely ghost on the war-torn landscape, searching for Sebastian. When she couldn't find him, she sat on a rock beneath the canopy of a giant maple tree and agonized. Now that she was here, the weight of her situation fell heavily upon her. She'd lost her totem. She'd let Sebastian down. How could she have been so selfish? She hadn't thought about him once the whole time she was looking for Poe. She was so caught up in herself, in her memories of her human life. She couldn't think straight when it came to Poe. Just thinking about him made her crazy. She was messed up, a jumble of self-pity and shame. Tears filled her eyes. She covered her face with her hands.

"Oh, Sebastian. I'm so sorry."

After several minutes of crying, she heard a voice.

"What ails you, child?"

Skylark raised her head with a loud sniffle. "Hello?"

The wind rustled the leaves of the tree. She was utterly alone. Now she was hallucinating on top of everything else. The tears began again.

"Why do you cry?" the voice asked.

Skylark sat upright. "Who are you?"

"Ask me what I am."

"All right. What are you?"

"I am Sugar Maple."

Skylark twisted around to look at the tree. Its bark was scarred with bullet holes. Several limbs lay broken on the ground, blown from their sockets. "I'm sorry," she said. "I don't mean to be impolite . . . but am I sitting next to you?"

"I'm sitting next to you," the maple corrected her.

"Oh."

"What are you?"

She wiped the tears from her face. "That's a good question. Maybe you can tell me."

"Well . . . you're too small for a Warrior. I've seen many of those over the years. And you're too big for a sylph. I give up. Tell me."

"I honestly don't know."

"Is that why you cry?"

Her shoulders sagged. "I'm not right," she confessed. "I didn't transform properly. I'm stunty and my appendage is . . . wrong." She held up her bound arm for the tree to see. "The worst thing of all is that I can't let go. It makes me do . . . questionable things."

She traced the edge of a bullet hole in the tree's trunk. "You've been hurt."

"*So have you.*"

"I've lost someone." Poe's face flashed in her mind and the pain in her soul reared up again. She pushed it down, chastising herself. Sebbie should be her main concern.

"*A little guy . . . ?*" the maple asked.

"Yes . . . my totem. A mouse. I left him behind earlier."

"*I remember.*"

She stood. "You've seen him, then?"

"*He's right above you, sleeping.*"

The mouse was curled in a ball on a branch over her head. Skylark was so overjoyed, she gathered him up and kissed him. "Sebastian! Are you okay?"

The mouse stretched. "Ah, it wasn't so bad, once I dodged all the feet." He looked at her closely and knew immediately that she was different. The certainty of her memories had changed her. But he said nothing.

Skylark felt calmer the moment she placed the mouse on her shoulder. She didn't feel crazy or angry anymore. His energy grounded her. Now she understood what the pewter being had meant during the training exercise. Her totem was a part of her. She nuzzled Sebastian affectionately before addressing the tree again.

"I want to thank you for taking care of my friend."

"*I didn't do a thing,*" the maple said.

"Well, I'd like to thank you anyway." Skylark extended her hand toward a branch.

The tree howled with laughter and Sebastian giggled.

She blushed. "What's so funny?"

A majestic being stepped out from behind the tree, its robes and beard a bonfire of red, orange and gold. It laughed again when it saw the look of amazement on her face.

"*I am the spirit of Sugar Maple,*" it said. "*I am the lifeblood that flows through the heart of each and every Sugar Maple tree.*"

Skylark covered her mouth in embarrassment. "I didn't mean to offend you."

"*Nonsense!*" The spirit took her hand and shook it.

It was warm to the touch, and she could taste a sweetness on her tongue. "Are there many like you?" she asked.

"*Millions. As many and varied as plants on the earth.*"

She looked at the trampled grass and the broken tree limbs. "The war . . . it hurt you—all of you. Do you ever fight back?"

"*We choose not to concern ourselves with the lives of men.*"

"But their actions affect you."

"*They affect everything.*"

"What if they destroy everything?"

The spirit stroked its beard. "*We hope that day will never come.*"

"It isn't fair that so many are affected by so few," she said.

"*Our world is unseen by the eyes of men. It has been for a very long time. We are waiting for the day when they see us again.*"

The mouse tugged on her hair. "We must go."

"I hope that day comes soon, for all our sakes," Skylark said. "And I hope we meet again."

The tree spirit smiled, its light gleaming around it. "*I have no doubt we will.*"

"You may want to step back when this one jumps," the mouse advised the spirit. "She's fiery."

"Just hold on this time," Skylark said. "I don't want to have to come looking for you again."

They jumped, and the second they touched down in the garden, Sebastian admonished her.

"You have to be more careful. You let your emotions run away with you."

Skylark plucked the mouse from her shoulder and looked him in the face. "That's the problem, isn't it?" She pointed to her chest.

"It's all still there. And it won't let go. I had a good life, once, with friends and family and a—" She stopped before she said the word *boyfriend.* Maybe it wasn't a good idea to mention Poe. "I was popular," she said instead.

Sebastian screwed up his face. "You chose to hold onto your memories. That life is over now, so you'd be wise to forget it. Remembering will only make things harder for you."

"I never want to forget. I liked being human."

"You have to let go of your old life—every part of it." He looked at her pointedly. He was alluding to Poe.

She lowered her eyes. How could everything be so final?

The mouse took pity on her. He climbed up her arm and lovingly stroked her hair. "It will get easier," he soothed. "In time you will come to understand and embrace the importance and necessity of your new life. A butterfly does not curse its wings, child. It takes to the air without a moment's grief for the time it spent crawling upon the ground."

Skylark wished she could believe him. The pain she felt said otherwise. "What will become of us?"

"We will become what we become."

She picked a pink lily from beside the bench and sniffed it. "What should we do now?"

"Go to your quarters, I suppose."

"Where are my quarters?"

The mouse sent her an image of a low white building at the edge of the practice field. "Those are your quarters. See if you can transport us there without too much aggravation."

Skylark tucked the lily behind her ear and jumped, landing right in front of the compound.

"Excellent," Sebastian praised her. "You're getting better at this."

She smiled, then looked at the uninspired building and pouted. It was ugly—just a stack of white blocks, one on top of the other. With all the ornate buildings in the city, this was all they could come up with? Just looking at it made her feel more sorry for herself than ever.

"Which room is mine?"

"Again, use your mind," the mouse said. "Everything has a unique energetic print."

Skylark closed her eyes, and in an instant they were standing before a white door that looked like every other door in the building. She searched for the handle. "How are we supposed to get in?"

"Ask the door to open—gently," Sebastian said.

"Please open," she said in her sweetest voice.

The door slid open.

The mouse winked. "Now, was that so difficult?"

"I used my real voice," Skylark said. "It works better for gentler tasks. I don't have the control in my mind yet for delicate things."

"Best not to get used to that," the mouse said. "It's the kind of habit that sticks."

"Just for now," she promised. "Until I get the hang of things." She asked the door to close and it did, sealing them inside the small square room.

The quarters were as mundane as the rest of the building. Like everywhere in the city, it seemed to be lit by some kind of inner power source. Though that was all it had going for it. There was a simple white bed, a small desk with a large brown leather book, a window overlooking the practice field . . . and nothing else. It was little more than a prison cell, Skylark thought. And it may as well have been, given the life sentence the mouse had just dumped on her. Her old life was gone, forever. And nothing would ever bring it back. It was so unbearably sad.

"What should we do?"

Sebastian shrugged. "Study, I guess."

Skylark wrinkled her nose at the book. "I don't think I've ever been any good at that."

"Why do you say so?"

"Because I don't really feel like it now, and I can't imagine I'll feel like it later. There are so many other things I'd rather do. Maybe we should go out and see what's going on. Anything would be better than sitting around here."

The mouse scuttled down her arm, jumped onto the bed and nestled into the pillow. "I think we've had enough excitement for one day."

"But I don't want to study," she said. "I'm pretty sure about that."

The mouse closed his eyes.

Skylark flipped half-heartedly through the big brown book. It had no title and appeared to be empty. "What's the good of that?" she grumbled.

The mouse ignored her. She sat on the edge of the bed, took the lily from behind her ear and twirled it between her fingers, kicking absently at the footboard with her heel. She would go crazy if she had to stay in this prison cell doing nothing. If she couldn't be with Poe, if she had to accept the stark reality of her new life, the least they could do was go out for a walk or something. She needed a distraction. She let out a loud sigh.

Sebastian cracked an eye and trained it on her. "Must you?"

"I'm so bored, Sebbie."

The mouse's whiskers twitched. "You're kidding."

She made a face.

"Fine," he conceded. "We can go out—but just for a bit."

9

POE

Caddy stared at Poe through the filtered light of the barn, trying to make sense of things. What was he doing here with these people? She was completely stunned to see him—and utterly grateful. It eased her fear to know she was not alone. There were so many things they needed to talk about though it would have to wait. Poe was already slipping into the dream. He squeezed her hand and closed his eyes.

The Dreamer's note was a sorcerer's spell. It lit on the back of Caddy's neck, worked its way to the base of her spine and set her bones singing. She sighed, her mind nudged by the rhythmic waves of sound. The tide rose, and there was a powerful surge as her consciousness linked to the collective like a boxcar coupling to a train. The visions began to come—not in the old way, the burnt toast way. They ebbed and flowed, colours blurring from grey to yellow to green. She could feel the cool earth beneath her and smell the musky scent of life pushing through the soil. Her light merged with the light of the Dreamers. Her vision became part of the whole. Together they twined upward, reaching for the sun.

The track suddenly shifted and Caddy found herself separate from the others in a strange room. It was a derelict hotel, despair clinging to the curtains and bedclothes and broken linoleum floor. There was a man on the bed, hunched in the sooty light of the window, a gun glistening on his knee. He raised it to his forehead and pressed the muzzle to his temple, his finger trembling against the trigger. Caddy reached for him with her mind and his face fell into focus.

It was her father!

There was another man, standing beside the bed, impeccably dressed, his eyes the colour of ice. A soft tinkling sound enveloped him as he leaned toward her father, whispering something. Her father sobbed and squeezed the trigger. Caddy panicked and screamed, breaking the vision. The train lurched and her mind uncoupled, tumbling back into the barn where the Dreamers hummed, stitching the sound into a single seamless note.

Caddy pressed the heels of her hands over her eyes. What had she seen? A shadow from the past? A glimpse into the future? Or the here and now? Was her father still alive? Or had he killed himself in some grimy hotel room? And who was the other man? The one with the suit and the frozen eyes? There was no way to tell. She'd broken the connection before the vision could completely unfold. Now she might never know.

She dropped her hands from her face and looked at Poe. He was deep in the dream with the others, their bodies stretched out like fallen soldiers across the loft. Except for Hex. She sat up and slowly turned toward Caddy. Had she seen the vision of her father too?

The humming slowed, the note hanging in the air long after the Dreamers stopped. They surfaced, stirring softly in the hay. Caddy watched Poe's eyes flutter open. He met her gaze and held it.

"Meg," she said, unable to sustain the silence.

He took her hand and gently explored the bandage with his fingertips. This simple act of tenderness made her want to cry. A lump formed in her throat. What was to happen to her? What was to happen to them all?

The Dreamers stood, moving toward the ladder with trance-like familiarity. Poe pushed himself up from the floor.

"We need to go," he said.

"Where?"

"We never sleep where we dream." He looked over his shoulder.

Caddy did the same and saw Hex watching them, her face cold as stone. Poe ducked his head and walked toward the ladder, lowering himself down. He didn't wait for her, joining the other Dreamers as they moved in a line out the door of the barn.

Caddy was reaching for the ladder when someone gripped her arm. It was Hex. She pulled Caddy into the shadows, speaking in a low voice so the others wouldn't hear.

"You saw something during the dream," she hissed.

"No," Caddy lied.

Hex squeezed her arm, her face inches away. "Maybe you saw something about your father?"

Caddy struggled to free herself. Hex squeezed harder.

"If you do discover something about him, I hope you will tell me. We are all very concerned for his safety."

"I didn't see anything," Caddy said.

Hex smiled, cunning as a snake, and released her grip. Caddy stumbled through the hay to the ladder. She searched for the rungs with her feet, Hex watching her, and climbed down, hoping to catch up with Poe. When she reached the bottom, the barn was empty. Caddy quickly walked outside and discovered a large cube van idling in the lane, lights off. A man stood by the back door, assisting the Dreamers into the truck. The wind had died and the grass was a pale lake of green. In the sky, a fragile crescent moon rested on its side among the stars. How long had it been since she'd seen a sky so wide, so uncluttered by buildings? It would have moved her in different circumstances. But she had no idea where she was, or how far from the city, or if she'd ever see home again. She didn't even know if her father was alive or dead. Only this morning she was worrying about a Physics quiz at school. Now she had no way of knowing if she'd make it through the night alive. She rubbed her arm. The pinch of Hex's grip lingered. Caddy thought about Red and wondered what he'd meant when he said he was trying to protect her. From what? The Company? Or Hex?

And then there was Poe. Where did he fit in all of this? She couldn't deny that she felt comforted to see him. Surely he wouldn't be part of a group that abducted and murdered people . . . would he?

Caddy looked back at the barn. She expected to see Hex standing in the doorway. Or Red. Neither was there. Were they staying behind?

"Please, hurry," the man at the truck said, taking her hand to help her up and over the metal grate.

Inside the truck, the Dreamers were hunkered like animals, some in the dark, some sitting in the triangle of starlight on the dusty plywood floor. Coughs punctuated the scuffling of feet. Caddy found a spot and sat, searching the faces. There was no sign of Poe. Where was he? She tried to count the number of people but it was impossible. In the low light, the bodies were a confusing shadow of heads and arms. She took a guess, and came up with thirty-five, maybe forty.

The door of the truck banged shut and the Dreamers were swallowed by darkness. No one spoke. No one moved. Caddy worried that she would need to pee. How long would they be trapped inside? She heard the driver check the door, ensuring the lock was engaged. His boots crunched over gravel as he walked the length of the truck and climbed into the driver's seat. The cab door closed, the engine revved, and the truck bucked forward. They rolled down the lane, the Dreamers bumping against each other, as unsuspecting as cattle to the slaughterhouse. Caddy flipped up the collar of her jacket and hunched her shoulders. Holding her safe stone, she sang her song soundlessly to herself, praying her father was alive and that they would both find a way home.

After an hour or so, the truck ground down, grumbling loudly as it slowed and turned. The gears groaned and they jerked to a stop. Caddy listened as the driver jumped from the cab and walked to the back. The door rolled open and the cool air rushed in. Without a word, the Dreamers disembarked, sleepwalkers shuffling into the night.

As soon as she was out of the truck, Caddy allowed herself to breathe. They were further in the country. An old farmhouse leaned against the spangled sky, dark fields rolling in every direction. And still no glimpse of Poe.

The Dreamers walked in a trance to the house. No one was paying attention to her. If ever there was a chance to escape, now was the time. She'd bent down to tie her shoelaces, steeling her courage to run, when a young woman came up beside her. Caddy stood up, fists clenched. The girl smiled. She was around eighteen or nineteen, with an angelic face and long, light brown hair. Had she somehow known Caddy was thinking of running? In any case, the moment was gone. They were surrounded by other Dreamers now, clustering together on their descent into the cellar of the house. She would have to wait for another opportunity.

Caddy followed the others down the stairs. On the threshold, she paused. The cellar was damp and stank of mould. The others brushed past, forcing her inside. Someone closed the door. A match was struck and the Dreamers' faces leapt in and out of the gloom. The man with the match carried it to the centre of the room and lit a candle. It sputtered to life, the flame lapping at the dark. The Dreamers gathered around it. Caddy found a spot with a good vantage point and looked for Poe. She could see the girl sitting between a man and woman across the room. They were focused on the candle as if they expected something important to happen.

An older woman handed out blankets. When she reached Caddy, she squeezed her shoulder and pushed a blanket into her arms. It was scratchy and smelled of cigarettes and mildew. Caddy thanked her and copied the others, folding the blanket into a small square to sit on. There was the clatter of tin on concrete as a bucket was placed in one corner of the room. A small bowl containing a slosh of soup was pushed into her hands. She looked at the man next to her. He was older—her father's age, maybe. He motioned for her to pass the bowl along. After three or four bowls he indicated for her to stop.

Caddy cupped the bowl in her hands and raised it tentatively to her lips. The soup was thin and tepid, little more than a watery broth with a few chunks of carrot and onion thrown in. She sipped it slowly, despite her hunger, letting her gaze drift across the faces in the room. Most of them were older. In fact, all the Dreamers seemed to be around her father's age except for the girl, Poe and herself. She wished she knew where Poe was. If he'd somehow managed to slip away then she would do the same the first chance she got. She'd have to keep an eye on the girl, make sure she wasn't watching.

After everyone was settled, a man stepped into the candlelight. "I want to thank you all for being so organized," he said. "These are emergency measures. You all know we've been preparing for something like this for a very long time. That time is upon us. No one is allowed to go out—not now. There's a bucket in the corner of the room. Use it if you need to. I apologize for the rustic conditions. Please pass your bowls back when you're finished and try to get some rest."

Emergency measures? Caddy turned to the man next to her. He was staring into his empty bowl. He gave a faint smile once he realized she was looking at him, and collected her bowl from her hands. He passed them to the next person then arranged his blanket and lay down. The others did the same, and so did she, bunching the top of her blanket into a makeshift pillow. She used this chance to look around again for Poe. Against the far wall she saw what she thought to be his silhouette. She made a note of his position and reclined, eyes open. She would wait until the others were asleep then go to him. It wouldn't be difficult to stay awake. Insomnia was no stranger to her, even in the best of times.

There was a general restlessness at first, and frequent trips to the bucket with mumbled apologies as people stepped over each other. Caddy lay motionless, staring into the candle flame as the heavy rhythm of sleep took over the room. Some snored lightly, a few moaned in their sleep, while others coughed against the damp. The floor was cold and her shoulder ached but she refused to roll over and face the dark. Her hands started to shake and she gripped the blanket, the smell of burnt toast coming on before the dark took her down into the Emptiness.

Caddy came to, confused and disoriented. She found her bearings, realized where she was, and was relieved to discover the Dreamers were still sleeping. Had anyone seen her go? She raised her head slightly. No one was looking back at her. Resting on the blanket, she subdued her hands and slowed her breathing. She needed to go to the bathroom, desperately, but couldn't fathom using the bucket. Instead she flexed her calf muscles—careful not to kick the person sleeping at her feet—and thought about her father. Was he dead? Or sitting in some low-rent hotel room with a gun on his knee? And her mother—would Caddy ever know the truth about her? It was too much to bear—all of it. She stifled a sob in her blanket. Squeezing her eyes shut, she forced her mind clear. Opening them again she saw a figure stand. It was Poe.

He picked his way through the bodies, stopping several times to check his footing. At first Caddy thought he might be going to use the bucket, but then she traced his trajectory to the cellar door. He fumbled with the hasp, covering it with his hand to dampen the sound of the latch as it clicked. With a jerk, he popped the door open. Watery starlight spilled across the floor and receded as he slipped out, closing the door silently behind him.

Caddy rose and crept across the room, stopping to steady herself the way he had. At the door, she felt for the latch, covered it with her hand and opened it.

Caddy snuck up the stairs, peeking out like a groundhog to search the landscape. Outside, the air was crisp and clean. No trace of Poe. Or Company men. She stepped onto the grass and followed a narrow path that ribboned lazily along the length of the house toward a stand of trees brooding in the distance. Empty fields rambled on both sides of her, their hummocks and gullies a moonscape under the stars. She breathed in deeply. Exhaled the cellar damp from her lungs. It was such a relief to be in the fresh air, even if it was dangerous to be out alone. She would take the risk for another opportunity to speak with Poe. First, she had to pee.

A clump of milkweed provided privacy enough. Caddy squatted behind it. Zipping her pants up afterwards, she caught the bandage on her hand in the metal teeth, cursing softly. The bandage pulled away, so she decided to unravel it. Then she unravelled the other, too, rolling the gauze into a ball and stashing it between the sticky milkweed stalks. Her palms were spotted with scabs where the glass had pierced the skin. But she was alive. She was more than thankful for that.

Stuffing her hands in her jacket pockets, Caddy slunk along the path, searching the barren fields as she went. Why hadn't they been planted? They should be thigh-high with green by now, she thought. And where was Poe? It was foolish to be wandering out in the night, chasing after him. She couldn't go back to that musty dungeon of a cellar. Not yet. She would walk until she reached the trees, and maybe keep going until she found her way home. She turned to look at the house. A faint light glowed on the horizon behind it. Was that the city? It seemed so far away. She could run right now—it was the perfect chance—

A hand clapped down on her shoulder.

Caddy jumped and withered with relief when she saw it was Poe. Had he been watching her the whole time? His dark eyes glittered in the low light. He appeared so much taller than she remembered.

"I didn't mean to scare you."

"It's okay. I'm just . . . tense."

"We really shouldn't be standing out in the open," he said, turning and walking toward the trees.

She shadowed him, nearly stepping on his heels as they slipped into the woods. Poe found a wide tree stump and offered it to her. She sat on the edge of it.

He crouched next to her, and she was taken aback when he cupped her hands tenderly in his.

"Do they hurt?" he asked.

"No." She was trying to be brave.

"They look like they hurt."

"Yeah . . . I guess they do," she admitted.

He smiled. It was the first time she'd ever seen him smile. It was disarming. She pulled her hands away.

"You should have left the bandages on," he said.

"They were dirty . . . and getting in the way."

"Yeah, I could see that."

He stood and leaned against a tree, staring into the forest. She hoped he was searching for a way to explain things to her. After several minutes of silence it was clear she was going to have to start the conversation.

"I can't believe you're here," she said. "Did they take you the way they took me?"

He folded his arms and studied her face with such intensity it made her look away. "I came on my own."

"Oh." She kicked nervously at the ground with the toe of her sneaker. "How long have you been involved with these people? I mean . . . the whole time at school . . . I never knew."

"How could you have known? We never really talked."

He had a point. She continued poking at the ground with her foot. "It's not because I didn't want to talk to you . . . I just didn't know how."

"I know," he said, letting her off the hook.

"Do you believe what they're saying about the Dark and our purpose here?"

"I don't have to believe anything they say. I know it's true."

"So, you trust Hex?"

"Of course I trust her."

He was so confident. It was comforting in a way, to know that he wasn't confused by doubt. "How can you be sure?"

"Because I've seen the visions."

Caddy was unable to mask her astonishment. "You've been to the Emptiness?"

"The place of lost souls? Yes. Once . . . but only fleetingly, like the others. We've all heard the stories, though, of the ones who've gone much, much deeper."

He was referring to her. It made her feel exposed. She clenched her hands, hoping they wouldn't shake. "And now you believe the world is going to end and nobody has a clue except us."

"It's not that simple, Cadence. These forces have been in play for a very long time. I know it's hard to take in all at once."

He'd called her Cadence. Only her father ever called her that. She was amazed he even knew her proper name—and more than a just little confused that he appeared fine so soon after losing his girlfriend. Meg had been killed by the Company men. Yet he seemed so calm about it all.

"What about Meg? Was she just a casualty of war?"

His mood darkened and she immediately regretted her words.

"People are going to die," he said. "We have to accept that. It's for the greater good."

It sounded so cold, so matter-of-fact. "You honestly believe that?"

"Yes."

"I'm sorry, but I think that's crazy."

"The world is on the edge of total destruction. That may be difficult for some people to comprehend."

Some people? Did he mean her? "Maybe they don't want to comprehend," she said. "Maybe they want things to stay the way they are. I'm one of them. I don't want anything to do with any of this. I want to go home." Her eyes welled with tears, betraying her.

Poe shoved his hands in the pockets of his jeans. Caddy wiped away the tears, feeling remorseful for her anger. It wasn't his fault the world was unraveling.

"I'm sorry. I'm just scared."

Her candor had an effect on him. His voice softened. "It's okay."

"I'm just so messed up about it all," she confessed. "I can't believe there are Company men out there killing innocent people. Why would they do such a thing?"

Poe looked away, and the night stretched out forever between them. When he spoke again, it was in a whisper. "It's my fault Meg's dead."

"Your fault? How?"

Grief clouded his face. "I had no right . . . I should have never seen her in the first place. They told me the risks. I tried to break off with her but she refused . . ."

"You're not the one that killed her, Poe."

"They killed her because of me. The Company—it does whatever it can to get to you—to break you. If it can't break you, it takes the ones you love. Meg didn't know anything about any of this. I told her nothing. I thought it would protect her . . ."

The anguish in his voice was heartbreaking. Caddy understood his pain all too well. "My mother . . . Hex told me Company men killed her to get to my father. When that didn't work, they killed him . . . at least, she thinks they did."

"They killed my mother and father too," Poe said.

His admission struck her like a fist. They'd hardly exchanged a word all those years in school, and now here they were, laying their souls bare to each other in the middle of nowhere. It made her feel closer to him, knowing he understood what she'd gone through. It made her reconsider if Hex had been telling the truth after all. Maybe her father *was* killed by Company men. What had her vision meant, then? Why had she seen him sitting on a bed in a hotel with a gun in his hand? Hex had said she suspected he might still be alive. Maybe he was. Maybe he'd missed when he pulled the trigger. This gave her the smallest feeling of hope. She vowed not to give up on her father. She vowed to uncover the absolute truth. As for Hex, she would remain cautious. She had no reason to trust her. Especially after their exchange in the barn. That part she'd keep to herself for now.

"I'm sorry about your parents," she said.

"My father knew the dangers."

"Did he try to hide the dreaming from you?"

"No. He prepared me from the time I was a child. He couldn't keep secrets from me."

For some reason she envied this. Her father had taught her to do things for herself, to solve problems, to be observant, aware, to question everything, to know things. He was adamant about it, pointing out trees and plants and animals anywhere he could, telling her the names. Showing her how to gather seeds, how to grow them. Teaching her how things worked—old knowledge.

Every game was an opportunity to learn, even hide-and-seek. He'd scold her if she was found too easily. He never spoke openly of the dreaming or its purpose. He never talked about Company men and the dangers waiting for her out in the world.

"My father told me nothing."

"Maybe he thought you'd come to it on your own," Poe said. "Maybe he was waiting for you to figure out what you are."

"And what am I?" she asked.

"You're a Dreamer, Cadence. A very special one. I knew it from the first minute I saw you."

The blood rushed to her face. Was that the reason why he was always looking at her in class? How could she have been so stupid, so self-absorbed? The whole time in school she'd thought that he liked her. And she'd allowed herself to like him too—more than she cared to admit. He wasn't interested in her that way. He'd just been waiting for her to figure out that she was a Dreamer—like her father.

Talking to Poe, it was clear now that her father had tried to help her understand her visions—or simply deal with them. Her mother too. They were both so patient. She should have figured it out long ago. The visions weren't about her. They were so much bigger than that. Poe must think her a snivelling child. Well, it was time for her to grow up and face the truth. She pulled her necklace from under her shirt and held up the green stone.

"It's a piece of fluorite—for psychic protection. My father gave it to me."

"So did mine." Poe produced an identical necklace from inside his shirt.

Caddy stared at it in wonder. It was too fantastic a connection to be a coincidence. "Do you really think we can change things by dreaming?"

"Yes, if we work together."

Caddy tucked her necklace back under her shirt. "It seems

so futile. The Company men are murderers. How can dreaming stop them?"

"It's the energy we're trying to change. The murders, the intimidation, they shift the energy on the planet toward negativity, toward the Dark. It fills the world with fear and despair. It allows the Dark to take over and control our thoughts. If they control our thoughts, they control everything. We can counter that by dreaming the Light together, by pushing against the Dark as a unified force with our visions of hope for the future, like a million candles lighting the way. Our dreams have power, Cadence, but only when the many dream as one."

He made it sound so easy. What good were ephemeral dreams of the future—even unified ones—against the reality of murder and torture?

"Hex's eye . . ." she said.

Poe picked up a pebble and rolled it between his fingers. "The Company took it. The left eye is the conduit to our dreams. By taking her eye they stole her ability to connect to the collective, to dream."

The idea of it made Caddy sick. "Why didn't they just kill her?"

"It was a warning. They mutilated her, took the dreaming away, but let her keep her right eye so she can witness the end of days. She was one of our strongest links. They thought they could break us all if they got to her."

"She's so young . . ." Caddy lowered her head. "I can't even imagine . . ."

"We're stronger because of it," Poe said. "When they broke Hex's link they lost the ability to trace her. It was a tactical error. We're safer as a result."

"Did you know her before? When she could still dream?"

Poe pushed the pebble into the earth. "No. She came to us after. She helped us organize. We had no real leadership before her. The Dreamers have always gathered in small groups and worked in secret to avoid detection. But the Company has grown too powerful. The men have depleted our numbers. Fractured us. Filled our hearts with fear. We heard stories of a woman—the daughter of a Dreamer—who'd started organizing, started gathering the Dreamers together. She'd discovered that the children of Dreamers could substitute for their parents. We heard she'd been tortured by the Company. That they'd taken her eye. This didn't stop her. When she found us, we were scared and nearly broken. She gave us hope again."

Caddy looked at the scabs on her hands. Her pain was nothing compared to Hex's. "If something like that happened to me . . . I'm not sure I could be so strong."

"You'd be surprised," he said.

She shook her head. "I'm not like you."

"We're not so different, Cadence. I've just had more time to adapt. My father prepared me for the worst from the beginning. He wanted me to know the truth. The Company men—they pick up on our emotions. They use them against us, to track us down. They've been doing it for centuries."

He was being so kind. She didn't deserve it, really, not after the way she'd judged him. Still, she welcomed his patience. "Who are they?" She wanted to hear his version, to see how it compared to Hex's.

Poe thought for a moment before he spoke. "They're an organization dedicated to the destruction of the Light. Some say they're connected to the one they worship, that they're lower forms of demonic energy made manifest on earth. Others say they're just people, willing to give everything for the cause they believe in."

"Even at the expense of their own lives?"

"They consider it an honour to die for their master."

"I'm not that dedicated," Caddy said. "I don't think I can do what Hex needs me to do."

Poe looked at her with alarming resolve. "We have to, Cadence.

Everything depends on us. But we're not alone. We have each other." He came to her, rolling up his sleeve to reveal a bandage on his arm. "I want to show you something."

He pulled the bandage back. There was a raised mark the size of a silver dollar on the underside of his forearm—a tattoo of some kind—in the shape of a mandala. It was raw and red. Newly acquired. The ink was unusual. Not black, like a regular tattoo, but iridescent, like a pearl. She'd seen one like it, though more faded. She'd thought it was a scar or a burn of some kind that her father was trying to hide. When as a child she'd asked him about it, he'd refused to explain it. Now she understood why he wore long sleeves all the time.

"This is how we recognize each other," Poe said. "The mark is only carried by Dreamers. It can't be forged. The secret of the mark is deeply protected. If someone tells you they're a Dreamer, make them show the mark as proof. If they can't . . ." He gave her a foreboding look.

She traced the mark lightly with her finger. It felt electric to the touch. "My father has one."

"Yes," Poe said. "And you'll have one too . . . if you decide to stay."

"I didn't know I had a choice."

"There's always a choice. I was uncertain at first too. Now there's real hope that we can win against the Dark." He moved closer. He had a strange light in his eyes. "Hex told us you were coming, Cadence. I got the mark because of you."

Caddy stepped back in shock. How could he make such a claim? Who was she to inspire that kind of commitment? She was just a person, a nobody. She couldn't give hope to anyone. She had no hope of her own. Hex had no right to put this on her. What kind of game was she playing? The last thing Caddy wanted was the responsibility of someone else's expectation and trust, especially Poe's.

She was about to tell him as much when they heard a branch snap. In the shadows of the trees, something was moving.

THE GUIDES

S kylark and Sebastian took to the streets. The city was as busy as ever with beings going here and there. What were they all doing? Skylark wondered. Nothing fun, that was for sure. Nothing even remotely interesting or human. Everyone was so serious all the time. And if you've seen one shiny crystal gold-domed building, she thought, you've seen them all.

What she really wanted was to flip through *The Book of Events* again. But she'd be hard pressed to convince Sebastian that staring at images of her human boyfriend was a good idea. She was actually formulating a plan to ditch the mouse and come back out on her own when she heard laughter. Not just one voice— many voices—all laughing at some great joke. It sent a spontaneous wave of euphoria through her body.

"Who do you think that is, Sebbie?"

The mouse sighed. "I don't know. But I'm sure we're about to find out."

Skylark glided toward the sound. "Listen," she said as they drew closer. "Is that music?"

"There's always music in the city," the mouse quipped.

"Not like this, Sebbie. I hear dance music!"

The mouse gripped her hair and held on as Skylark sped toward the sound. Rounding a corner, she sailed head first into a group of beings hanging around in front of a red-brick building. These beings were different. They weren't wearing robes. They were wearing real clothes. And they weren't tall like the Spectrals. They were various heights—like real people. Skylark couldn't help staring.

The group fell quiet when they saw her, stepping respectfully aside. She nodded politely, making sure to keep her lips clenched for fear of being condemned as a mouth-talker. She could feel their eyes watching her as she passed. Cruising as casually as possible, Skylark moved to the back of the building to check things out. When she was sure no one was watching, she looked through the window.

"Look, Sebbie! There are hundreds of them!"

The place was filled with beings of every shape and size. They sat at tables and stood at a long bar, drinking and eating and laughing. In one part of the room, some were even dancing. What's more, they were talking with their mouths! It was glorious!

"What is this place?" she asked, her nose pressed against the glass.

The mouse clucked his tongue with disapproval. "It's a bar."

"I want to go in."

Sebastian tugged on her hair. "No. This place is for Guides. Your kind sticks to its own."

"Why? They look friendly enough."

"It's just the way things are done."

"I'm practically one of them," she said. "Look at my shape—and my size. They're stunty, like me. They won't even notice my arm in there. I'll keep it close to my body." She demonstrated for him.

Sebastian twitched his nose. "They will know you are not one of them. They're not the same Frequency as you. They're not even on the same level. We shouldn't be here."

The mouse was determined to spoil everything, that was clear. Skylark pulled him from her shoulder and looked him in the face. "I won't do anything stupid, I promise. I just want to go in and look around. Only for a minute. They're having so much fun in there."

"They're not your kind, Skylark," the mouse said. "Their place in the order is not the same as yours. The sooner you accept this, the happier you will be."

The sound of her name caught her off guard. "You called me Skylark."

"Yes, I did."

She smiled. "I appreciate that."

"I know it means a lot to you."

"Yes, it does. Thank you."

"You're welcome. Now, can we leave this place?"

Her shoulders dropped. "Yes. But I want one more peek."

Skylark watched the Guides through the window until the mouse insisted they go. She turned from the bar unwillingly and glided away.

"Who are the Guides?" she asked as they moved through the streets.

"They work with people, to help them in their life's journey."

"I thought the Advisers did that."

"Yes . . . but Advisers don't manifest on the earth plane," the mouse explained. "They simply offer options and provide guidance as to the best choices during the in-between time."

"What's the in-between time?"

"The time between earth lives."

"What's that?"

"It's where human souls go to get advice and readjust their life's trajectory before they reincarnate on the earth plane. They spend the in-between time talking to their Advisers so they can make good decisions when they return to earth."

"And then they become people again?" she asked, swishing to one side to let a group of silver beings go by.

"Yes."

"And their Guides help them when they're on earth?"

"Yes. They provide guidance to help keep people on track."

"Oh." This was the most exciting thing Skylark had heard since she'd arrived. She needed to learn more. "Do Guides always have so much fun? I mean, how come they're not working and training like us?"

"Because their role is different," the mouse said. "They train through remote observation. In fact, most of their work is done remotely, through dreams and projected ideas, though they often appear to humans in times of great distress to offer comfort and guidance."

"Is that why they look like people—in case they need to appear?"

"Yes. They're energetically connected to humans. It helps them to communicate if they pattern their form and energies to match those of people. Some assume other likenesses—dwarves, elves, rangers and such. It depends what their human feels most comfortable with."

"So . . . they have shape, like me," she said.

"They don't have to. They just like to. Their true form is amorphous."

But the Guides have a choice, she thought. Which made them as close to human as she would ever find in the city. "How do they change their shape?"

The mouse clucked. He'd grown tired of her questions. "They just rearrange their particles. It's not difficult for them, though it does take practice. Guides evolve over many lifetimes. They spend quite a few tours of duty in the corporeal world."

"If their true form is amorphous, why do they assume human shape when they're here?"

The mouse didn't answer right away. "It helps to keep them connected to their human charges," he finally said. "And for fun. Guides are allowed to enjoy human pleasures and interests—to some degree—to help them understand the ones they work with."

Skylark sighed. Why couldn't she have been a Guide? She swerved to avoid an Adviser, nearly gliding over its wolf in the process.

"Just keep your eyes on the road," the mouse admonished. "It doesn't help to dream about being something other than what you are."

"But I—"

"Enough talk," the mouse said. "We need to get back to your room."

Skylark folded her arms. What was the point of being out if she couldn't have a good time? If the mouse really expected her to give up everything she loved, he could relax a little. She was so frustrated with his rigid rules and constant strictness that she jumped home in protest, landing with a deliberate thump to rattle his teeth to the roots.

"Door open," she growled, and then she slammed it closed after they'd entered the room.

Sebastian leapt from her shoulder onto the pillow and nestled in as before. She moped on the edge of the bed, staring angrily at the big brown book. The mouse wasted no time falling asleep. With nothing else to do, Skylark glided begrudgingly over to her desk and thought the book open. "Show me your purpose," she said.

The book's pages immediately filled with weird symbols and drawings and the tiniest writing imaginable. Skylark flipped through several pages, each one more excruciating than the last. She read a few lines. It was a manual of sorts, from what she could understand, written in the most laborious style. Something specifically for Warriors. She touched the page with her finger and the words enlarged in front of her. A voice recited the contents. It was the same stuffy narrator from *The Book of Events*.

Skylark clapped the book shut. She was not in the mood for learning—she would never be—especially after seeing the Guides having so much fun at the bar. She thought about what the mouse had said, how the Guides rearrange their particles to change form. Closing her eyes, she stood with her arms at her sides and imagined what that would feel like. After several moments, a funny tingling stirred in her fingertips. Her eyes popped open and she looked at her hands. They appeared the same. She glanced warily at Sebastian. The mouse was still asleep on the bed.

Closing her eyes again, she relaxed her mind and it opened like the petals of a flower. She imagined the molecules of her body moving apart and dancing slowly around each other. The tingling returned to her fingertips. It moved up her arms and across her chest. It crept to her scalp and down the length of her body, through her legs, across her knees, and all the way to her toes. She could feel her energy reaching beyond her shape. Slowly opening her eyes, Skylark saw a misty outline glowing around her form. At the centre of her body was a birthing star, pulsing and expanding. This must be her soul light!

"Mirror," she whispered to the ether.

A mirror appeared and hung in the air before her. She allowed her mind to go deeper still, watching as her form turned to fog, breaking up around her. Her features blurred, and her body took on the appearance of luminous smoke. She conjured an image of the girl she used to be, and her particles danced slowly around each other, rearranging. To her amazement, her human self stared back at her in wonder from the mirror. She was wearing jeans and a white T-shirt with blue suede sneakers. Her heart-shaped face was surrounded by a mass of blond curls. Only her eyes didn't change. They remained the same deep colour of violet. Skylark gazed at her reflection. How she loved her face. Her lips were full and her eyes were as big as a deer's. It thrilled her to look human again. But what would it be like to have straight hair? she wondered. Her blond curls instantly relaxed and hung in a thick curtain over her shoulders.

"How about red?" she whispered, and her hair turned red.

"Shorter."

Her hair halved in length.

"Frizzy."

It looked like a halo.

"Longer."

It tumbled down her back.

"Straight."

It instantly relaxed again.

"Black," she said. "The colour of raven wings."

Skylark turned her head from side to side, admiring her shining mane of dark hair. She really liked what she saw. It made her want to go out again, to see how it would feel to move through the city in her new form.

She would have to change her clothes, though. Trying out a bunch of outfits, including half a dozen dresses, she eventually decided on pants, ankle-high brown leather boots and a black shirt—form-fitting and buttoned up the front with a collar and long sleeves slightly flared at the wrist. She changed the colour of her pants several times before landing on black as well. Scrutinizing her reflection, she concluded she needed something more, and gave herself a studded brown leather belt that clung to her hips. And fingerless gauntlets, laced at the wrists and dark brown, to match the belt. When she was happy with the results, Skylark closed her eyes and imagined her form solidifying and holding its shape. Opening one eye, she was astonished to see that it had worked. Well, most of it. The healing cord on her floppy arm was still visible through the shirt, though its colour had deepened to a shimmering brown. She puzzled over this for a while, decided she liked the look and went with it.

Throughout this process, the mouse slept peacefully on the bed. Would he approve? She wasn't going to wake him to find out. I'll only be gone a little while, she told herself. What harm could it possibly do?

Swishing softly to the door, Skylark whispered for it to open, glided out and closed it quietly behind her. She wanted to stroll through the city in her new form, take her time, and gauge the reactions of other beings. But that would take too long. What if the mouse woke up? Or she ran into someone she knew? Best to jump instead, she thought.

Skylark hid behind a tree on the edge of the practice field and imagined the bar where the Guides gathered. The roar filled her ears and the stars started to slipstream. She felt a tremor in her body and to her dismay, her robe snapped back into place. "Oh!" She'd ruined all her hard work.

Calming her mind, she focused on her new outfit. The robe dissolved and the new clothes reappeared. She centered herself, to jump again. As soon as the roar began, her robe returned. She'd have to glide to the bar after all.

Moving as gracefully as possible, Skylark floated through the city, avoiding eye contact with the beings she met along the way. She could feel them watching her. Were her seams showing? Could they tell she'd changed her form? If they could, no one said anything. They're only staring because you look so awesome, she reassured herself. When she reached the bar, she gathered her courage and glided up to the door.

"Open," she thought.

The door didn't move.

"Open," she said with her mouth.

Nothing.

Skylark grabbed the handle, yanked the door open and stumbled backwards. Straightening herself, she cruised into the bar and was met by a wall of music, laughter and conversation. It was so exciting! She cased the room, trying to look like she belonged. Every table was full and everyone seemed to know each other. Where was she going to sit? There were a few empty seats at the bar. She would take one of those.

Several Guides greeted her as she passed. She was definitely drawing attention. She nodded, maintaining her cool. What she really wanted to do was stare at everything—the way the Guides were dressed, the things they were drinking and eating, the way they talked with their mouths. It was hard to contain herself. She chose a seat one away from a casual-looking Guide. He was sitting alone, leaning over some bluish-looking drink, tapping his fingers absently to the music. She absorbed as much of him as she could from the corner of her eye. Blond hair. Blue jeans. Hooded shirt. Cute. She felt guilty for thinking that last thought. What would Poe say? She stifled a laugh. She was having so much fun.

After several minutes of sitting, she was approached by an affable being behind the bar. It was tall, formless, little more than a face reflected on water. It smiled and small lights sparked at random intervals through its energy field.

"What'll you have?"

Skylark shifted in her seat. "Umm. Pardon me?"

"To drink. What would you like to drink?"

She'd paused too long. She hadn't had anything to drink since . . . she couldn't even remember when. The being waited expectantly. She cleared her throat, speaking in a low voice. "I'll . . . uh . . . I'll have whatever he's having." She pointed surreptitiously to the cute Guide beside her.

The being reached beneath the counter and produced a heavy-bottomed glass. Pushing a lever on one of the taps, it filled the glass with a viscous blue liquid and placed it in front of her. She thanked him . . . it . . . lifted the glass to her lips the way the other beings were doing and took a sip. The blue liquid burned all the way down to her toes. She coughed. It felt good, and deeply familiar. Like whiskey. Only blue. And thicker. It filled her body with the most incredible sensation of warmth.

"Hey, it's good," she said, raising her glass.

The blond Guide shot her an amused look.

"Cheers," the bartender said.

After several sips of the blue liquid Skylark felt confident enough to swivel in her chair and check out the scene. How amazing it felt to be part of so much commotion. This was a joyful place—it was easy to see that. The Guides were fun to watch, too. They assumed every shape and size—some old, some young, some fantastical, like gnomes and druids and elves.

Tapping her foot to the music, Skylark threw her drink back and ordered another. Raising it to her lips, she caught a Guide staring back at her from a shadowed corner of the room. He was tall, Japanese by the look of it, twenty, maybe, with short black hair, a long overcoat and black pants and boots. She liked his style. He was wearing sunglasses, even though the light in the bar was far from glaring. She watched him for a while. Then he stood and walked toward her. Oh no. Skylark spun around in her chair and faced the bar, her cheeks burning. Seconds later the Guide appeared, leaning casually next to her.

"I haven't seen you here before," he said.

She fiddled with her glass. "That's because I've never been here before."

He smirked. "That's a surprise. You don't look like a Guide."

An elvish-type character stepped up to the bar, ordered a drink and returned to the crowd.

"What do you mean?" she asked.

"Your EP—it's different."

She contemplated the blue liquid in her glass, hiding the fact that she didn't have a clue what he was talking about. He leaned closer.

"Your energetic print, in case you were wondering."

Skylark threw back her drink and wiped her mouth with the back of her hand. Smacking her glass down on the counter, she ordered another. He took this as an invitation and claimed the seat next to her, ordering two more drinks. She stole a glimpse of him. Was his energetic body bleeding around his human form? Or were her eyes playing tricks on her? She looked at her glass. It was empty again. And there was another drink waiting. How many had she had?

He held his hand out. "My name's Kenji."

She stared at his hand for a moment, then shook it. She still couldn't bring herself to look him in the eyes. "Skylark."

"Seriously?" He held her hand, his energy pulsing up her arm. "Pleased to meet you, *Skylark*."

"Hey, what are you doing?" She pulled away. "Keep your vibrations to yourself."

"It isn't usual to see your kind in here," he said. "In fact, I don't think I've ever seen anything quite like you before."

She pressed her scarred arm against her side. "Is that right?"

He leaned closer. She could feel the energy snapping off him.

"So . . . why are you here?" he asked.

She turned at last to engage him and was surprised to see her reflection in his glasses. She'd almost forgotten she'd changed herself. "I don't even know where *here* is," she said.

He smiled. She planted her elbow on the bar, resting her head in her hand. She felt deliciously relaxed.

"You have very nice teeth."

He laughed. She let her guard down.

"What's it like being a Guide?"

He raised his eyebrows and took a sip of his drink. "Complicated. Like people."

"Is that why you all look so different?"

"Nah. Guides just like to have fun. Actually, Guides are kinda weird . . . As a matter of fact, people are weird."

"I like people," Skylark said. "They're interesting. Spectrals all look the same except for their colour . . . and their totems. They're so . . . boring."

"What about you? You don't look like a Spectral."

She avoided the question. The blue liquid was making her feel bold. "Do you always get to hang out and have fun?"

"Pleasure is our principle," Kenji said. "The soul's purpose is to be happy."

Skylark scoffed. "I don't believe that."

"Why not?"

She flicked her hair over her shoulder. "Because I don't feel happy. Ever since I got here it's been nothing but rules."

"It's not that bad, is it?"

She dismissed him with a wave. "I wish I were a Guide."

"No you don't."

"Yes, I do."

"No, you don't. Guides aren't really good for much. Nobody listens to them. Nobody sees them. And when they do make an effort and appear, people spend half the time convincing themselves that what they saw was nothing out of the ordinary. Why do you think they're all here drinking and hanging out?"

"Well, you seem to fit right in."

He burst out laughing. "You're not the only one who feels that way."

She smiled. It was so good to talk to someone.

He placed his drink on the bar. "I think you should come meet some of my friends."

"Really?" She'd answered a little too eagerly. So uncool. She straightened her face. "Where are your friends? And why should I meet them?"

"Come on," he said. "Let's get outta here. You can see for yourself."

11

HUNTED

The shadows of the trees stirred, and the Company men appeared, their grey suits illuminated in the gathering light.

"Run!" Poe said. He took Caddy's hand, pulling her forward as she ran to keep up with him.

In the distance, several stars on the horizon quavered. They grew brighter, multiplied and broke into a convoy of headlights. In the opposite direction, another set of lights appeared. Caddy pointed to the road.

"Someone's coming!"

When they reached the house, Poe dropped her hand, dashed down the stairs and crashed the cellar door open. There were shouts, cries of terror. The Dreamers poured from the building like mice unearthed by a fox in the snow. The first truck arrived, careening up the lane in a cloud of dust. Caddy stood paralyzed, the Dreamers racing past her. The girl from earlier ran up and grabbed her hand.

"The bus is here," she said. "Across the field—run!"

Caddy spun on her heels and the two girls ran. The soil in the field was heavy and deep. Their legs jarred in ruts and their feet caught on clumps of dirt.

The trucks roared to a stop by the house. The Company men swarmed out, knives glinting. They singled out the weaker people, culling them from the group as they went.

"Don't look back," the girl said.

Caddy turned and saw the flash of a blade. A woman screamed and fell, tackled to the ground. The Company man's knife gleamed and arced, swung and struck, and the woman's blood sprayed in a crimson plume against the morning sky.

"Keep going!" the girl yelled.

They passed the man who'd taken Caddy's bowl in the cellar. He reached for her, their eyes locking for a lightning count before his face twisted and he stumbled, the air punching from his lungs. A Company man caught him and went to work. Caddy screamed as another grabbed her jacket, pulling her off her feet and tearing her away from the girl. The girl bolted to the right. The Company man rushed in, knife raised. Caddy covered her face. There was a guttural shout and the man fell beside her. She rolled out of the way and saw Poe, kicking the man repeatedly in the face and chest. "Get up!" he told her. "Run for the bus!"

Feet flying, Caddy trained her eyes on the road. The first Dreamers had reached the fence. They sprang over the wire and helped those behind them. Several jumped onto the bus. A woman took up position at the front doors, another at the back. Caddy hit the fence, falling against it. It dipped wildly, nearly throwing her to the ground. Two men grabbed her and hoisted her up and over by her arms. She touched down and was pushed toward the bus. More hands lifted her onto the vehicle. She tumbled in, collapsing into the first free seat she found. The driver revved the engine.

The last of the Dreamers—a man and two women—cleared the fence, Company men on their heels. The bus driver hollered and the emergency doors slammed shut. The two women clambered through the front door. Reaching for the stairs, the man tripped and the Company men fell on him like dogs. Their knives danced as the bus pulled away, the man's cries filling the air. No one looked back. No one witnessed the slaughter. The Dreamers stared straight ahead as though nothing was happening, their bodies jostling with the movements of the bus. Caddy covered her ears, blocking out the screams. She couldn't fathom the fate of the man and the others left in the field. Was Poe one of them? Or the girl? She hadn't seen either of them get on the bus.

Whipping around in her seat, Caddy searched for their faces. With great relief, she found the girl sitting halfway down the bus, head lowered. Poe was at the back, distant, absorbed. The bus swayed, dipping dangerously close to the ditch. It righted itself and lurched forward, the driver turning off the headlights as they roared down the road. Caddy grabbed the seat in front of her, her shoulders bumping those of the woman next to her. Moments later, the Company trucks could be seen, leaving the lane in a reckless convoy. The bus accelerated, bucking and rocking over the gravel. They took a hard turn onto a side road and then another, the driver hitting the gas once they rounded the corner.

Someone on the bus was moaning. A man stood, steadied himself, and walked along the aisle, searching for the source. There was shuffling and lowered voices, and the moans eventually stopped. Caddy checked the road. The trucks were no longer behind them. Had they outrun the Company men? She caught a glimpse of her sneakers. Red marks stained the fabric. Was that blood? Her hands started to shake, worse than ever, and the puncture wounds were open again and raw. What would Poe think of her now? She couldn't even save herself, let alone anyone else. Had he really meant what he'd said when he told her that she had given him hope? She hardly knew him. How could she trust a word he said? One thing was certain: if it hadn't been for him, she'd be dead in the field with the others.

Caddy dropped her hands in her lap and stared vacantly ahead like the rest, too horrified even to cry. Was this how her father had met his end? She couldn't bear to think about it, couldn't stand the idea of him dying in such an awful way. She chased the images of the knives and the blood from her mind, the shouting and screaming. They returned, relentless.

The bus bumped and rolled along the road. Eventually, the fields gave way to trees, the land slowly revealing itself with the rising sun. The driver relaxed, slowing to a less dangerous speed. Were they out of harm's way? A couple of people opened windows, letting the air in. It felt cool and sweet. Caddy looked at the woman beside her. She was asleep, mouth open, her head bobbing against the window with the movement of the bus. She was thin—fifty, maybe—her grey hair pulled back in a loose ponytail. How could she possibly sleep? So many of the Dreamers were sleeping. Poe wasn't, though. He was looking out the window. Caddy wanted to go to him and thank him. She wanted to sit beside him and stay close because that's the only way she would feel safe.

The bus ground its gears, pulling into a narrow lane. They rumbled through the trees to a small clearing in the woods and stopped. The Dreamers sat up and looked around. Eyes ringed with exhaustion, the driver stood and cleared his throat.

"This is where you disembark." He pointed to a man at the front. "He'll take you to the new location."

Caddy left the bus and lingered on the edge of the group, doing a head count while she waited for Poe. There were twenty-eight people remaining, including herself. Sixteen men and twelve women. They must have lost at least a dozen in the field.

As soon as Poe appeared she moved next to him. She didn't want to lose sight of him again. The man in charge raised his hand to make an announcement.

"We have a long hike ahead of us," he said, and without further discussion, walked into the woods.

The Dreamers followed obediently, snaking in a line through the trees. The forest was cool and moist. The soil was spongy with green moss. Caddy swatted at the mosquitoes that whined in undulating clouds. Several deer flies orbited her head. She was so hungry. She pressed her hand against her stomach to stop the noise.

"There will be food when we get there," Poe said.

It was a relief to hear his voice. "Do you know where we're going?"

"No. Only the leader knows."

"Is he always the leader?"

"We take turns. That way no one is a direct target. We keep knowledge to a minimum to prevent disclosure."

"You mean, in case we get caught?" she said.

"Yes."

Caddy thought about this. "The people back at the field . . . they weren't asked any questions. They were just . . . killed."

"We can't take any chances."

The line suddenly stopped. Someone had fallen. They waited while the woman was helped to her feet.

"Have you seen many people die?" Caddy asked.

Poe clenched his jaw. "This was my first experience," he confessed.

She looked at him in surprise. He spoke with such authority, she had just assumed he'd seen it before.

"I've never travelled with the Dreamers like this," he said. "I waited before I made the decision to really commit. But after Meg . . ." His voice trailed off.

"And how do you feel now?"

"If you're asking if I've changed my mind, I haven't."

"Even if people are being murdered right in front of you?"

"Especially then. Things have shifted for the worse. The Company is attacking with greater frequency. Now more than ever we need to stand together against the Dark."

"I'm not sure I could ever get used to seeing people murdered," Caddy said.

"We never get used to it."

"Then why has no one said anything about the ones who were killed? Everyone's acting like nothing happened. Do we even know how many people died back there?"

He spoke to her as though she was a child. "I know it's hard to understand, Cadence, but we do what we have to. It's important that we don't become overwhelmed."

"Overwhelmed? Why hasn't anyone called the police?"

He laughed derisively. "The police won't help us. They're part of the problem. The Company infiltrated them long ago. They're everywhere—governments, institutions—anywhere they can have the most control."

"Why don't the Dreamers fight back, then? Why does everyone just run away? Can't you arm yourselves? Can't you prepare?"

He smiled. It made her feel so naïve.

"Ours is the way of peace, Cadence. *Thou shalt not kill.* It is our most sacred covenant, strictly enforced. The sin of the one is the sin of the many. If we fight, if we take up arms, we're no better than them. You can't create peace through violence. You can't fight the Dark with more darkness."

It sounded so rote, like he was delivering lines. She turned it around on him. "You fought back."

His face hardened. "I shouldn't have done it—for so many reasons. We don't engage them. It just gives the Dark more opportunities. And that puts everyone at risk." Then he dropped the rhetoric, his mood softening. "It was stupid," he admitted. "I just couldn't let anything happen to you."

Caddy was taken by his honesty. She placed her hand on his arm. "If you hadn't done it, I'd be dead in that field. I'm indebted to you."

The line moved again. They walked in silence until she spoke.

"Are there other groups of Dreamers?"

Poe sighed. "There used to be. The Company men killed some and scattered the others. Hex has been gathering those who are left to keep us strong."

Caddy looked at the weary group trudging through the woods. How could Poe feel anything but despair? There seemed to be endless numbers of Company men and so few Dreamers. Surely they hadn't a chance against such odds. Why didn't the Company shoot all the Dreamers and be done with it? "Why do the men use knives?" she asked.

"You mean, why don't they use guns?"

"Yes."

"Knives are quieter. Guns draw too much attention. That would put them at a disadvantage."

It made sense. "Maybe that's why the One-Armed Bandit uses a knife," she said.

Poe gave her a funny look. "One-Armed Bandit?"

"It's what the paper's calling him—the guy who killed those people . . . the ones with the missing arms."

Poe smiled to himself. Obviously she'd said something that amused him.

"There is no One-Armed Bandit, Cadence."

"I read it in the paper . . ."

"It's the Company men. They left bodies where they knew they would be found. It was a threat to anyone who would bear the mark. They know we're recruiting so they're trying to dissuade those who would join the Dreamers by chopping off the left arm of their victims where the mark would be. The media created the whole One-Armed Bandit thing. It's a catchy name and I'm sure it's selling lots of papers. They haven't got a clue who the real perpetrators are."

"Oh." She felt stupid for mentioning it.

"The threat is real," he said. "The Company uses the paper to do their work because they know the Dreamers eschew technology to limit detection."

It would certainly explain her father's bizarre devotion to the newspaper. She was learning more about her own life every minute. "My father reads the paper. I thought he was being old-fashioned."

Poe smiled again, though this time he wasn't making fun of her. "Mine too. They read it for information. It's one of our communication streams, a way to send hidden messages. We post fake ads. You have to know what to look for, like clues. We don't do it very often because we don't want the Company to figure it out. They know we read the paper and sometimes they use it to spread fear."

"Do they always take the arms of the Dreamers they kill?"

"No one knows. They don't normally leave the bodies."

The idea was gruesome, either way. Caddy looked at her sneakers. The blood had dried to a dark patch. You couldn't really tell what it was, but she would never forget how it got there. If she didn't need her shoes she would kick them off and leave them in the woods.

The path took an upward turn, curving through the trees. She was so tired. And her legs ached. But how could she complain? Most of the Dreamers were more than twice her age and they seemed to be managing okay. She looked for the girl. She was ten people ahead, marching with her head down. Caddy wished she could speak to her. Maybe later, she thought. She was wondering if they would stop soon when the leader announced they'd reached their destination.

The log cabin squatted in a clearing among the trees. It had one small window beside a door pieced together from boards of various widths. The cabin was rustic and low, a strange mushroom, with a mossy roof and a tilted stone chimney. It looked damp and dark. Still, it had to be better than the cellar they'd occupied the night before.

The leader raised his hand. "This is it," he said. "We have proper facilities this time—an outhouse and a stream with running water." He gave a weak smile. "The stream is behind the cabin. If you wish to wash up, please do so now. Keep it brief and don't leave anything behind. We want to get inside as soon as possible. There's food to prepare and watch to keep. I need some volunteers."

Half a dozen hands were raised. Four people were chosen and the rest dismissed.

Caddy stayed beside Poe as the group walked to the stream. They wound down a rock-studded slope, stepping over the polished bones of tree roots. At the river, the men drifted off on their own, moving toward a cluster of smooth grey stones that reclined like seals at the base of a low waterfall. Poe leaned toward her.

"Stay with the women and watch the trees for movement," he said.

Caddy followed the women farther downstream. They searched for a quiet pool and found one in a wide curve of the river. It looked so deceptively peaceful, she could almost convince herself that nothing was wrong. The women mutely shed their clothes, as though it were the most natural thing to do. Caddy peeked shyly at their naked bodies. They were as varied as the coloured pebbles in the stream. Yet each one bore the mark on their arm, even the girl who had helped her. They stepped into the pool, undergarments in hand, and sank up to their necks. Dunking their heads, they scrubbed their hair. Some pulled water methodically up their arms and over their shoulders. No one talked.

Removing her jacket, Caddy folded it neatly and placed it on the riverbank. She did the same with her shirt and pants. Everything else she left on—her bra, her underwear, even her sneakers and socks, because she wanted to wash the dirt and blood from her shoes. Folding her arms across her chest, she slipped into the water. The cold energized her skin. She navigated over the slippery stones to a flat spot. When she was in over her hips, she inhaled and dunked below the surface. The river burbled in her ears. The water felt so good, she wanted to stay under forever. Bobbing up for air, Caddy blinked the stream from her eyes and worked off her undergarments. She scrubbed them together and pulled them back on, floating lightly on her toes. Next, she rubbed her sneakers with a handful of small stones until they were clean—as clean as she could get them. No matter how hard she scrubbed, the blood left a faint stain on the fabric.

The women eventually emerged from the water and Caddy did the same. When everyone was dressed, they walked together up the slope. Caddy trailed behind the girl, sneakers squeaking with wet, hoping to speak to her. The right opportunity never presented itself because the women remained silent, so she did too.

Inside the cabin, the smell of fried onions and bread dough tugged at Caddy's appetite. The men were already there, sitting on the floor. The girl took a seat between two older women. Poe was reclining against the wall on the far side of the room. There was no space beside him so Caddy took a spot on the edge of the group.

The cabin was dark, the one small window providing little light for the cooks to prepare food. They worked, stacking strips of fried bread into a small teepee on a wooden board. A woman offered them around the room along with a pitcher of water and a single glass. No one took more than one piece of bread, Caddy noticed, though they must have been as hungry she was. When the bread came her way, she did the same, taking only one piece. The woman beside her took two and gave the second to her. The last thing Caddy wanted was preferential treatment. She accepted the bread out of politeness and looked around to see if anyone had noticed what the woman had done. They were all focused on the bread in their own hands. She felt too guilty to eat two pieces, so she pushed one into her jacket pocket for later.

After the bread, the group relaxed. Small circles were formed with people speaking in soft voices. Caddy looked at Poe. He was resting against the cabin wall, his eyes closed, the diffuse light from the window highlighting his cheekbones. He covered his face with his hands and shuddered, and Caddy realized he was crying. She wanted to go to him, to comfort him and tell him it wasn't his fault—no matter what he thought—he wasn't responsible for Meg's death. As if reading her mind, he dropped his hands to his sides and his eyes locked on hers. The door to the cabin opened and everyone turned. It was Hex and Red.

12

KENJI AND CO.

S kylark glided alongside Kenji. He walked, one foot after the other, like a human. It looked so fun.

"Do you always move with your feet?" she asked. She was still feeling the effects of the blue drink from the bar.

"Yeah, most of the time. Why?"

"I don't know. I just thought everyone glided or jumped around here."

"I jump," he said. "And sometimes I even glide. But I like walking. That's what legs are for. Besides, I don't want to attract any unnecessary attention."

"What do you mean?"

"People don't glide on earth. Whenever I'm there, I walk so I don't stand out any more than I already do."

"Do you go there often?" Skylark asked, trying to contain her excitement. If she were a Guide, she'd never leave the earth behind.

"Often enough."

She stopped, looked at her feet, then looked at Kenji. "I don't think I know how to walk anymore."

"It's easy. Watch me." Kenji took several steps, turned like a runway model, and walked back.

Skylark took a tentative step, wobbled dangerously, straightened herself and stopped. She was as graceful as a store mannequin come to life.

"Try again," he said.

Lifting her chin she slowly stepped forward, placing one foot in front of the other like a geisha. "Hey . . . I think I'm doing it . . ." She flashed a huge smile just before she tipped, her arms flying up to regain her balance. When she did this, her robe popped up in place of her clothes and reverted again.

Kenji smirked. "What was that?"

"What?" she tried to deflect.

"Your clothes. What happened there?"

"Oh . . . uh . . . sometimes that happens when I try something new . . . It's nothing, really." That didn't sound very convincing, even to herself.

"Do it again."

"Why?"

"Because it's a neat trick."

Was he making fun of her? He smiled back.

"Okay, fine," she said. Closing her eyes, she loosened her particles and slipped back to her robe state.

He clapped his hands. "Very cool."

"Really?"

"Yeah. Seriously. I'm impressed. My friends are going to love you. Now, try walking again."

Skylark reverted to her street clothes and walked, slow and deliberate. Staring at her feet, she took fifteen steps, attempted a turn, made it and walked back to Kenji. "Was that good?"

"Yeah. Now do it without looking at your feet."

Skylark squared her shoulders. Fixing her eyes on the building in front of her, she took ten steps, turned, focused on Kenji and walked back, a big smile on her face.

"Perfect," he said. "You're a pro."

"Hey, don't make fun of me."

"I'm not."

"Yes, you are."

"Honestly. I think you're amazing. Truly."

"Really?"

"Sure."

No one had called her amazing in a very long time, certainly not since she'd arrived here. It felt so good. Kenji was nice. Hanging out with him was fun. She hoped his friends were as enjoyable.

They continued toward their destination, Skylark biting her lip with concentration, hands held out at her sides as she walked unsteadily beside Kenji. Every once in a while she'd pitch, exclaim under her breath and right herself. She didn't give a thought to where they were going or who they would meet.

"Walking takes a lot of effort," she said.

He laughed. "Even more when you've got training wheels."

"Are we almost there?" she asked.

He pointed to a modest red-brick building. "This is HQ." He opened the door for her, grabbing her hand as she tripped over the threshold.

Skylark looked around. It didn't belong with the rest of the city. It was dusty and old and cluttered with stuff—books, piles of papers, a worn couch. "Your friends live here?"

He ushered her toward an office, jiggled the door open and towed her in by one hand. Behind a worn wooden desk, an old cowboy reclined, eyes closed, hands clasped across his chest, black cowboy boots crossed at the ankles on the desktop. He wore a big white hat, white T-shirt and blue jeans, his grey beard quivering as he muttered to himself. Skylark wanted to laugh when she saw him, he looked so comical.

Kenji let the door bang shut. The old man started awake with a grunt, jackknifed in his chair and crashed his boots to the floor. "Kenji, you big—" He cut himself short when his blue eyes landed on her.

Kenji grinned, presenting her like a trophy. "Francis, I'd like you to meet Skylark."

The old man dropped his jaw, speechless. He cupped his beard, looking at Kenji for confirmation. Kenji nodded.

Skylark felt suddenly shy. What was going on here?

"Go ahead, Skylark," Kenji said. "Say hi to Francis."

She waved and smiled. "Hi. You've got really blue eyes."

Francis smacked his hand on the desk, sending papers flapping into the air. "Unbelievable!"

"I found her at the bar," Kenji gloated. "She just learned how to walk."

The old man pushed away from his desk and cowboyed over to her, the heels of his boots clomping loudly over the wooden floor. "Say something else, sweetheart."

She looked at Kenji, who smiled encouragingly.

"It's nice to meet you," she said. "Are you a Guide too?"

Francis guffawed and shook his head. "What'd you tell her, hotshot?"

Kenji shrugged good-naturedly and slouched into an old red easy chair. He folded his hands lightly in front of him, one foot jiggling. She stood, monkey in the middle, looking back and forth between the two men.

"Okay, Skylark," Kenji said. "Show him your true colours."

"What do you mean?"

"Do that thing you showed me on the way over."

"Walking?"

"No—that other thing—with your clothes."

She hesitated. Maybe it wasn't a good idea to go showing her true colours to strangers. But here was Kenji, nodding her on. And they both seemed so interested in her. It was nice to have the attention. She closed her eyes and concentrated, and her real form took shape. She held herself there, letting her robe wave around her for full effect before returning to her street clothes.

Kenji tilted his head at Francis. "Neat trick, huh?"

The old cowboy raised his eyebrows. "Does Timon know?"

"Nope. I wanted you to see first."

Francis took her by the hand and spoke as though addressing a three-year-old. She couldn't help smiling at the way his beard jiggled when he talked, he was leaning so close.

"We're going to go see another friend of ours who would love to meet you. We can jump together. Are you game?"

It had to be better than moping around in her room. "Sure."

"Shouldn't you call first?" Kenji said. "You know how the old codger hates it when we arrive *unannounced.*"

Old codger? Skylark tried to hide her disappointment. She was hoping Timon was young.

Francis brushed Kenji off. "This is too important. Skylark and I will meet you there—don't get sidetracked. Skylark, you're going to hold my hand and let your mind go completely blank. Can you do that?"

"I think so."

"Good."

It was actually a relief to let someone else do the jumping for a change—especially with her track record. Skylark took Francis's hand. With a bright clap, they vanished. Seconds later, they were standing in an ornately decorated Victorian-era room, books lining the walls, fire roaring, stately wingback chairs strategically placed to allow for the most heat. It was a nice place. Much nicer than Francis and Kenji's. And she hadn't reverted back to her robe state when they jumped. Probably because Francis had done the driving—she'd hardly needed to use any energy at all. Certainly not enough to make her return to her etheric form. In any case, she was feeling quite pleased about it all until an irritated voice addressed them.

"You know how I dislike it when you arrive unannounced," one of the wingback chairs said. It had a heavy English accent.

Francis took a step toward the fire, her hand still clasped in his. "I'm sorry, Timon. But I think you'll be interested in seeing this."

A ribbon of smoke curled above the chair, followed by several languid puffs. "Well . . . what is it?"

Francis lead Skylark over to the chair. She was anxious, wanting to make a good impression, except that the toe of her boot caught on the edge of the carpet and she nearly tumbled headlong into the fire. Kenji materialized at that very moment, caught her, and helped her up.

"You should have let me bring her," he said, giving Skylark a wink.

She smiled, brushed the hair from her eyes and found herself in front of a man in his late sixties. He was clean-shaven, with a thick head of bronze hair and two great hairy caterpillars over his blue eyes. He wore a rumpled brown tweed jacket with a matching vest and pants, and brown leather loafers with crepe soles. A pipe hung from his mouth as though it had grown there. He peered disparagingly at Skylark through a cloud of smoke.

"Kenji found her," Francis started right in.

Timon clenched his teeth on the stem of his pipe. "At the bar, no doubt."

Kenji ignored the comment, addressing Skylark instead. "Show him your little trick."

She was starting to feel like a trained seal. Still, the attention was delightful. She closed her eyes and concentrated, the way she had before. Her robe and true form appeared for a moment, then slid away again as her human form reappeared. She opened her eyes. Francis looked hopefully at Timon, who puffed on his pipe, then plucked it from his mouth and sighed, clearly unimpressed.

"A parlour trick, easily learned. We've seen this kind of aberration in Spectrals before."

"Only fleetingly," Francis said. "Skylark's the real deal. Look at her EP."

Timon pointed the stem of his pipe below one eye. "There's nothing wrong with my vision, Francis." But he allowed his gaze to slowly drift over Skylark all the same.

Francis grew impatient. "Tell me you see it."

Timon stuffed his pipe back in his mouth and nodded begrudgingly.

"It's strong, isn't it?" Francis said. "Stronger than we've ever seen before."

Timon snatched the pipe from his mouth again and pointed it at her as though she were a piece of furniture. "What's going on there . . . with her arm?"

"It's not my fault," Skylark blurted out. "I was transformed this way."

Timon paused, lips open with surprise. He turned to Kenji. "A mouth-talker too?"

Kenji nodded.

Timon turned back to Francis. "Is she capable of telepathic communication?"

Francis looked at Kenji. Kenji looked at Skylark.

"I'm getting better," she said. For some reason she really wanted them to like her, though she didn't know why. Maybe it was because they were the closest thing to human she'd met since arriving. And they seemed so excited to have found her . . .

"What about weapons training?" Timon asked.

Skylark took a step toward his chair. "I've done a lot of marching . . . None of the swords would have me . . . I really just got here."

Francis raised his hands. "Did you hear that?" he said cheerfully. "None of the swords would have her."

Obviously, he thought that was a good thing. Skylark hoped Timon would think so too.

"Yes, yes," he said, dismissing Francis with a wave of his pipe. "Does she know what we do here?"

Francis and Kenji answered simultaneously. "No."

"What about her Frequency? Do they know she's here?"

Kenji and Francis looked at Skylark. She shook her head.

"My totem doesn't even know," she said.

Timon tapped the stem of his pipe against his teeth. "Figure it out and get back to me. And for heaven's sake, let the girl know what she's getting into."

Francis saluted. He took Skylark's hand and prepared to jump.

"And Francis . . ." Timon interrupted them. "This isn't anything close to a pass. We need to know more before she becomes a full-fledged member."

"Of course," he said. And before Timon could say anything more, Francis and Skylark snapped from the room. They landed in the office with a neat pop, Kenji arriving on their heels. Francis ushered Skylark to a paper-littered seat, brushed the papers to the floor, plopped her down and pulled up a chair beside her. Kenji chose to prop himself against the wall, arms folded. Francis gave him a look.

"Why don't you have a seat, Kenji, you're making her nervous."

"I'm okay," she said.

Kenji sneered. "Just get on with it, old man."

Francis grew thoughtful. "What we do here . . . it's—"

"Very dangerous work," Kenji interjected.

Francis scowled at him. "It's top secret. Nobody really knows what we do here. It's for safety reasons."

"We hunt bad guys," Kenji said.

"One bad guy," Francis corrected him. "We've been chasing one very bad guy for a very long time."

"Centuries," Kenji said. ". . . if you consider time relevant."

"They do on earth," Francis said.

"Right."

Francis tipped his hat back. "We're a dark operations group, working independently from the Legion of Light. We have unique skills, so to speak, a special energetic orientation that sets us apart from the rest. We're just a bunch of misfits, really. But we can do things and go places others can't. And we don't answer to anyone."

"Except Timon," Kenji added. "He's the founding father of our little glee club."

"And he's all right," Francis said.

Kenji shrugged. "For the most part."

Skylark blinked back at them. They were making her dizzy. "You just look like Guides to me."

"Is that so?" Francis stood, his hands at his sides. With a slight tremor, he slipped from his human form. He beamed back at her, silver hair and beard flowing, his skin and robe glowing. Skylark straightened in her chair, mouth gaping, and turned toward Kenji. He, too, had changed into an ethereal being. They were just like her! He smiled when he saw the look on her face.

"What are we?" she asked.

Francis winked. "We're a whole lot of confusion, it seems. We have a set ethereal shape, like a Spectral, but we can slipstream our form and hold it like a Guide. That makes us pretty special." He leaned toward her. "I can't tell you how thrilling it is to have found another one of our own. That makes four of us now in the City of Light, including Timon. And I think you're even more special than the three of us combined. I just feel it."

"Where are your totems?" Skylark asked.

"I never had one," Kenji said. He pointed to Francis. "He lost his."

"Don't go there," Francis warned him. "You know that's a tender bruise."

They reverted back to their human forms. Francis took her hand. "We wouldn't expect you to start right away. You'd have to train. You'd have to familiarize yourself with the way we do things around here."

"You could get hurt," Kenji said.

Skylark frowned. What did she have to lose? Anything would be better than trying to fit in with the Spectrals.

Kenji and Francis looked at her hopefully, waiting for her answer.

"I'm supposed to be a Warrior," she said. "I suppose I could get hurt either way."

Francis glanced at Kenji. "True, true. But we'd have to get approval from your Frequency."

"I don't think that'll be too hard. They don't seem to know what to do with me anyway."

"So, they won't mind then," Francis said.

Kenji pushed himself from the wall and stood in front of her. "We should at least show her what she's going up against."

"Oh, yeah." Francis sat back down in his chair. Concentrating, he projected a holographic image into the room. It wavered in the air, taking form. The image sharpened and Skylark gasped in disbelief. It was the well-dressed man—the one with the ice-chip eyes. The sight of him made her scarred arm spike with pain.

Francis enlarged the image. "We call him the Speaker. I won't lie to you. He's one mean desperado. This guy's been messing things up since time immemorial. He didn't start out so tough. He was small potatoes. But he's been getting dirtier and meaner with every offence. Timon had an inkling about him from the beginning—call it a gut feeling. No one else cared about him around here so they pretty much let us do what we want. Anyway, we've been watching him for a very long time. And Ol' Slippery Tongue's picked up all kinds of fans on earth over the years. We're getting close though. Real close. We've got intelligence now—good sources."

A series of scenes scrolled by and Francis narrated. The Spanish Inquisition. The slaughter at Nanking. The Chicago fire. Hitler's armies. The Salem witch trials—hundreds of tragedies across time. Scene after scene, the Speaker was there, his frosty eyes gazing indifferently upon the altar of human suffering. Skylark gripped her bad arm, the pain growing with every image.

Francis rattled on. "He's got a neat trick he does with his voice." He zoomed in on the picture. "Watch this."

The Speaker raised a small, intricate metal funnel to his perfect lips. Skylark watched in horror as the demon moved his mouth and a dark tendril wormed from the end of the funnel into his victim's ear.

"I've turned the volume down so you can't hear him," Francis said. "He uses his words to convince people to do bad things. When they do bad things, the Light diminishes on the earth plane."

"Which gives the Dark a chance to take hold," Kenji said.

"He gets up real close to his victims," Francis continued. "He uses that dark tendril to transmit his ideas into people's heads. He trades in hopelessness and despair. Madness and greed. He feeds off the vulnerable and power-hungry in equal measure, preying on those who have fallen into the grips of desperation or moral corruption. We've noticed the tendril is getting longer the stronger he gets. Who knows how far he'll be able to reach. Maybe he won't even need it if he keeps going."

"He's a soul collector too," Kenji said. "A trophy hunter. He keeps the souls of all his victims trapped in little glass vials— thousands of them. For every vial he keeps, there's one less soul in the universe. One less flicker of Light."

Skylark thought she would swoon. It was all so dreadful. "What happens to them . . . the trapped souls . . . ?"

"Well . . ." Francis scrubbed his beard. "They're lost between the frequencies. They stay there, unable to evolve or see the Light."

Between the frequencies. Skylark shuddered. She'd been there. During the initiation ceremony. What a dreadful, lifeless place. She winced, the pain in her arm blistering. What did this demon, this taker of life, want with her?

"I've seen him before," she confessed, her voice a whisper.

"What?" Francis turned his head so quickly, the image was lost.

The pain in her arm thankfully left with it.

"I've seen him before," she said again.

"Where?" Kenji demanded.

"On the earth plane."

Francis and Kenji exchanged looks.

"Could you find him again?" Kenji asked.

"I think so . . . I don't know. I found him by accident . . . during a jump. There's some connection between us—something from my past. I just don't know what it is."

Francis took her hand. "We need to talk to your superiors right now, get things arranged. Can you take us where we need to go?"

"I can get us to my dorm. My totem's there. He may be able to help."

"Your totem . . . right." Kenji screwed up his face at Francis. "You know how I feel about working with animals."

"He's not that bad," Skylark said. "He's just a mouse."

Kenji looked skeptical. "It's not the size that worries me. It's the moralizing."

"He's a bit boring," Skylark said. "Other than that, he's okay."

Francis pursed his lips at Kenji. "What do you think?"

"I guess we can work around him." He took Skylark's hand. "Ready to rock and roll?"

Francis stood and took her other hand. "Let 'er rip!"

Skylark called up an image of the dorm building. The roaring started, and she saw Francis and Kenji exchange split-second looks of horror before the blast. All three came hurtling down in a heap in the middle of the practice field. They were nowhere near the dorm. Kenji adjusted his glasses and looked sardonically around.

"This is all very pretty, Skylark, but . . ."

She scrabbled to her feet, slipped back into her human form, and began picking the grass from Francis's beard. "I'm so sorry. Do you want to try again?"

Francis stood and offered Kenji a hand. Kenji accepted it with a measure of reproach.

"Try to get us in the right ballpark, Skylark," Kenji said. "And go easy on the rocket juice."

Skylark concentrated again, this time imagining Sebastian inside her room. There was the roar, and the flash, and they crashed down on her bed, Sebastian leaping to the desk in terror.

"Please! Watch where you're going!" he shouted.

Kenji eyed the mouse with amusement. "Nice totem."

Sebastian stood on his hind feet, his pink nose twitching. "I see you've made some friends." He sniffed in disgust. "You smell like the bar."

Kenji smelled the lapel of his jacket. Francis clumped down from the bed. He approached the mouse, getting in close.

"We'd like to talk to you about Skylark."

13

THE MARK

Hex and Red entered the cabin. She wore sunglasses and a brown silk scarf tied over her hair. In her hands she carried a thin grey river stone, the shape and size of a dessert plate, and a brown leather pouch tied with a cord. They greeted no one, moving quietly into the shadows to wait. Poe sat beside Caddy.

"They're here for the ceremony," he said.

The eyes of the woman next to her flashed with hope.

"What do you mean?" Caddy asked.

Poe pointed to his arm. "It's time to choose, Cadence."

He was talking about the mark. He wanted her to be tattooed. Had he known all along this was coming? Was that why he'd confided in her? To gain her trust? The blood pounded in Caddy's ears. How dare he single her out and make her choose like this? Everyone in the room was staring at her. She didn't want the mark. She wasn't ready to make that commitment—she might never be.

"I don't want to do it, Poe."

"It's a great honour to bear the mark. The Dreamers need you. We can't survive without you."

"No, I don't want it. I don't want to end up like the rest."

Poe persisted. "You've seen what we're up against, Cadence. These people have been holding the dream for generations. If we lose this, if the link is broken, your vision of the future will become reality."

Caddy stared at the floor. Maybe she was being paranoid. Maybe she was just afraid. She wished she could share Poe's conviction. But his intensity paralyzed her. "I can't."

"You don't have to stay," he said. "You can leave if you want."

This made her angry. Stay and be marked, or go—were those her only options? "You keep saying that. What do I have to go back to? My father's missing. There are Company men everywhere. I'll be killed like Meg."

His eyes clouded at the mention of her name. He didn't need to be reminded that his girlfriend was dead. Surely the guilt he carried was deep, even if he hid it well. For her, it was crippling. "I'm so tired."

He took her hand in his. "I know. We're all tired. But we must keep going." He drew her close, and she allowed herself to rest her head against his chest. He held her in his arms, speaking softly in her ear. "I know how hard it is. It's too much for one person to bear. That's why we have to stay together, so we can help each other carry this burden."

She shook her head. "All those arms . . . I can't stand the idea of it."

"That's what the Company wants—to scare you, to break us apart. The mark connects us and makes us stronger. It's what the Company fears most."

He held her closer. She could hear his heart beating and smell the river on his clothes. Could she trust him? Could she trust anyone? She wanted to. She wanted to let go, to surrender to the tide and let it take her so she wouldn't have to make choices. The truth was, she was terrified of dying alone. Better to belong than not belong and be forsaken. Raising her eyes, she could see the dark curve of his lashes against his cheek. She clung to him, her resolve waning. He squeezed her hand.

On some imperceptible cue, the Dreamers created a circle around them. Hex kneeled in front of her, holding the stone and leather pouch. Red lurked in a corner of the room, watching. Poe left her, taking a seat with the others.

Hex placed the river stone on the floor and removed her glasses, the empty socket a dark shock against the life in her sky-blue eye. Unwinding the leather cord, she worked the pouch open with her fingers and extracted a handful of wood shavings, setting them in a neat pile on the stone. She produced a needle, a spool of thread, a box of matches and a smaller fabric pouch that glistened as though sprinkled with fairy dust.

The Dreamers hummed, the note pulsing rhythmically down Caddy's spine. Her eyes grew heavy. Hex drew a measure of thread from the spool, threaded the needle and twisted the strand around the length of it until only the tip was exposed. She struck a match, lit the wood shavings, and pulled a penknife from her pocket, running the blade back and forth through the flame.

"Give me your hand," she said, the fire dancing in her good eye.

Caddy felt hypnotized, transfixed. Somewhere deep in her mind, she didn't want to do what Hex asked. Yet she was powerless to resist, as if the note and the expectation of the Dreamers were controlling her through some form of witchcraft. She inhaled sharply as Hex made a quick cut on her finger and squeezed several thick red drops onto the stone. Caddy held the wound to her lips to stem the flow of blood then cradled her hand in her lap. The Dreamers' voices ascended. Hex opened the small fabric pouch and pinched a bit of shiny dust from inside, sprinkling it over the blood.

"Roll up your sleeve."

Caddy removed her jacket and rolled her sleeve to her elbow. Her skin looked so pale and vulnerable. It made her want to cry.

Against her volition, she offered up her arm. Hex slapped it several times to numb the skin, sterilized the tip of the needle in the flame and dipped it in the blood and powder mix. Caddy caught her breath when the needle punctured her skin. Hex worked, evenly, methodically, and the mark took form. From the depths of her trance, Caddy struggled in vain to free herself. The humming mounted, pushing her deeper and deeper beyond the shoals of her will. She could hear Hex's voice hissing faintly inside her head.

"You will contact your father," she thought she heard her say. "You will bring him to me."

Hours later, Caddy surfaced from the murkiness of a troubled dream. She was lying on a blanket in the middle of the cabin. Her head was heavy. How long had she been out? Had she even gone through with the marking ceremony? Her eyes darted to her left arm. It was wrapped in a clean cloth bandage. There was a faint red outline where the mark had bled through the fabric. She looked around the room. The Dreamers were sitting quietly. Hex and Red were gone. Poe saw that she was awake and came to her with water in a wooden cup. He helped her to a sitting position and held the cup to her lips. She gulped. She was so thirsty. He brushed the hair from her face.

"We are forever bound, now," he said.

And so it seemed to be true. Caddy could feel the bond between them, an energetic cable from him to her—to all the Dreamers.

"Can you stand?" he asked.

Taking his hand, she stood and followed him to a corner of the cabin. The Dreamers beamed at her. She sensed their gratitude. And their relief. It made her feel important. Poe helped her to the floor, carefully, and sat beside her, her head in his lap. His energy flowed with hers.

"I can feel you so close to me," she said.

"Now I can never hide from you."

He laughed and to her delight, his happiness rang inside her. It was so intimate, so personal. It made her want to stay like this with him forever. She tried to decipher her emotions, to rationalize her feelings. Was she falling in love with him? Was the feeling real? Did she even care? After all the fear and misery of the last few days, this joy was a welcome drug. She reached up and touched his lips. "In the Emptiness, there is no laughter."

He kissed her fingertips, sending a shiver through her body. "It's a place beyond the vibration of life."

"Why would anyone want that?" she whispered. "How could we ever allow it?"

"So many have given up. People have lost their way. There is very little hope in the world."

"Is that the source of the Emptiness?"

"Yes, in part." Poe sipped from the wooden cup and passed it to her. "There is a Darkness that abhors the Light and the life in it. It has existed since the world began."

"If it's always been here, why destroy the earth now?"

"We're at a crossroads. The Darkness is taking advantage of the hopelessness."

Caddy let her mind linger over this and was suddenly moved by a revelation. "They're the ones who are scared. They're afraid of us."

Poe smiled. He was so beautiful when he smiled. "Yes. The balance could tip in either direction. The veil over human consciousness is lifting. We are only just realizing how powerful we are."

She was elated by the idea. Anything was possible. Then she looked at the Dreamers lying on the floor and her euphoria faltered. They seemed so tattered and worn. Several were coughing. What could a handful of terrified people do against such powerful forces? The joy in her heart waned and doubt crept in its place. She could hear Hex's voice, telling her to contact her father. Telling her to bring him here. Had she really said those words? Or had Caddy imagined it? She hadn't considered the danger to him when she'd allowed herself to be marked. She could see now that it was a mistake. Maybe this is what Hex had wanted all along. Maybe she'd even used Poe to trick her ...

Outside the cabin, the sky darkened with gathering clouds, and there was a muted sound like someone weeping.

"Do you hear that?" Poe asked.

Caddy held her breath and listened. "It's starting to rain."

The drops fell, tapping lightly at first—then pounding on the roof in a fury of fists. Caddy withdrew into herself, resting her head on her hands. She felt so tired again. And the mark on her arm was starting to burn.

14

THE SPEAKER

"The Council was more than fair," Sebastian said, clinging to Skylark's hair.

"Fair?" Trust the mouse to take their side. "They said I couldn't come back if I decide to work with Kenji and Francis, and that I'm no longer a member of my Frequency."

Kenji snorted. "Those guys are about as fun as a bag of knives."

Francis clomped backwards in front of her. "Slow down, honey. What are you so angry for? You said yourself you didn't fit in with them."

Skylark crossed her arms. "I can't believe they were so happy to dump me."

"They didn't know what they had. We appreciate what you are." Francis pointed at her feet as she walked. "Look how good you are at that now." He turned to Kenji for support.

"Fast learner," Kenji said.

"It's not the most comfortable way to travel," Sebastian complained.

Kenji raised an eyebrow at the mouse. "Have you seen her jump?"

Francis stopped, forcing her to stop as well. "So, how about it, Skylark? What do you say? Are you going to work with us?" His sapphire eyes blazed at her.

She looked away. She didn't want to give in so easily. Sebastian busied himself tickling the hairs on the back of her neck. "Yes," she grudgingly agreed, pouting at Francis. "You knew I'd say yes."

Kenji held out his hand. "Welcome to the island of misfit toys."

Skylark took it and they shook, sealing the deal.

Francis pushed his Stetson to the back of his head. "Well, now, that's good news," he said, and got straight to business. "Okay, first assignment—figure out how you know the Speaker."

"Whoa, Tex," Kenji intervened. "Let the girl settle in."

"It's all right," Skylark said. "I don't mind. We'll need to go to the Hall of Records."

"Fine. I'm flying the plane this time." Kenji touched her sleeve and with a bright flash, they landed in front of *The Book of Events,* Francis appearing right behind them.

"Okay, honey, show us what you've got," he said.

Skylark called up her memory of the Speaker, wrestling to control the fear and pain she felt when she thought of him.

Sebastian murmured in her ear. "Relax your mind. Imagine the scene without the emotional investment."

She closed her eyes, envisioning the car and the girl beneath it. The book flew open, its pages flapping wildly.

"Easy . . . easy," Francis soothed.

Skylark tipped her head back, letting the images flow. The book slowed and came to rest. She opened her eyes and looked down at the page.

"Is that it?" Francis asked.

She nodded.

"Put it on-screen."

The image sprang into the room, three-dimensional and life size. The scene unfolded and Skylark's pulse quickened. Sirens wailed. People shouted. The girl lay beneath the wheels of the car, as twisted and broken as a discarded doll. Pain seared along the lightning strike on Skylark's arm. She clenched her teeth in agony.

Kenji pointed to the man behind the wheel. "Would you look who it is. . . . a grey guy."

They watched the driver leave the car, brush off his suit and walk away.

Francis clucked his tongue. "Tsk, tsk, up to no good as usual."

"I don't see the Speaker," Kenji said.

The pain blistered through Skylark's body. She doubled over, clutching her head. Kenji elbowed Francis, who rushed to her side.

"What's happening?" he asked.

"My head . . . it's splitting open . . ."

"Try to relax . . ." Francis looked at Kenji for help, but he just made a face and shook his head.

The mouse massaged the back of her neck. Francis patted her shoulder, one eye on the scene. "Keep relaxing . . ."

"Hey, there he is," Kenji said. "On the right."

The Speaker blipped in and out of the scene.

"Go back," Francis ordered the screen.

The recording rewound and began playing again.

"There!" Kenji said. "On the sidewalk."

"Stop," Francis said. "Go back—slowly."

The image reversed, clicking frame by frame. When the Speaker reappeared, Francis told the recording to freeze. The demon stood, his frigid eyes casually watching the turmoil on the street. Skylark straightened, the pain in her arm mercifully subsiding once the image had stopped. Francis sauntered up to the Speaker and followed his line of sight. "Who's he talking to, I wonder?"

Skylark tentatively approached the car, her pulse hammering in her ears as she drew in close to examine the girl. The bloodied hair. The impossible angle of the arm. The sneaker in the middle of the road. Her eyes. Soft. Grey . . .

The icy finger of memory pushed a shiver up her spine. She was the girl beneath the car! She'd been hit while riding her bike to school to see Poe! This was the part of her memory she'd been missing. This was why she was overcome with pain whenever she saw the Speaker.

Skylark moved into the demon's line of vision and stared into his dispassionate face. "It's me," she said in a hushed voice. "I was standing on the sidewalk after she got hit by the car . . . after I got hit. The Speaker was the one who told me I was dead."

No one said anything for the longest time. Francis chewed the fringe of beard along his bottom lip.

"You know what this means," he finally said. "Skylark was a priority target."

She looked at him in shock. "A priority target?"

"That's right." He gestured at the driver. "These grey ones are assassins. They work for this guy." He jerked his thumb at the Speaker. "They even dress like him. They don't kill just anybody. They pick their targets. They're very deliberate. The Speaker only shows up if the target is extra important. He must have really wanted you gone."

"She was just a high school kid," Kenji said.

Francis rocked on his heels. "Was she?" They both turned to Skylark.

Why would anyone have wanted to kill her? She was popular. She had so many friends. She had Poe! Her memories were happy, for the most part. Why would someone want her dead? "I don't understand . . ."

The mouse patted her neck. "Don't let it upset you. These images can no longer harm you."

Francis cupped his chin, musing. "This is a real puzzle . . ."

Kenji pretended to brush some invisible lint off the Speaker's shoulder then pointed his finger like a gun and pulled the trigger. "We've got you now, buddy."

"What about the grey ones?" Skylark asked. "Why aren't you hunting them?"

"They're out of our jurisdiction," Kenji said.

Skylark looked at Francis to explain. He scrubbed his beard.

"We're not allowed to meddle with the Natives. Humans are strictly off limits. They need to fight their own battles. It's all about free will and the growth of the individual soul as part of collective enlightenment and whatnot. They have the power to change their world in a heartbeat." He snapped his fingers. "But they have to figure it out for themselves. We can't tell them anything. Oh, we can guide them here and there, but ultimately, they're on their own. Our job is to make sure things don't get outta hand on this side." He turned on the heels of his boots and mulled over the scene. "Do you think we should run through this again, just to see if there's anything we've missed?"

"What about Skylark?" Kenji asked. He held his hands to his head, miming her pain.

"Oh, right."

The mouse reared up, pressing his small fingers on her temple. "I'll send light to deflect the pain. Move away from the scene, Skylark. It may help."

She stood to one side of the room as Francis and Kenji rewound and gesticulated and discussed. Over and over. Maybe it was the mouse's light, or the repetition of the images, but with each pass she found herself less involved. The pain in her head and arm had subsided and she was actually growing bored with the endless analysis. Until he showed up. Francis had finally allowed the scene to scroll through to the end when Poe burst through the crowd, as wild-eyed as a panicked horse.

"Stop the image!" Skylark shouted, and the scene froze. She walked through the crowd, past the police and the emergency workers, past the car and the broken body of the girl. When she reached Poe, a longing, deep and primitive, took hold of her. She raised her hand—she couldn't stop herself—and touched his face. A charge ran through her body. Her particles raced. Balancing on her toes, she closed her eyes and kissed him. A fever consumed her when her lips met his. The room and everything in it fell away. It was just her and him, the way it used to be . . .

Francis coughed. "Skylark?"

The sound of his voice wrenched her from the moment. She turned on him. "What do you want?"

"We should wrap this up. Close the image," he ordered the book.

The book slapped shut and the image disappeared.

Skylark flew at the podium. "Bring him back!" she cried. "You can't take him away from me!" Her soul raged, the pain of loss tearing through her body. Her power arced in a braided coil of crackling light, snapping and skipping wildly to the ceiling before everything went black.

Skylark woke in her robe on a couch back at headquarters. She must have reverted when she passed out. The mouse was sleeping on a pillow next to her. Kenji slouched in an overstuffed chair, feet jutting out in front of him. Francis paced, worrying his beard. They were speaking telepathically so as not to wake her, no doubt. Skylark eavesdropped on their conversation.

"Why was the Speaker at her death?" Kenji asked.

"I don't know."

"I heard the Prism sounded every fork at her initiation ceremony."

Francis folded his arms. "Who told you that?"

"I have my sources. I heard she fell between the frequencies too."

"That's bunk and you know it. No being has ever returned from between the frequencies in the same form."

"That's just what I heard."

"Yeah? What else did you hear?"

"That she's an energetic aberration, capable of tipping the balance either way."

"What?" Francis nearly fell over. "Now, that's just stupid."

Kenji pitched an eyebrow. "Is it? Nothing about her is normal. You saw what happened back there. She nearly blew the Hall to smithereens—and us with it. If we hadn't laid down that neutralizing blast—"

"All right, all right," Francis said, cutting him off.

Kenji wouldn't let up. "Her EP's off the charts. She jumps like a rocket. She's got more power than you and me combined. Admit it—she's the strangest thing you've ever seen."

Skylark had heard enough. She didn't care what they thought. She had to get back to Poe. She tried to sit up, but she felt so weak. Francis flew to her side.

"How are you feeling, honey?"

"I have to get out of here."

Francis placed his hand on her shoulder. "Easy now."

She pulled away from him and the pain shot through her arm. She looked in disgust at her scar and the healing cord winding from her shoulder to her wrist. She hated it—everything about it. And her robe too. She glared at it, the fabric softly fanning around her body like the wings of a manta ray. "Why did they do this to me? Why didn't they just let me die?"

Francis looked at a loss. "It's all part of the plan . . . There are markers—in our energetic imprint—that determine where we go. Some are Guides, some are Spectrals, some cycle endlessly through the human code . . . and then there's us. We're something entirely different."

Skylark lay back on the couch. She didn't want an explanation. She wanted to be alive and human so she could be with Poe. She looked Francis in the eyes. "What's an energetic aberration?"

He gulped air, feigning innocence. "Now, where'd you hear that?"

She stared back at him, unflinching. He rubbed his beard self-consciously.

Kenji stepped in. "Eavesdropping is a bad habit. And you shouldn't listen to rumours either."

She gave him a scathing look. "I won't if you won't."

"Okay, okay," Francis said, patting Skylark's arm. "You just rest, honey. Collect yourself. We'll give you some space. We can continue this conversation when you're feeling better." He turned to Kenji. "Let's go, hotshot."

They politely dematerialized. Sebastian was still asleep, no doubt exhausted by her power overload, too. There was no reason to wake him. Rising from the couch, Skylark steadied herself and tiptoed to one side of the room so as not to startle the mouse when she jumped.

She dropped down in the Hall of Records, skittered across the threshold and nearly decked a Carrier. Smiling apologetically, she got a blank stare in return as the Carrier glided past. Drifting over to *The Book of Events*, she checked to make sure she was alone, then cooled her mind and decided what she wanted to do. She could go back in time to a place when she and Poe were together. Then again she was curious about what he did after she was gone. Did he suffer greatly? Did he pine away for her the way she pined for him? She hoped so. She concentrated and the book fanned open.

"Show me what happened next."

The page turned. Poe was in a small cabin crowded with people. He was sitting against a wall, talking to a girl—a beautiful, hazel-eyed girl. Skylark's soul immediately pinched with jealousy. She leaned in to get a better look and realized she knew this girl. It was Cadence, that pretty loner from her high school—what was Poe doing with her? Were they together? Had he forgotten about her already? She wasn't going to wait another second to find out.

With a sonic boom, Skylark jumped, landing like an angry cat on a rafter inside the cabin. Poe was sitting on the floor next to Cadence just as the book had shown. Skylark seethed with resentment and desire. She should be the one beside him. It was torture to see him smile at another. Did he love this girl? The thought of it made her want to obliterate herself, it was so painful. She wished she could tear that other girl from his heart. Breaking down, she collapsed on the rafter, buried her face in her hands and wept. The clouds gathered around the cabin and the sky grew dark.

Poe tilted his head, listening. "Do you hear that?"

Caddy paused, holding her breath for a moment before she spoke. "It's starting to rain."

15

BLOOD

The cabin door burst open and the man on watch ran in. "They're coming!"

The Dreamers fled. Caddy skittered down the hill toward the river. A woman screamed behind her and the bright ring of a knife blade cut through the woods. Caddy slid on her heels down the bank, crashing like a frightened animal into the water. Her sneakers slipped over the slick stones and she fell. The current grabbed her, whisking her away. Her clothes weighed her down and she thrashed to keep from sinking, flailing at tree branches that sped past. At last she caught one and held on, kicking her feet and pulling herself to shore, scrambling up the muddy riverbank on her hands and knees.

Another scream split the forest and Caddy saw a black mastiff charge down the hill. It bowled a man over in a snarl of teeth and black fur. A flash of grey between the trees drove Caddy forward.

The Dreamers had scattered in every direction. Caddy followed a woman running in front of her. It was the girl, flying over the ground, her gold hair streaming behind her. She was fast—too fast for Caddy to catch soaking wet. Her clothes made her clumsy. She pumped her arms—she didn't want to lose sight of her—chasing the girl into a stand of maple saplings. Several more screams pierced the air. The saplings lashed at Caddy's skin, leaving angry welts on her face and neck. Her sneakers snagged on the stems and she fell, a maple whipping against her throat as she hit the ground. The girl didn't even look back. She kept running, up and over a hill, and was gone.

Caddy freed herself, ran to the top of the hill and scanned the woods. The girl seemed to have vanished. In the hollow of a moss-covered boulder something moved. Caddy ran to the rock and discovered a crevice, grinning like a jagged mouth in the stone. Had the girl crawled inside? It was narrow—maybe too narrow. Where else could she have gone?

A man's shout echoed through the trees. The Company men were getting closer. Arms outstretched, face turned to one side, Caddy wiggled into the rock mouth. The stone was cool and rough as a cat's tongue. Now that she was inside, she could see that the mouth opened into a small cave, its throat narrowing before it widened. She inched forward, the opening growing tighter and tighter, restricting her breathing. Caddy panicked and pushed herself back, wedging herself deeper and dislodging one of her sneakers. There was no way to turn around. She would have to go forward. Gritting her teeth, she gripped the stone and pulled, her fingers cut and bleeding by the time she reached the edge of the opening and fell to the cave floor.

The girl was there, arms clasped around her knees, eyes wide in the dark. Caddy crawled in beside her, her breathing laboured. She shivered uncontrollably, her wet clothes clinging to her. A shadow darted across the mouth of the cave. The girl grabbed Caddy's arm. Caddy picked up a rock the size of a softball from the cave floor and held it. She would use it as a weapon if any Company men came calling. Her hands started to shake and the rock fell from her grasp. The bad feeling was coming. She wanted to stop it, to derail the train before it hit, but it charged over her, dragging her into the Emptiness.

The first thing Caddy saw when she returned was the girl's distraught face.

"Are you okay?" she whispered, her eyes more frightened than before.

Caddy struggled to sit up. The girl helped, propping her against the cave wall.

"Thanks," Caddy murmured, her tongue a handful of dust in her mouth. "I just need some time to pull myself together."

They sat in silence, Caddy waiting for her hands to stop shaking, the girl watching her closely.

"Was I out long?" Caddy eventually asked.

"I thought you were going to die. What is it? Epilepsy?"

"No . . . visions." She could have lied and saved herself a lot of trouble. She had to trust someone.

"Bad ones?"

"Yes."

The girl looked so concerned, Caddy worried she'd made a mistake being truthful.

"You were moaning pretty loudly," the girl said. "I thought the Company men would find us."

The heat rose in Caddy's face. "I'm sorry."

"Does it happen often?"

"Often enough."

Caddy expected condemnation. The girl surprised her with kindness.

"We were told about you," she said. "I've never seen anyone in the vision before. I didn't know what was happening. Does it hurt? It looks like it hurts . . ."

Caddy considered lying this time, to save the girl further anguish. But what was the point? "Yes."

The girl frowned sympathetically. "That's awful. I hope you're okay." She extended her hand. "My name's April."

They shook. She seemed genuinely kind. "I'm Caddy."

"I know." April noticed the welts on her face and neck. "You're beaten up pretty badly."

"Yeah." Caddy drew back her sleeve. The mark was bloody and raw from her trip through the stone. The bandage was shredded. She dabbed at the blood with the cuff of her jacket, then pulled her sleeve down and explored the welts left by the maple saplings. They were hot and tender to the touch. They would heal and fade with time. The mark wouldn't, though. It was hers for life—however long that would be. And now she'd outed herself to this girl. She was relieved, really. She wouldn't have to pretend anymore. Not to April anyway. She looked at the stone lying next to her.

"Did anything happen while I was out?"

April shook her head. "Do you think they're gone?"

"I don't know."

"Is it bothering you?" April pointed to Caddy's blood-stained sleeve. "The mark, I mean."

Yes, Caddy thought. In so many ways. She shrugged. "It stings."

"We can take care of it once we find the others."

"If there's anyone left." The look of horror on April's face made Caddy retract her words. "I didn't mean it . . ."

April tucked her knees under her chin. She looked like a lost child. "I wish we could just stay here."

"Me too."

"How old are you?" she asked.

"Seventeen."

This made April happy. "I'm nineteen. It's nice to have someone my age around."

Even a freak like me? Caddy wondered. "What about Poe?"

April's face lit up. "Oh, yeah. He's really nice. I'm kind of shy to talk to him, he's so smart."

"I know what you mean. We went to school together."

"Really?"

"Yeah." Caddy caught a glimpse of her sock foot and thought of Meg. She would never forget the image of her lying beneath that Buick. "I saw his girlfriend killed in a car accident."

April's smile fell. "Oh."

"I'm sorry," Caddy apologized again. "It's just . . . I guess I'm kind of in shock about everything."

"No . . . it's okay. I didn't even know he had a girlfriend. He never said anything. What was she like?"

Caddy massaged the back of her neck. She'd wrenched it crawling through the opening to the cave. "Meg? She was beautiful. Popular. I didn't know her very well but she seemed nice."

"How sad."

"I know." Caddy studied her hands. They were banged up pretty bad. Thankfully, they'd stopped shaking. It was going to hurt like hell to go back through the rock. She'd be smarter this time though. She'd remove her jacket and go slowly, try not to freak out. "We should probably go."

April shrank with fear.

"I'll go first," Caddy volunteered. "Wait until I'm through before you start. I'll give you the all-clear."

April clutched Caddy's arm. Her voice was earnest. "I promise not to tell anyone . . . about the visions."

It was a comfort to hear her say it, even if Caddy knew everyone would find out soon enough. She smiled. "Thanks. I'm really glad you're here."

She peeled off her jacket, and looked through the rock. The sun was shining on the other side. If there were Company men lurking out there, so be it, Caddy thought. They couldn't stay in this cave forever. She exhaled and reached into the mouth of the stone, pulling herself in. Flattening against the rock, she inched along, pushing her jacket in front of her. It was a tight squeeze, but not as tight as before. And she was moving toward the light so she could actually see where she was going. Her fingertips burned as she gripped the stone, but the fear of what might be waiting on the other side kept her mind focused.

When she reached her shoe, Caddy freed it and held it in one hand as she crawled. At the opening, she shoved the shoe and her jacket out of the mouth and waited several seconds. Nothing. She shimmied from the rock like a lizard and looked around. The woods were quiet. A light breeze moved through the trees. No one would ever guess people had been killed here. With a wave of her arm, Caddy signalled to April, then crouched beside the rock and quietly pulled on her damp shoe and jacket. She checked the woods for movement. After several minutes, April squirmed from the rock and squatted next to her.

"We can call the others with the mark," she whispered.

Caddy nodded, even though she didn't want to use it. If her father was alive, she didn't want to risk his safety. She couldn't explain this to April. All she could do was hope that everything would be okay. "We should find a safer place. We've been here too long."

They walked, searching the trees as they went. At a thick clump of cedars, Caddy stopped.

"We'll be well hidden here."

They crept into the cedars. April faced her, taking her hands. "Concentrate on the mark and they'll know where we are." She closed her eyes.

Caddy hesitated. Her mind was a whirlwind, spinning from her father to the Company men to Poe. Had he made it to safety? She would have to use the mark to find out. She hoped her father was smart enough not to answer the call, wherever he was. Reining her thoughts in, she held them still and called up the mark, a sparkling mandala in her mind's eye. She imagined herself walking its path, weaving around and around, in and out. There was a buzzing at the back of her neck and the sensation of her body lifting. Within minutes, the Dreamers arrived, gathering in the cedar grove. Caddy waited for Poe. He didn't come with the others.

"There are only twenty-two of us," she said. "Who's missing?"

The Dreamers stood, too afraid to answer.

"We do not dwell on the past," a man said. "We must always look forward. It is the only way to stay whole."

"What if some are injured?" Caddy asked. "What if they need help?"

"We can't risk the safety of those who are here—for the sake of the dream, we must carry on."

"There'll be no one left to dream if we don't take care of each other." Caddy petitioned the others for support. "Who have we lost?" she asked again.

The man flew into a rage, spitting through his teeth. "Attachments are dangerous. They'll get you killed. Hex would want us to move forward."

"We can't leave people behind."

The man took a threatening step toward her. Caddy thought he was going to hit her until a woman intervened.

"Nicholas," the woman said, her voice quavering. "I saw him fall to the knife."

The man glowered at her. There was an uncomfortable silence. Another Dreamer spoke.

"Theresa. I saw her fall."

"Prita," another said.

"Christophe."

"Madelaine."

Caddy held her breath, waiting for his name. "What about Poe?" she asked. "Did anyone see him fall?"

The man exploded. "Enough! We have to move to safety and wait to be contacted."

"We can't leave without Poe," Caddy insisted. "If no one saw him fall, we have to look for him."

"Can't you see the trouble you're causing?" the man said. "Hex will not be happy with you." And then he calmed himself and smiled as though everything were fine. "It's time to move."

Caddy didn't care what Hex or anyone else thought. She wasn't going to abandon Poe. If he was alive, she would find him. She only wished she could do the same for her father. "I won't go."

"Then stay," the man said. "It's your choice."

Caddy hoped April would stand beside her, but she was already mingling with the other Dreamers. They moved, quiet as deer, into the forest. As soon as they were gone Caddy started to question her decision. What made her think she could possibly help Poe? What if he was already dead? She couldn't leave without knowing. If it had been her who was missing, he wouldn't stop until he found her. She believed this.

Searching the ground, Caddy found a branch with a thick knot on the end. It was a good, strong stick, a heavy club. It made her feel better just to hold it. She stayed close to the trees, mouthing the words of her song, moving from shadow to shadow. Before long, she was clearing the hill and could see the river.

On the bank, she discovered a dark, wet stain. She touched it, rubbing her fingers together. Blood. Around the stain were the signs of struggle—torn grass, an upturned stone. But no body. Caddy looked closer and caught something glinting in the grass. It was a thin gold chain with a small green stone. A lump formed in her throat. It was Poe's fluorite talisman, the same as hers. She picked the necklace up, holding it in her hand for a moment before cleaning it in the river and pushing it into her pocket for safekeeping. It didn't mean he was dead, she told herself. Maybe he'd dropped it while running.

Downriver, Caddy found more blood on some boulders. She kneeled, cupped her hands in the water and washed the stones. "I will remember," she promised the one whose blood had been spilled. When the stones were clean she crossed the river, jumping from rock to rock so as not to get her feet wet again. At the last stone she leapt onto the bank. The cabin was at the top of the hill, its door ajar. Everything was quiet.

With small fox steps, Caddy crept up to the building, club raised. She peeked through the window. The cabin was empty, except for the blankets abandoned on the floor from when the Dreamers had escaped. Now what? She stared down at the river and wondered if Poe hadn't run with the others after all. Maybe he'd doubled back and gone in the opposite direction.

Caddy set out, away from the cabin and the river. Creeping through the trees, she nearly shouted when a partridge burst from a bush in front of her, its wings a drum, beating in her chest. She hid in a thicket to collect herself, checking carefully several times before moving again.

At a stone outcropping she stopped. It looked like a reclining giant, its shoulders sharp and angled at the end and easily fifty feet high. It wore a beard of mud-swallow nests, and the birds flitted in and out, undisturbed. This would be a smart place to hide, she thought. Good vantage point. Substantial cover. And the birds would give warning if anyone came near. Caddy was thinking this when she suddenly spied Poe's face shining out among the bushes at the edge of the cliff. Her hand shot into the air to grab his attention. He pointed ominously to something behind her.

Caddy's blood froze. Less than fifty feet away was an enormous black dog.

She bolted, the swallows erupting in a blur of wings. Poe burst from the bushes, scrambling along the edge of the cliff toward its base. The beast was on her in seconds. It leapt and she cranked around, wielding the club. With a bone-crushing thud, she hit the dog in the head. The animal yelped and rolled. It shot to its feet, mouth frothing, teeth flashing, and attacked, hitting her in the chest with its paws. Caddy fell, blocking the dog's deadly jaws with the club. It snarled and snapped, over and over, inches from her face.

Poe jumped, clearing the last eight feet of cliff, a rock held in his hand. Swinging his arm, he smashed the stone down, crushing the dog's skull, killing it instantly. A Company man crashed from the trees, knife gleaming. Caddy screamed. Poe hurled the stone at him and charged, hitting him in the stomach and knocking the blade to the ground. They fought, a flurry of fists and feet. Poe managed to snatch up the knife and drive it into the man's throat. The man grappled and clawed, blood spitting from his lips. His face contorted with confusion. Poe pushed the knife deeper, pressing with all his strength, until the man went limp.

From the shadows, a raven appeared. Then the shadow itself congealed and took form. Caddy watched, convinced it was a trick of the light when the shadow shivered over the ground and hung above the dead Company man. The man's body convulsed violently, and the shadow darkened before dissolving between the trees.

"Did you see that?" Caddy whispered.

Poe was staring at the blood on his hands.

16

O L' S I L V E R

F rancis, Kenji and the mouse were waiting for Skylark when she returned to the room. No one said anything, but she could feel the weight of their concern. She hoped they didn't know where she'd been. She thought she saw something in the old man's eyes, but if he did know something, he was keeping it to himself. Kenji was inscrutable behind his glasses, as always. The mouse scuttled up her arm and groomed himself. She decided to act casual.

"What's up?"

"Target practice." Francis didn't wait for her response. He took her hand and with a quick clap, the four of them were standing in the middle of a large green space. A bull's-eye stood at one end of the field.

"All right," Francis said. "Aim your light at that target over there and see if you can hit it."

"What do you mean?" Skylark asked.

Francis raised his hands to demonstrate. "Channel your energy through your hands and fire it like a weapon." He fired a short burst of light at the bull's-eye, hitting it right in the middle.

Skylark straightened her back and fixed on the target. Holding her hands at heart level, she blasted a beam of light so powerful, it hit the target like napalm, her robe reverting with the impact. The bull's-eye exploded, along with an innocent line of trees in the background, leaving a curtain of orange flames and black smoke rolling against the blue sky.

"Whoa whoa whoa!" Francis hollered. He shot a dousing ray to extinguish the fire.

A charred crater smoked in the pristine carpet of green where the target had stood. Kenji shot a wry look at Skylark. She turned from the smouldering hole, tugging on her robe with disappointment.

"Why do I keep reverting like this?"

"It's the power," Francis said.

"You don't revert."

"Sure I do. When we battle, when we exert a great effort, we need all the energy we've got to make our shots count. That's why it's essential not to go in half-cocked. Once we revert, the Speaker can pick up on our energetic signature and the rodeo starts—whether you're in the saddle or not. You've got more power than anyone I've ever seen, so it's not a surprise you revert so easily."

Skylark pointed at the gaping hole in the ground. "What good is all this power if I can't control it?"

"Now, don't get hasty. These things take practice. Let's try reining it in a bit. Cup your hands next time."

"Clear your mind," the mouse advised her. "Beaming is a surgical art. It requires an equal measure of precision and power."

Skylark shook her hands as though preparing for a piano recital, and cupped her palms. She looked at Francis for approval. He plucked at his beard and nodded.

"Aim for the hole."

Skylark fired. Another wall of light blasted from her hands, reigniting the smoking crater and the scorched trees.

"Subtle," Kenji said.

Francis rocked back on his heels, mulling. "We can't go around blowing things to blue blazes all the time," he instructed. "Our work requires more . . . delicacy."

"You're the one who told me this takes practice," Skylark said.

"Not to worry," the mouse soothed, patting her neck. "You'll get the hang of it."

"What about the Ephemeral?" Kenji suggested.

"You mean Ol' Silver?" Francis hooked his thumbs in his belt loops. "Now, that's an interesting thought . . ."

"Tell me you don't mean the Elusive Ephemeral," the mouse said. "You're going to need permission for that."

Kenji ignored him. "She may give Skylark more control."

Francis squinted at Kenji. "When's the last time we knocked on her door?"

"Not since we got in trouble."

"Who are we talking about?" Skylark asked. They just kept going as though she wasn't there.

"They may not bond . . ." Francis said.

"We won't know unless we try."

Francis and Kenji nodded at each other, and finally acknowledged her.

"We're going on a field trip," Francis said.

Skylark shrugged. "Okay." It had to be better than standing around demolishing things and feeling foolish.

In a heartbeat they were standing in a hushed, dimly lit room. Its pink marble walls were lined with illuminated glass cases holding all kinds of treasure—gold boxes and bowls, swords, shields, urns, vases, gauntlets, shoes, scrolls, illuminated manuscripts. It was the coolest place Skylark had ever seen.

"What is this?" she asked, her voice swallowed by the ambient energy in the room.

Francis smiled. "The Museum of Relics and Artifacts."

He walked over to a case that looked like a magician's prop. It was tall and thin, with gold borders and a filigreed, antique padlock securing the door. Inside the case, a bright cloud of mist hung, captured and held by an alchemist's trick. Skylark peered through the glass to get a better look and was startled when the holographic image of a glistening bow and quiver jumped into view beside her.

"The Elusive Ephemeral," a scholarly voice narrated. "Also known as the Bow of Ages. Believed to bestow extraordinary precision upon its owner. Characteristics—scrolling colour and light polarity serve as a form of communication and camouflage. Origin—unknown."

Skylark couldn't believe her eyes. The Elusive Ephemeral was exquisite—all glimmer and mystery. "How beautiful."

"One of a kind," the mouse said.

"Whose was it?" she asked, tapping on the glass. "And why is it hidden in that mist?"

Francis ran his hand along the length of the case. "As far as I know, Ol' Silver has never been anybody's. No one's had the right touch. And that mist . . . it's hers. She creates it and hides in there like a cuttlefish."

"She's never been held?" Skylark asked.

"She's skittish as a filly."

"I held her, once," Kenji said. "But not for long."

Skylark studied the hologram. "So . . . why should I be any different?"

"Why shouldn't you be?" Francis said.

She thumbed the gold padlock. "They've got her locked in."

"Then we'll have to ask the curator for the key—politely." Francis cocked an eyebrow at Kenji.

"Oh, I doubt they'll give it to you," the mouse said.

Kenji reached into his trench coat pocket and produced a small gold key.

The mouse squeaked with shock. "Where did you get that?"

"Yeah, *where did* you get that?" Francis asked.

Kenji smirked. "It's a miracle." He turned the key in the lock. There was a satisfying click, and the arm of the padlock popped up and swung to one side. He opened the glass door. The mist retreated cat-like to the back of the case.

"I don't like this one bit," Sebastian sniffed, clinging to Skylark's hair.

"Go on and reach in there," Francis said.

She hesitated. What if the Ephemeral didn't like her?

"Go on. She won't harm you."

Skylark raised her hand, pausing for a moment longer before sticking her fingers in the mist. It felt cool and strange. It swirled around, pushing against her hand at first then wrapping around her wrist and drawing her in. "Hey!" She yanked her hand out. "It grabbed me." She looked at Francis.

"You're doing good," he said.

"It feels funny."

Francis winked. "She's just being playful."

Skylark poked at the mist. It curled around her finger. She laughed and offered her hand again, this time allowing the mist to take it.

Francis nodded with approval. "Feel around a bit—gentle like."

She felt around. Nothing. Then her hand brushed against a string of sorts. It sent a charge through her fingers and she had to force herself not to pull away. "I can feel it," she said. "It feels alive!"

Francis laughed. "She is alive. Keep going."

Skylark reached deeper and found the bow. It shivered lightly against her palm. She traced the arc of its spine with her finger. It rose and dipped in a French curve. Mustering her courage, Skylark clasped the bow. It gripped back, forming to fit her hand. She drew it into the light, the bow trailing a veil of mist from the case. The Ephemeral scrolled through its rainbow of colours, humming in her hand like a honeybee. Skylark was ecstatic. She turned to Francis, triumphant. "I got her!"

Francis slapped his thigh with excitement. "You did it!"

Kenji whistled. "What did I tell you?"

"Ohhhh . . . so beautiful," the mouse sighed.

"Keep looking," Francis said. "There's more."

Skylark reached in and found a finely carved quiver made from the most fantastic material. It looked like leather, but shone like the belly of a fish. The quiver held a sheaf of silver arrows, straight and true. They hummed and glistened like the bow. Francis and Kenji exchanged astonished looks.

"Go on," Francis encouraged her. "Try it on."

Quick and light, Skylark swung the quiver onto her back. It hugged the curve of her spine, mimicking the colour of her shirt so that it rested nearly invisible between her shoulder blades. Its energy pulsed, bonding with her own, and she was struck by a profound sense of love and wonder. "I can feel its life against me! I think it's . . . *breathing*." She looked to Francis for confirmation but he seemed as surprised as she was.

The mouse shivered. "I can feel it too."

Skylark tested the tension on the bow, plucking the string. It responded in a pure, high voice.

"There's more yet," Francis said. "Reach in there one more time."

Skylark searched the mist. There *was* something else—a fingerless leather glove and laced armguard. When she took them from the case, the last of the mist came with them and dissipated. Without hesitation, Skylark stripped the gauntlets from her wrists and pulled the glove onto her right hand, pressing the hollows between her fingers until it was snug. She squeezed her other hand into the armguard. It wrapped around her skin, as cool and elastic as a snake. To her amazement, the ties retracted on their own, tightening the brace. She was delirious with joy. Could it possibly be true? Did this magical creature belong to her?

Francis clapped Kenji on the back. "Would you look at that!"

"It appears you are its owner," Sebastian said.

"How does it feel?" Kenji asked.

Skylark thought she would burst with happiness. "Like I've found a long-lost friend!" She worked her hands, clasping and unclasping her fingers. She marvelled at the bow—she couldn't take her eyes off it—its colours scrolling from blue to red to purple then green and every colour in between, including silver. *Will she really help me control my power?* Skylark wondered. Holding the bow close, she felt the weight of the moment pressing down on her. The bow had chosen her over all others. They would be together, forever, joined in united purpose against evil. She was no longer an outcast. She belonged. And with that great honour came great responsibility. "I hope I do right by you," she said.

"Why don't we go to the practice field and try it out," Francis suggested.

Skylark slung the bow over her shoulder and it disappeared, matching the colour of her shirt as the quiver had done. Francis reached for her hand but she stopped him.

"I can't wear training wheels for the rest of my existence," she said.

"Right. I'm so happy for you." He winked again and vanished.

She smiled at Kenji, expecting him to jump too, but he didn't. He had the oddest look on his face, as though wrestling to find the strength to say something. He removed his glasses. It was the first time Skylark had really seen his eyes. They were blue—not like Fran's sapphires—but dark and simmering.

"I know how hard it is," he said.

She laughed. "What? This is the best day of my life."

He took a step toward her. "I know where you were, Skylark. You have to let him go."

"Who?" she asked. Then it clicked. He was talking about Poe. She turned her back to him, her throat tightening. "Don't."

The mouse stiffened. "Oh dear. This isn't good."

"It's nothing," she deflected, but she couldn't hide the anger in her voice.

"You can't have him," he said. "He's lost to you. You must accept it. If the Council found out . . ."

How dare he threaten her with the Council? How dare he get in the way of her love? She whirled around to face him. "And who's going to tell them?"

The mouse groaned. "Let's all just take a step back."

Skylark stared Kenji down. He held her gaze.

"I know how you feel," he said. "But you're just torturing yourself. It'll be easier if you make the decision to let go—especially now. The minute you held the Ephemeral, the minute she accepted you, the contract was signed. You have an obligation to her. You have to be more responsible now. You can't go chasing after some human boy."

The bow shimmered in collusion, scrolling through its colours again. The quiver nuzzled against her back. Skylark was unmoved. "You haven't got a clue what I'm going through."

"You're wrong." Kenji stepped closer. "I know all too well. It's doomed, Skylark. Nothing can ever come of it. You have to pack up your feelings, put them in a box, and never open it again."

"I can't."

"You're forcing his soul into a loop. This boy you love . . . he's only one incarnation of that soul. When you hold him so close, he can't evolve beyond what he already is. He can never experience the full breadth of his soul's expression. By being with him, by tying yourself to him outside of time, you're preventing him from living out his life's natural cycle. His soul will never grow beyond that personality. He will never reincarnate and become what he is meant to become. He'll be trapped, a butterfly inside a jar, for all eternity. You have to set him free, Skylark. It's the right thing to do."

She glared at him. "So he can end up like me? I don't want him to evolve. I want him to stay the way he is."

"It isn't right to interfere with another soul's journey!" Sebastian blustered, taking sides.

"You don't mean what you're saying," Kenji said.

Skylark scoffed. She didn't need his sanctimonious advice. "I mean exactly what I'm saying. Stay away from me, Kenji, or you'll regret it."

He wouldn't stop. "You're being selfish, Skylark. Think about what you're doing. It's wrong and you know it." He reached for her arm. She ended the conversation by jumping in a burst of light and thumping down beside Francis in the practice field. Her robe furled around her. She hated that she reverted whenever she jumped by herself. She angrily popped back into human form.

"What took you so long?" Francis said. "I thought you got lost."

"Ask Kenji."

Kenji showed up an instant later, glasses and cool demeanour in place. Francis gave him a look, tugging at his beard. Whatever question he was formulating he dropped and got back to business. "Okay. Let's get to it." He jerked his head toward a new target standing next to the scorched crater where the old one had been.

Skylark drew an arrow from the quiver. It hummed and flickered in her hand. Fitting the arrow's notch against the string, she pulled back, channelling her anger at the target. Francis nodded and she released. The arrow shrieked as it flew, ripping through the bull's-eye and driving into the blackened trunk of one of the scorched trees, its fletching shaking like a feather duster. Skylark's soul surged. She turned to Francis victoriously.

Francis and Kenji stared at the impaled tree. The old man cleared his throat.

"That was good."

"Beginner's luck," Kenji said.

Skylark sneered. "Of course, you would know."

"Now, now," the mouse soothed.

"Can you do that again?" Francis asked. "Only this time, ease back on the throttle."

Skylark drew another arrow from the quiver, secured the notch, pulled the bowstring and released. The arrow sang, hitting the target square in the eye with a satisfying thwack. She gave Kenji a self-satisfied look.

Francis beamed at her. "You're born to it."

"It was my idea," Kenji said.

"Oh, you're full of good ideas," Skylark snapped.

Francis pushed back his hat. "Go ahead, hotshot, take credit. It was Skylark who pulled the trigger. The girl's got innate skills."

"Or was it the bow?" Kenji said. "The real test is whether she can keep her head and not do anything stupid under pressure." He folded his arms. "Firing at targets is one thing. Shooting at demons—that's a different story altogether."

"Bring it on," Skylark challenged him. "Silver and I are ready."

"Ah, it'll come with practice," Francis said.

"Yes," Sebastian chimed in. "Practice makes perfect."

Skylark narrowed her eyes at Kenji. "I'm happy to practise." She lined up and fired, the arrow streaking through the air and lopping off the top of the only tree behind the target that hadn't been torched. She frowned.

"Don't let him get to you," Francis said. "He's just jealous."

"Am I?" Kenji stared smugly back, then jumped, leaving Francis and Skylark alone in the field.

"Good," Skylark said. "I thought he'd never go."

Francis grunted. "Who put a bee in his bonnet?"

"I thought she was doing fine," Sebastian said.

"Sore loser," Francis muttered. "Shall we continue?"

MURDER

Poe washed his hands in the river, the blood streaming from his fingers in loose red ribbons. He pulled off his shirt, plunged it into the water and scrubbed. Caddy sat on a stone, watching.

"How did you get separated from the group?" she asked.

He wrung the water from his shirt and examined it. The blood was stubborn, staining the fabric with pink splotches. He dunked the shirt back in the water and scoured it against a rock. "I ran in the opposite direction to make the Company men chase me. There were a lot of them and they split up. I doubled back to find the others and they tracked me. I hid and waited for an opportunity. Then you found me."

And here we are, Caddy thought, searching for a way to begin the conversation neither of us wants to have. "That man . . . you killed him . . ."

Poe clenched his jaw. "Yes."

"But the covenant . . ."

"Thou shalt not kill—you think I don't know that? I wasn't expecting you to show up, Cadence. I thought I was on my own. It came down to you or him. Which would you have preferred?"

It was her fault. He was right. If she'd listened to the other Dreamers, Poe wouldn't have blood on his hands. "I couldn't just leave you."

"I would have been okay. You have to start thinking about your own safety. Things are worse than ever."

"What do you mean?"

"They've never used dogs before. Something has changed. They're more aggressive. The attack today . . . it was a full-scale assault."

Caddy felt a twinge in her fingertips. The bad feeling was near. Please, not now, she silently begged. "Do you think they're still out there?"

"If they were, we'd have seen them by now." He inspected his shirt and kept scrubbing. "You can't put yourself at risk for me, Cadence. It's not good for you—or the group."

The group. How could she tell him what she really felt? The group scared her, almost as much as the Company men. "What's going to happen to you—with the group."

"I'll be punished."

Her jaw dropped. "Punished?"

"The sin of the one is the sin of the many."

"Those are just words."

"Not to us."

"What does being 'punished' even mean? What will they do to you?"

"I don't know. There will be a judgment. This is a very serious offence."

"I'm the one to blame," Caddy said. "I should have never come after you. Surely they'll understand the circumstances."

Poe shrugged. "I knew the rules and I broke them."

He was being so pragmatic. The whole thing was absurd. "Is that you talking . . . or Hex?"

He stopped scrubbing and stared into the water. "Hex is only doing what she has to."

"And punishing you is part of that?"

"Yes, if need be. The Dreamers are on a set course. We've been following this trajectory for centuries."

"Things have changed—you said so yourself. The Company men are using dogs now. It won't be long before they kill us all. Then where will we be?"

"We have to follow the directive." He wrung out his shirt and pulled it on, faint pink blossoms marring the fabric.

Caddy stood. "Something is really wrong with this, Poe. What good does it do to punish you? You did what you thought you had to. We can't all run like scared rabbits and hope the dreaming will change things."

Poe faced her, his eyes as dark and deep as oceans. "Our dreams are powerful, Cadence. Don't ever doubt that."

The mark on her arm began to ache. It filled her with disgust. "I don't doubt it. But I do doubt Hex—and the wisdom of anyone who blindly follows her." She thought this would make him angry. He just smiled.

"The Dreamers' eyes are open, Cadence. When you look with your heart, you see clearly, and there is no room for doubt."

More rhetoric. She didn't want to hear it. "I wish I shared your conviction."

Poe moved closer. She could feel the heat off his body.

"I can't let anything happen to you, Cadence. I couldn't forgive myself if I did. I'll take whatever punishment I have coming to me."

She searched his face, and at last she understood. "I'm not Meg, Poe. Killing a hundred Company men won't bring her back."

He lowered his head, hands clenched, and for the first time she appreciated how truly vulnerable he was. In the years she'd known him at school he'd seemed so aloof, so immune to everyone and everything. Now here he was, standing in front her with his heart exposed. His wet shirt clung to his skin, accentuating his broad shoulders and the chiselled muscles of his stomach and chest. He was strong—strong enough to kill a man. He couldn't save Meg. But he could save *her*. And he was willing to, no matter what the cost. This realization stirred something in her heart. She reached for his hand.

"Poe . . ."

He pulled away. "We should find the others."

Caddy followed him, wanting to continue their conversation. The moment was lost, so she spoke around it. "The knife the Company man carried . . . it was strange."

He walked in silence, and she thought he wouldn't answer, but then he spoke as though nothing had changed. "It's called a punyal. It's a type of dagger."

He'd gotten his edge back. This was the Poe she knew from school. Caddy skirted around some tree roots.

"It looked old."

"It is. The Company men come from a very old order—as old as recorded time. They have their traditions, one of which is to pass weapons from man to man. We've seen them with every-thing—scimitars, bayonets, Second World War trench knives—even blades of fractured obsidian."

"Obsidian . . . that's a type of stone, right?"

"Volcanic glass," he corrected her.

They cleared the hill, moving toward the jagged mouth of the rock where she'd hid with April.

"And the Dreamers?" she asked. "Are they as old?"

"Yes. As long as there have been those who embrace the Dark, there have been those who anchor the Light." He pointed to a clump of cedars. "Is that where you and April called the Dreamers?"

"Yes."

They pushed into the stand of the trees and he took her hands. His energy flowed through her like a current. It made her feel light-headed. "Poe," she said, trying to bridge the distance between them. "I won't tell the others about the Company man."

"I'm sure they already know." He closed his eyes. "Concentrate on the mark."

After everything that had happened, after all her misgivings about Hex and the judgment Poe said she would enforce, Caddy didn't think she could summon the mark. Yet it appeared as readily as before, sparkling in her mind. She traced its pathway, and the faces of the Dreamers emerged. When she opened her eyes Poe was looking back at her.

"You saw them," he said.

"Yes. I know which way to go."

"We have to hurry. Using the mark leaves us exposed."

Caddy's connection to the Dreamers was palpable. It drew her toward them by an invisible cord, growing stronger with every footstep. Eventually, she found them, standing in a group among the trees.

April's face brightened when she saw Poe. "We waited when we felt the mark," she said. She squeezed Caddy's hand and whispered, "I'm so glad you found him."

The Dreamers set out through the woods, the sun casting long shadows behind them. At a cluster of sheltered stones, they stopped and took their places for the night, hunkering in small groups between the rocks. A man and a woman kept watch. There would be no fire.

To Caddy's relief, Poe stayed close, curling next to her. April did too, taking a place next to Poe. Caddy secretly hoped April didn't like him too much. This thought made her feel selfish and she pushed it away. She drew her hands into the sleeves of her jacket. The ground was cold. There were things crawling beneath her. She was hungry. It was the first time she'd thought about food in hours. She checked her pocket for the bread she'd stashed from the cabin. It was a soggy mess from her swim across the river. She tossed it and settled in. Her hands started to shake, and the smell of burnt toast filled her nostrils. She moaned.

Poe put his arm around her as the bad feeling took her under. She tumbled alone into the Emptiness, Poe's voice calling her from somewhere far away, telling her everything would be all right.

When she returned, shivering and dazed, Poe was still holding her.

"Are you okay?" he asked.

She nodded. If only she could stop shaking. He held her close, the warmth of his body a comfort against the cold.

"Sleep," he said. "You're safe now. I'll watch over you."

At dawn, Caddy woke to someone jiggling her shoulder. It was Poe, red rimmed with exhaustion. Had he slept at all?

"It's time to go."

Caddy pushed the hair from her eyes. "You should have woken me earlier."

"I thought you could use the rest." He gestured at some bushes. "If you need to go, you should do it now."

Caddy squatted half asleep behind the bushes before joining Poe and April with the others.

"Do we know where we're going?" she asked.

"No."

For hours, the Dreamers walked, stopping only when they reached a gravel road that cut a parched swath through the trees. They hid in the underbrush, mosquitoes swarming, relentless. Caddy retreated like a turtle inside her jean jacket. The sun pressed against her back. She was dirty and hungrier than ever. They all were. Poe kneeled next to her, watching. April looked tired and nervous.

After a while, an engine could be heard grinding down the road. A yellow school bus rounded the corner, dragging a small tornado of dust behind it. One of the Dreamers waved, signalling the driver. The bus slowed and stopped, and the door flapped open. The Dreamers boarded, weary and wordless. Caddy stayed close to Poe, taking a seat at the back by a window. April shadowed her, sitting on the other side of Poe. When everyone was on, the driver closed the door and shifted into gear. A woman took charge, handing out glass mason jars of water and knots of white bread from a cloth sack.

"There's more if you need it," she said to Caddy.

Caddy politely declined. She wouldn't take more than the others again. No more special treatment. She held the bread to her nose. The sweet smell of yeast and flour made her feel faint. She wanted to stuff the bread down, but her stomach was sour, so she took small bites and chewed thoroughly before swallowing. The water was warm and tasted of metal and glass. She sipped it, slowly, and secured the lid, holding the jar in her lap as she rested her head on the window. Poe reclined beside her, legs stretched out in front of him. April slouched next to him. They slept, the three of them, rocked by the movement of the bus.

The sun was high by the time Caddy woke. Poe and April were already up. The bus was trundling along a dirt lane through an expansive meadow of wildflowers and waving grass. It cranked to a stop where the lane narrowed into a meandering footpath. The driver opened the door and the Dreamers straggled out. Caddy stepped down into a sea of green and gold. Where were they?

Caddy and April trailed in Poe's footsteps, snaking single file with the rest of the Dreamers to a small hill that rose above the ground in a low arc. The path curved down a set of stone stairs to a strange house that peeked out from the hillside like the bleached eye socket of a half-buried skull. Inside, there was a single, large room with floor-to-ceiling windows overlooking the meadow. It was cool and subdued, the smell of incense and wood smoke hanging in the air. At the centre of the room was an open stone fireplace. The floor was terracotta tile, with several rugs dotted here and there. The Dreamers sat, claiming places on the floor. Caddy, Poe and April sat together in a corner, an inseparable group now. When everyone was gathered, the woman who had handed out water and bread on the bus stood and spoke.

"There's food and a shower with hot water. Let's make ourselves comfortable."

Hot water. Caddy felt hopeful for the first time in days. Maybe there was even a toothbrush. If there was, she would steal it. She laughed to herself at the idea. The door to the house opened and Hex and Red walked in. Red's expression was as bleak as a winter sky. Caddy tensed warily. What was coming?

"It's me she's looking at," Poe said. "Not you."

Caddy's eyes skipped to the bloodstains on his shirt. "Do you think she knows?"

"I'm sure of it."

18

A RARE AND UNEXPECTED
OPPORTUNITY

Francis and Skylark returned to headquarters to find Timon sitting behind the desk, brow furrowed. He launched in immediately.

"Where's Kenji? He's not picking up."

Francis grunted. "Did you check the bar?"

Timon glowered at Skylark, the Elusive Ephemeral clinging to her, its presence reduced to a band of near-visible energy. "What the deuce is that?"

"What do you think it is?" Francis answered.

Timon's eyebrows practically leapt off his forehead. "Don't be impudent. I know exactly what it is. How the devil did she come upon it?"

Francis deflected. "Isn't it great? It likes her."

The bow glistened. Skylark hunched her shoulders, making herself as small as possible beneath Timon's caustic stare. Apparently he didn't share the old man's enthusiasm.

"That's a precious artifact," Timon said. "Who gave you clearance?"

Francis pushed his Stetson back on his head. "Come on, T, this is incredible. No one's ever carried the bow before." He pointed at Skylark. "You should see her shoot. She's a natural." He gave a high whistle.

Timon flipped. "We'll discuss this later! There's been an unforeseen development. One of the Nightshades procured a soul—a grey man. We were able to extract some information before it was interred." He conjured a slip of paper from his vest pocket and held it out between two fingers.

Francis took the paper and opened it. "What's this?"

"A date, obviously. A very important one. Intelligence went to great effort to secure it. The Speaker will appear at that time, at those coordinates. I want you and Kenji there immediately." He gestured at the paper. "Destroy that."

Francis burned the paper with a quick motion of his hand. "I'd like to bring Skylark."

She looked at him in disbelief. Sebastian gripped her shoulder.

"The girl?" Timon blustered.

"We've been practising," Francis said. "You should see her with Ol' Silver. It's like she was born to it."

Skylark shrank. She wasn't prepared to be put on the spot. And Francis failed to mention the incinerated trees and the targets she'd already ruined.

"Ol' Silver?" Timon said disdainfully. "I wish you wouldn't call it that. The Elusive Ephemeral is a mystical creature."

Francis didn't let up. "It's like it was made for her, T. Look how it fits . . ." He spun Skylark like a doll.

Timon waved him quiet. "This isn't a practice session. This is a rare and unexpected opportunity. We lost half a dozen men transporting that soul, not to mention the three others obliterated during its interment." His eyes grew distant. "Such evil I have never seen . . ." He shook it off and collected himself. "There's only room for two on this trip. The portals have already been arranged. We've been given a very small window of time. You're to take Kenji."

"This is kind of last-minute," Francis said.

Timon slammed his fist down on the desk. "Don't test me, Francis!"

The cowboy rocked back on his heels. Skylark made herself even smaller, wishing she could disappear.

"No more arguments," Timon said. "Just find Kenji. And don't botch this up." He vanished with an angry whip crack.

The moment he was gone, Skylark turned to Francis. She knew by the look on his face what he was thinking even before she spoke, but she asked anyway. "What are we going to do?"

"You and me—we're going to meet the Speaker together."

Sebastian jumped in. "What about Timon? Did you listen to a single word he said?"

Francis addressed Skylark overtop of the mouse, ignoring him completely. "The Speaker won't be expecting you. We'll have the element of surprise on our side. He's familiar with Kenji's signature—with both our signatures. If you show up, it just may throw him for a loop. That'll be the advantage that wins the match."

"I don't like this," Sebastian protested.

Skylark couldn't believe what she was hearing. The cowboy really intended to go through with it. "But . . . I don't have a clue what I'm doing. I've never done any of this before. I didn't even finish basic training."

"This is suicide," the mouse groaned.

Francis squinted at her. "From what I've seen, you don't need much training. You've got what I'd call 'natural proclivity.'"

"Natural proclivity!" The mouse nearly fell off Skylark's shoulder. "She has no experience with demonic entities!"

Francis kept going. "We'll have to get you suited up. Best to go in prepared. We haven't got much time. Come on."

This must be a joke, Skylark thought, but Francis was already tramping out the door and down the hall to a cluttered room that looked as though it hadn't been cleaned in a millennium. Kicking boxes aside, he cleared a path to the closet. He opened the door and dragged a large black wooden chest from inside. The chest was a plain steamer trunk with a big brass latch and thick leather straps securing the lid. He unfastened the buckles and popped the latch. The hinges creaked. A waft of musty air rose from inside. Skylark looked at the contents. All she could see was an unimpressive jumble of old leather pads.

"It may not seem like much," Francis said. "But this kept me safe when I was starting out." He reached in and produced a worn, medieval-looking chest guard.

The mouse scoffed. "You've got to be kidding."

Skylark stared at the chest guard. The mouse had a point.

Francis held it up to judge the size and a strap fell off. "Oh." He turned it around and the chest guard flopped like a wilted carrot. "You won't win any fashion shows with this, but it's not so bad . . ."

The mouse scrambled to the top of Skylark's head. "Not so bad? It's dismal!"

Skylark couldn't mask the look of dismay on her face. Sebbie was right. Francis caught the look and tossed the chest guard back into the trunk. He kicked the lid shut with his cowboy boot and exiled the trunk back to the closet with his heel.

"How about we get something a little fresher?"

"I think that's a good idea," Skylark agreed.

"I know just the place."

"Great," the mouse said, his voice dripping with derision.

Francis was unfazed. He reached for Skylark's hand, then stopped himself. "I'll give you the coordinates if you want to jump on your own."

She took his hand. "It's okay."

They touched down in the middle of a busy studio, silver beings sewing and measuring while groups of sober-faced Warriors waited to be outfitted with new armour, their lions lying patiently at their feet. There was an air of anticipation and urgency. Skylark kept her head down, hoping no one would recognize her.

"Must be one hell of a manoeuvre going on," Francis said.

Sebastian sniffed with indignation. "You'll never get served without an appointment."

Francis paid him no attention. They stood in the middle of the hubbub, invisible, until the old man finally approached one of the beings.

"Excuse me . . ."

The being whisked past, oblivious. Francis hailed another.

"Excuse me . . ."

This one didn't even make eye contact. Francis stepped in front of an imperious-looking being who regarded him as though he were daft. He confirmed this by speaking with his mouth.

"Can we get some help here?"

The being gazed around the room for full effect then trained its sights on the cowboy. "As you can see, we're quite busy," it telepathed. "Do you have an appointment?"

"Ha!" the mouse laughed smugly.

Francis raised his eyebrows, preparing to spin a story, and was cut off immediately.

"Take a number."

"I told you," the mouse quipped. "Some places have rules—and they follow them."

"We haven't got time for this," Francis yelled across the room, causing a scene. "We're on a special mission!"

Skylark withered with embarrassment as a different being materialized before them.

"Outbursts won't be tolerated," it snipped.

Francis strode off, muttering to himself with frustration, and snatched a number from the machine. When he returned, he pointed at the mouse and gave it what-for. "Not another word out of you."

The mouse retreated into Skylark's hair. Francis rocked impatiently on the heels of his cowboy boots, twisting the hairs of his beard. It made her feel guilty. She didn't want to make trouble for anyone. Besides, what good could armour really do? If the Speaker was as devious as everyone was making out, armour afforded little comfort to a recruit with zero experience.

"We can go without it," she said.

Francis punched his cowboy hat to the back of his head. "No way. I'm not throwing you into the mix unprotected."

"I don't understand why we have to get these guys to make something," she said. "Can't we just conjure it from the ether?"

The mouse clucked his tongue. "Oh, good gracious, no."

"Armour is different," Francis said. "It takes special care and precision."

The whole thing was getting far too serious. What Skylark really needed was a way out of this deal altogether. "Maybe you should just go with Kenji like Timon said."

"I can't get hold of him."

"Did you try?" the mouse asked.

Francis closed his eyes and attempted to contact Kenji, only to thrash back to the surface. "See? The guy is never around when you need him. He does this all the time. You don't know him like I do. He's not reliable." He was gearing up for a full-blown attack on Kenji's shortcomings when their number was called. "Ah ha!" he gloated, jabbing a finger at the mouse. "Never get served without an appointment, huh? Shows what you know." He took Skylark by the arm and hustled her over to where a silver being stood, tape measure draped over one arm. "We need armour, *stat*," Francis said. "The strongest thing you've got—but light."

The being walked around him, evaluating his physique. "What type of entities will you be engaging?"

Francis jerked his thumb at Skylark. "Not me. Her."

The being paused, scrutinizing her shape. Its eyes trailed along the healing cord on her arm. "How . . . unusual. I've heard about this one. Caused a lot of concern."

Skylark started to say something smart but Francis shut her down with a look. "We're in a hurry here."

The silver being advanced, tape outstretched. As soon as it got close, the Ephemeral lit up, scrolling through its colours. The being recoiled.

"What is *that*?"

Skylark clasped the string of the bow protectively. "It's my weapon."

"You'll have to remove it."

The bow clung to her, curling around her like a mink. "I can't."

The silver being looked to Francis for help. The old man scrubbed his beard.

"Is there any way you can do your measuring around it?"

The being thought about this for a moment. "What about the mouse?"

"Just knock him out of the way." Francis picked the mouse up by his tail and stuffed him into his pocket.

"Hey!" Sebbie cried.

Somewhat satisfied, the silver being pursed its lips, raised its tape and advanced as though Skylark were a rattlesnake. It measured in quick bursts, here and there and around, then zipped its tape shut. "What type of entities will you be engaging?" it asked again.

"The worst kind," Francis said.

The being stared at him, waiting for proper information.

"The kind that have a lot of dirty tricks up their sleeves."

"Weapons?"

"Energy bolts."

"I have an intuitive composite hyper-alloy membrane," the being said. "Very light and resilient."

"Perfect."

It waved its hand and another silver being arrived with the fabric, placing it on the cutting table. The two beings hunched over the cloth, cutting and discussing quietly between them. Occasionally, one or both would throw a look at her. Francis paced, arms folded, boots clomping back and forth across the floor while the mouse sulked in his pocket. Skylark trotted to keep up with him.

"I don't get it. Why are we in such a hurry?"

Francis snuffed through his moustache. "We're going back to a unique place in time."

"But . . . I've done that before," Skylark said. "A bunch of times. It's easy." Her eyes widened when she realized she'd just given herself away.

Francis gave her the fisheye but let it ride. "Not like this. This is different. We have to make sure we don't disturb the energetic imprint of the event so as not to alert anyone to our presence. The portals allow us to enter the moment unnoticed. But it's very precise. If we're late, or cause a ripple in the imprint, we miss the train—or derail it altogether."

"I thought time was of no consequence here. Everything is simultaneous."

"It is, sure. But things that happen on earth affect us here, and vice versa. If you change events, the consequence of those changes affects everything. That's what the Speaker is depending on."

She had no idea what he was talking about. He spun on his heels and tromped in the other direction.

"Time is simultaneous and unique, but never both at the same time," he explained. "It depends on your perspective. What seems like forever here is just a heartbeat on earth. It's like particle/wave duality, or the old woman and the lamp—it's both, but you can only perceive one or the other at any given moment, never the two simultaneously, and points of contact can cause smears in the paint."

Skylark puzzled over this. "Paint?"

"Just forget that," Francis said.

More confusion. Skylark shook her head. "Okay, whatever. Why didn't they just wait to make sure we were ready?"

Francis stopped pacing. "Once they get the intelligence, they have to line up the crosshairs for that point in time. If we wait, the information is corrupted and the bad guys will be all over us. As many of us as there are here, there are twice as many of them out there. They work overtime to mess with the works. They've got nothing else to do. They're just waiting for us to screw up." He started tromping again, working his way over to the cutting table like a persistent dog.

The silver beings shooed him away. Francis continued to pace until finally, they were ready. With more than a modicum of fanfare, they presented a breastplate, front and back. It was gold, with silver seams piped in the tiniest stitches.

"You'll have to put it on yourself, I'm afraid," the silver being with the measuring tape said to Skylark. It cast a cautious look at the Ephemeral.

She took the breastplate and started to put it on, but Francis stopped her.

"It has to go over your true form," he said.

Skylark reverted to her robe state. Nudging the bow and quiver to one side, she slid the breastplate on. The plate held itself in place while she secured the back. When the armour was fitted, the silver being used a small handheld implement to fuse the seams with a thin beam of light.

"How does that feel?" it asked.

Skylark shifted around to test the comfort level. "It's a little tight."

"It will stretch a bit as you wear it."

She fidgeted some more, adjusting the Ephemeral so that it rested comfortably on her back again. It whirled through its array of colours and assumed the texture and colour of the armour. Skylark returned to her human form. It took more energy to accommodate the breastplate but she managed to do it. The Ephemeral changed its colour accordingly, matching the black of her shirt.

When she was comfortably back in her civvies, Francis stepped in. "Great. We should get going." He tossed the indignant mouse on her shoulder and saluted the silver beings.

"Wait!" the one with the measuring tape said. "To whom do we send the paperwork?"

Francis and Skylark left it hanging without an answer. They landed in the Hall of Records, inches from *The Book*.

"Are you sure about Kenji?" Skylark asked. "Won't he be angry if you go without him?"

Francis clamped his hands on her shoulders. "Don't be nervous. You're going to be fine." He sent a thought message, dialling *The Book of Events* to the appropriate date, location and time.

"Here we go," he said, and they jumped.

19

UNFORGIVEABLE SIN

The Dreamers joined voices. The note was a rain-filled cloud hanging over the room. Poe and Caddy lay side-by-side, fingers almost touching. April lay on the other side of Poe. Through the humming Caddy heard soft, deliberate footsteps. Opening her eyes she saw Hex kneeling beside Poe. He stood robotically and followed her from the room. What was happening? Was Hex taking Poe away? Caddy raised herself on one elbow and saw Red looking back at her. He shook his head in warning, causing her to lie down again.

The note opened, tapping a persistent rhythm on Caddy's skin and seeping into her veins. Her eyelids drooped and she slipped beneath the membrane of her consciousness. Her concern for Poe, for whatever was going on between him and Hex, slid from her grasp and she joined the others inside the dream. Caddy generated Light with her hands to push back the Dark. She'd relaxed into it, making good progress, when she abruptly jumped. She wasn't in the dream anymore. She was in the rundown hotel room again—in the vision she'd seen before.

Her father was on the bed, gun in hand. The man in the expensive suit stood beside him. But something was different.

There were more people there—a young girl with black hair and the most beautiful violet eyes, and an old cowboy. They looked on as the man in the suit held the small funnel to his lips. His mouth moved, and once again the dark tendril twined from the funnel into her father's ear. Caddy forced herself to watch as her father pressed the gun to his temple. Finger trembling, he squeezed the trigger, and the cowboy shouted, "Now!"

In a brilliant flash, the girl and the old man transformed into strange beings with flowing robes and hair. The girl drew a bow and arrow. She aimed at the man in the suit, then suddenly turned her violet eyes on Caddy. *The girl could see her!*

Time stood still. Caddy was certain she saw recognition in the girl's eyes—and more than just a little anger. The girl curled her lips as if to speak but the old man yelled, "Shoot!" Then everything happened at once. The girl regained her composure and fired. The man in the suit returned volley, striking the girl down with her own arrow. A beam of light flew from the old man's hands. And Caddy's father pulled the trigger.

Caddy screamed, breaking the vision as before. Only this time she punched from the dream straight into the Emptiness. The wind howled around her. The faces of the dispossessed thickened and formed. "No . . . please," she begged. "I can't help you!" There was the sound of a giant sheet ripping in two, and she fell through the void, back into the house in the field.

Caddy crashed into the now with a gasp. The humming had stopped. The silence was crushing. The Dreamers were gathered in a nervous half-circle. How long had she been out by herself? Had they seen what she'd seen? April pointed furtively to the front of the room. Hex and Poe were sitting there. Poe looked like a man about to be hanged. Red was hidden in the shadows to one side of them. Hex had her glasses off. She raised her hand and the Dreamers held their breath. Her words were daggers, cutting through the quiet.

"There has been a transgression," she said. "Someone has broken the code."

No one spoke. No one moved. Caddy tried to get Poe's attention. His head was bowed, his face hard, resolute. Her mind raced as she anticipated what was coming next.

"There has been murder," Hex said.

Poe clenched his jaw.

"We all know the code," Hex continued. "There can be no blood. The sin of the one is the sin of the many. We are all equally guilty. We must vote."

The Dreamers shifted anxiously. Poe kept his eyes to the floor. If only he would look at me, Caddy thought. Shame and anger seized her. She should be up there next to him. He'd spilled blood for her—the Company man's life in exchange for her own.

Poe stood. She could tell he'd made a decision.

"I choose to leave," he said. "I will not burden the group further with the need to vote."

Hex agreed without hesitation, and Caddy suspected that this is what she'd hoped for all along. She wanted Poe to leave. She wanted to tear her and Poe apart. They were too strong together, too unpredictable. Poe cared more for her than his allegiance to the Dreamers and Hex's code. And now a Company man was dead. If Poe were allowed to stay, how many more Dreamers would be tempted to fight back? Maybe Hex wanted the Dreamers to die—Caddy's father included. Maybe she wanted them to fall passively on the Company's knife. Caddy's blood boiled. She would not sit idly by while Poe was made a scapegoat.

She moved to stand and April stopped her.

"Please," she said. "You can't intervene."

Caddy refused to listen. She stood. "I'm the one who should leave. It was my fault. Poe was protecting me."

The temperature in the room dropped. Hex tilted her head like a raptor.

"Your hand did not guide the blade."

"It was my mistake that put Poe in danger. My actions forced him to make a decision he should not have had to make."

Hex's voice was ice. "Thou shalt not kill. It is a law as old as time. The Dreamers are committed to peace at all costs, even at the sake of our own lives. Killing diminishes us. Killing diminishes the Light. We cannot save the world through violence. Murder makes us the same as them. It opens a rift in the Light and lets the Dark in. The blood will come back on us in ways we can not begin to comprehend."

"I can't allow Poe to suffer for my weakness," Caddy said. "I take sole responsibility. Banish me."

The sky in Hex's blue eye narrowed and Caddy was sure she saw a darkness gathering there. Hex hadn't expected her to protest. Caddy had thrown a wrench in her plans. She could see Hex's mind working as she searched for a way to turn the situation around. Poe beat her to it by moving toward the door. One of the Dreamers hastily wrapped some food in a cloth and handed it to him, along with a blanket roll tied with string. The others lowered their eyes. Caddy followed him but Hex intercepted her with a hand on her arm.

"You can not interfere with the judgment. Your role is here, with us."

Caddy pulled her arm away in contempt. "Your judgment holds no weight with me." She ran from the house and across the field, chasing after Poe. When she reached him, he spurned her.

"Go back, Cadence. You're not responsible for my offence."

"I want to leave with you."

"Your place is with the group. They need you."

Caddy grabbed his sleeve. "I don't want to stay with them. I don't trust Hex. She's trying to pull us apart. She wants the Dreamers to fail. She's the reason why we can't succeed—I know it."

Poe smiled patiently at her earnestness. "Hex has given

everything to the cause. All she's trying to do is keep you safe. There's blood on my hands, Cadence. The Company knows me now. They won't stop until they find me, and when they do . . . they'll kill you too."

Caddy wanted to scream. How could she make him understand? "Have you ever wondered where she goes? Why doesn't she stay with us? Why is she never there when the Company men attack?"

"She has her reasons," Poe said. "We can't afford to lose her."

"She's trying to find my father. That's the real reason why she abducted me. She wants him dead."

Poe squeezed her hand. "Caddy, stop . . ."

"I think Red suspects her too," she continued. "He told me in the beginning that he was trying to protect me. Why would he say that?" She gripped his arm. "Please, Poe . . . you have to listen to me. Hex can't be trusted. She has the darkness in her."

He removed her hand. "The Dreamers need you, Cadence."

She choked back a sob. If only she could make him see. But what did she have to go on? A feeling? A perceived darkness in Hex's blue eye? She had no real proof. Nothing concrete. No wonder he didn't believe her. "Where will you go?"

"I don't know."

He turned to leave.

"Poe, wait . . ." Caddy pulled his necklace from her pocket. Balancing on her toes, hands quaking, she fastened it around his neck. "Be safe."

"Dream well, Cadence," he said, lifting the blanket roll to his shoulder. He walked across the field, his silhouette blurring in the sunlight. With every footstep, Caddy's heart grew heavier, until she thought it would break in two.

The Dreamers were waiting when she returned to the house. Hex and Red were gone. Caddy hadn't seen them leave though she was sure Hex had witnessed her exchange with Poe. April made space for her in the circle, taking her hand as she sat. A woman across the room straightened and cleared her throat. She faced Caddy.

"Tell us where you go when you dream," she said.

20

A BIG MESS

Skylark lay on the hotel room floor, clutching the shaft of the arrow, ice filaments creeping up her hand. Things with the Speaker hadn't gone as the cowboy had planned. She'd let the old man down. If she hadn't allowed jealousy to get the better of her, if she hadn't hesitated when the girl showed up, they would have had the advantage. Her obsession with Poe had caused her to screw up the mission. She was so focused on Cadence that she gave the demon an opening. And he took it. Now she might never see Poe again. What was Cadence doing there anyway? What was her connection to the Speaker?

But there were more pressing things to worry about. Like Timon. He was going to be furious, that was for sure.

Skylark's teeth started to chatter. She must look ridiculous, she thought, lying on her back in some sleazy dive, her own arrow through her shoulder, freezing to death. At least the arrow had hit her left side. It shouldn't affect her shooting much—if she survived.

She lifted her head, just long enough to see the Speaker dissolve into a shapeless form that receded like the signal on an old tube TV. Someone pounded on the door.

"I'm calling the cops!" a man yelled.

Francis leaned over her, his blue eyes blazing, face crimped with worry. "Aw, hell, Skylark."

She shivered uncontrollably. "I'm cold, Fran." She saw the mouse lying next to her. His mouth was open, and his whole body was blue with frost.

"Sebbie . . ."

Swift as a sparrow, Francis pocketed the mouse and gathered her in his arms. She tried to tell him she was sorry, but the cold stole the words from her mouth. He wasn't in a mood for listening anyway. He lifted her from the ground and they jumped, landing in front of two gleaming doors. Francis didn't bother to announce himself but simply kicked the doors open with his cowboy boot and hurried in.

The building was all glass and glimmer like every other place in the city. And it was packed. There were beings of every Frequency and animal totems everywhere. They loomed past as Francis raced with her down the corridor. She wished he would slow down. He was making her dizzy. The pain in her shoulder spiked and she cried out, causing Francis to hustle even faster. He veered into an empty room and placed her lovingly on a stretcher, then put the mouse on his own stretcher beside her.

"Hold on, sweetheart," he said.

Several Healers and their falcons glided into the room, radiating compassion and calm. Two of them wheeled Sebastian away. The others gathered around her bed. Skylark could feel ice filaments crawling across her face. Her chest felt so heavy. She coughed, and a thick black ooze sputtered from her mouth. This upset Francis, and a Healer had to escort him from the room. She could see him standing in the hallway, worrying his beard. She felt awful for causing so much trouble.

The pain was growing in her shoulder, triggering small starbursts across her vision. Was she going to die? The Healers poured their emerald energy over her, concentrating on her wound. Several tried to remove her armour. The Ephemeral was being difficult, refusing to let go. Such a beautiful, loyal thing. Skylark would have told it so, if only her teeth would stop chattering.

By the time Timon arrived, the Healers had managed to remove her armour, and the Ephemeral was hovering in a cloud of its own mist beside the bed. A laser beam of green light was being trained on the arrow, with little success. It seemed to absorb everything. Skylark watched what was happening from a remote seat in her mind. The more the Healers tried to remove the arrow, the deeper its toxin crept through her body. At one point her soul light began to falter, and more Healers hastened into the room. Poor little light, she thought, though she was more concerned about Timon. He was glaring through the glass, disapproval pouring from every molecule in his being. His brow was permanently knit and he wouldn't even look at Francis. Skylark strained through her agony to hear their conversation.

"What's the prognosis?" Timon asked.

The cowboy shook his head. "They don't know. They've never seen anything like it before. They think there's some kind of poison in her system, messing with her energy."

"You've made a grave error in judgment this time, Francis. It's going to cost us dearly."

"She was ready, T. He pulled a fast one. Even I didn't see it coming."

"Meticulous fieldwork, Francis. We lost so many good men to acquire the information I gave you."

"We almost had him. Skylark severed the cord like a champ. We didn't know he'd learned some new tricks. He infected her arrow—turned it all black and evil. We'll get him next time."

Timon's eyebrows jumped. "I don't think you understand the severity of the situation. There may not be a next time. We've run out of options. It's as simple as that. If you'd taken Kenji instead of Skylark, as per orders, this may have ended in our favour. Now the Council will have to be involved. We will likely lose the assignment altogether—and Skylark."

Francis shot him a panicked look. "Skylark's strong, T. She's gonna pull through."

"If you'd listened to me, she wouldn't be in this situation!" Timon yelled. He walked away, leaving Francis alone with his guilt and worry.

The Healers produced a surge of energy and Skylark nearly passed out as the arrow crumbled to dust. Its black ashes were carefully brushed into an even blacker box and sealed with a strange gold liquid from a thin vial. The box was placed inside a larger gold receptacle, covered with a silver fabric, and carried from the room. The remaining Healers and their falcons circled the stretcher. They directed their light on Skylark, and sustained an emerald beam, causing the last filaments of ice to melt from her body. Using strips of ethereal cloth, they carefully bound the wound on her shoulder and wheeled her from the room. The Ephemeral followed like a puppy, floating in its mist. Francis chased after them, jogging alongside the stretcher.

"How're you feeling, sweetheart?"

Skylark reached for him and her arm sagged. He took her hand and held it the entire length of the hall. The Healers steered her into a quiet room. They lifted her with their light energy from the stretcher to the bed and made sure she was comfortable. One addressed Francis, communicating telepathically.

"She's had quite a shock. Please don't upset her in any way."

"How long before she's back on her feet?"

Francis asked this for her sake, she thought. He was trying to be optimistic. The Healer wasn't about to humour him.

"We don't know. Vital signs are faint though stable. We will have to wait and see."

The Healers glided from the room. Francis pulled up a chair

and sat beside her, careful not to thump his cowboy boots on the floor. Skylark watched him through half-closed eyes. He was riddled with remorse—she could see that. She wanted to tell him not to worry, that it wasn't his fault. But her eyelids were heavy and she drifted off.

She was immediately confronted by a confusion of images—the Speaker, the man on the bed, the landscape of ash, the girl with the hazel eyes. What was her name again? She saw herself fire the arrow and watched as it streaked back toward her. When it hit her shoulder, everything went black. She floated in the void, the arrow's dark poison taking hold. It was doing something to her. Creeping deep into the hollows of her system. Changing her energy. She could feel it. And there was nothing she could do to stop it.

After a very long time, a voice penetrated the darkness.

"Well, well, well. You really screwed up this time, didn't you, old man."

Skylark's eyes popped open. It was Kenji. He had a bouquet of orange chrysanthemums in his hand. She sighed with relief, thankful to have been rescued from the murky fluid of her dreams. Kenji held the flowers up for her to see, removing his glasses and studying her with concerned eyes.

"How you doing, kid?"

Her robe draped dull and lifeless over her legs. The arrow had really kicked it out of her. She was lucky to be alive. "I'm okay," she said, trying to be positive.

Kenji turned to Francis. "Does she know?"

"Know what?" Skylark asked.

Kenji gave the cowboy a reproving look. "How's the shoulder?" he deflected.

She touched her bandage and was surprised by how hot it felt. "It's fine," she said, not wanting to burden anyone anymore than she already had. "I don't know what all the fuss is about."

She attempted to sit up to prove it, and the pain in her shoulder ramped up, forcing her back onto the bed.

"Just relax, sweetheart," Francis soothed. "Give yourself a chance to recover."

Skylark smiled weakly. He was being so caring. "Where's Sebbie?" she asked.

Kenji raised his eyebrows at Francis.

Francis worked the muscles in his jaw. "Skylark . . . honey . . ."

That's as far as he got. Skylark did the math and broke down. "No, Francis, please . . ."

Francis stared at the floor.

"You're getting slow, old man," Kenji said. "Timon's taking Skylark out of the mix because of this."

"What?" Francis tore his hat from his head and smacked it across his thigh. "We almost had him!"

All of this is my fault, Skylark thought. She should just tell them what really happened and face the music. She was getting kicked off the case anyway. She owed it to Sebastian to come clean. Her actions had gotten him killed.

"There was a girl . . . " she began. The moment she started to confess, a voice whispered in her ear and the pain in her wound flared.

Kenji looked at Francis. "What girl?"

Francis shook his head with the slightest motion. Kenji folded his arms gravely. Skylark lay back on the bed. Whose voice had she heard? Her thoughts whirled. Maybe coming clean wasn't the best plan after all. Besides, if she told them about the girl, she'd have to tell Francis about Poe. And she wasn't willing to do that. Kenji already knew something was up. He just didn't know the details. She reached into the mist to stroke the Ephemeral. It arched like a cat to meet her hand.

Francis pushed his hat down on his head and turned on Kenji. "Where were you anyway? I tried to call you."

Kenji fired back. "Don't pin this on me, old man. You had this planned. Admit it. You wanted to make me look bad, and it blew up in your face."

Francis sprang from his chair. "I don't need to make you look bad. You're doing a great job yourself."

"Screw you." Kenji threw the chrysanthemums at him, clipped his sunglasses on, and left the room.

Francis slammed the flowers into the wastebasket beside the bed. "Jerk!"

The Ephemeral purred in Skylark's hand. She didn't know why, but she felt mildly amused by all the drama in the room. Francis was upset though. He sat on the edge of the bed, rubbing his eyes with his thumb and forefinger.

"Don't worry," she reassured him. "Kenji won't stay mad for long. He's probably gone to the bar to drink it off."

Francis patted Skylark's hand with distracted affection. "I'm sure you're right, sugar."

21

THE DARK ENTERS

Skylark reclined on the hospital bed, alone. She'd sent the cowboy away, convincing him she needed the rest. But she wasn't tired. She was surprisingly awake. And so was her robe. It smouldered around her, waving seductively. The whispering in her head had grown louder, too, as sure as the arrow's dark energy pushed deeper inside her. It made her feel distant. Removed. Strong. As nimble and strategic as a spider. She felt like she could see in every direction, hear the tiniest movement, catch the quietest, most secret of thoughts.

She touched the dressing on her shoulder. The wound was hot and festering. Lifting a corner of the bandage, Skylark peeled it back to take a look. The dark hole gaped at her, ragged and inky as the underside of a toadstool. She covered it with the bandage again and thought about Sebastian. Had he suffered when he died? She was sorry for the mouse, really, though she wasn't nearly as upset as she knew she should be. He was a casualty of war, she told herself. It was as simple as that. Her mind wandered to Kenji. She wondered if he was at the bar, drinking away his anger. Maybe she should go and see for herself. She was feeling restless, anyway, and could use a distraction.

Sitting up, she swung her legs easily over the side of the bed and dressed herself. First the breastplate, then the glove and wrist guard and, finally, the Elusive Ephemeral, which had been waiting patiently in its shroud of mist beside the bed. She slung the bow and quiver over her shoulder, triggering a sharp pain in her wound. This time, she embraced it, revelling in the feeling as she threw her head back and morphed into her human form. The Ephemeral scrolled to the colour of gun metal and vanished, concealed against her shirt. Skylark conjured a mirror to admire her reflection, turning her head from side to side. Her violet eyes had darkened to the richest colour of amethyst. "Beautiful," she said, tossing the mirror back into the ether and zeroing in on Kenji's energy.

"Take me to where he is now."

The lights began to blur, and with a jet engine roar Skylark shot from the hospital room. Touching down, she was delighted to see she hadn't reverted as before. She credited him, the one whose darkness flowed through her. He had made her stronger. She looked around. She hadn't landed at the bar. She was standing in a garden outside a teahouse in eighteenth-century Japan. There was music coming from the building. She prowled toward one of teahouse's translucent paper windows and peeped through a small hole.

"Well, well, what do we have here?"

A dozen Japanese men sat on the floor, transfixed. Skylark followed their line of sight to the front of the room where the most exquisite geisha danced. Her fan moved as delicately as a butterfly. Her voice was haunting, like the fluty song of a wood thrush calling through the trees. Skylark was spellbound. And then she saw him, standing at the back, bewitched by the geisha's charm.

The look of shock on Kenji's face when she entered the room was delectable. "So . . . this is where you go . . ."

"What are you doing here?" Kenji demanded.

He was cagey as a tiger. Skylark laughed. "Why? Afraid I'll upset your pretty girlfriend?" She walked around the geisha, appraising her kimono. "Nice dress."

Kenji gritted his teeth. "Get out, Skylark."

"Make me."

He lunged and she dodged him, the geisha's kimono ruffling in his wake. The geisha paused, recovered artfully and continued to dance.

"Careful," Skylark said. "You're leaving your grubby little energetic prints all over this place."

Kenji stepped cautiously toward her. "Let's take this outside."

Skylark shrugged. "They can't see us unless we engage them." She reached for the geisha's fan.

Kenji dove, hitting her in the chest and blasting her out the teahouse door. She grabbed his arm and flipped him, effortlessly, then pressed her boot on his neck.

"Looks like we have a problem, Kenji. The whole time you were telling me to put my feelings in a box, you were mooning over your little Japanese girlfriend. What about her soul's expression? Don't you want her to evolve?"

He fought to get up.

"Stay down," she growled. She pressed harder with her boot, enjoying his helplessness. He was pitiful. "I'm guessing you were here when we needed you the other day. That makes you responsible for what happened. I wonder what Francis would have to say about that?" Reaching under her breastplate, she tore the blackened bandage from her wound. She examined the stained cloth with mild curiosity then pitched it and leaned over Kenji.

"I feel him so close to me . . . I can see his eyes . . . I can hear his voice inside my head."

"Don't listen to him, Skylark. The Speaker's using you."

She kicked him aside. "Why would I take any advice from you? At least I have the guts to admit I'm weak." She imagined Poe's lips against hers. She would go to him, now. Nothing could stop her. Not Kenji or Francis or some girl with hazel eyes.

Kenji hollered as she jumped. In an instant she was standing over Poe, watching him sleep beneath a blanket on the ground. Her soul light nearly burst at the sight of him. There was someone with him—a young ranger. He stood when he saw her.

"I am this man's Guide," he said.

Skylark sneered. "Get lost."

The ranger approached, undaunted. "He is my charge. This is a very delicate time in this man's life's journey."

"That's why I'm here," Skylark said. "To help him on his way."

The ranger positioned himself between her and Poe. "Who are you?"

With a flick of her hand, Skylark incinerated him. "Boring." She turned her violet eyes on Poe and drank him in as he slept. He was so beautiful. She would never relinquish him to another girl—ever. Whatever it took, she would tear that girl from his heart. She closed her eyes and projected herself into his dream. In the liquid shadows of his subconscious she took his hand and held it to her chest. His mouth found hers and she breathed herself inside him.

Poe woke with a shout, scrabbling away from her. Skylark stared at him. He stared back.

"Can you see me?" she asked.

He looked confused.

"I didn't mean to frighten you," she said.

He staggered to his feet, checking over his shoulder.

She twirled a lock of her raven hair between her fingers. "It's okay. We're alone."

"How long have you been standing there?"

"Not long."

He scrutinized her clothes, following the healing cord up her scarred arm and coming to rest on her face. There was a glint of recognition in his eyes. Yet she could tell he doubted himself. He didn't understand who she was. She smiled, her skin tingling just to be near him.

"Your eyes," he said. "They're . . . purple."

"Do they please you?"

"I've never seen anything like them."

His candour was so charming, though his guard was quick to come up.

"Who are you?"

"What?"

"Are you following me?"

"No."

"Then what are you doing out here?"

She hesitated. She hadn't thought that far ahead. Inspiration suddenly came to her as if transmitted from someone else. She made herself look as small and vulnerable as a kitten. "I'm lost, I guess . . . What are you doing out here?"

Poe picked up his blanket, shook it, and worked it into a tight roll. He secured it with a piece of string. "I have to go."

Oh, he was spoiling the fun, she wickedly thought. "Where?"

No answer. His bewilderment delighted her.

"Don't go," she said.

He turned, his face set with anger. "Did they send you?"

"I don't know what you're talking about."

"Then what do you want?"

"I don't want anything. I just thought you'd like some company. It's scary out here. I'm alone. I have nowhere to go."

He tucked the blanket under his arm and grabbed a small cloth bundle from the ground. "Well, I can't stay here . . . and you can't come with me."

"Why?"

"It isn't safe."

Skylark looked around. "Who are you running from?"

"No one."

"Then why are you in such a hurry?" She perched on a nearby stone, savouring everything about him.

Their eyes locked. She was winning him over. He tossed the blanket to the ground, sat on a rock across from her and untied the bundle.

"Are you hungry?" He offered her a piece of fried bread. "It isn't much."

She took it, just to hold something he'd held, and gave it a sniff.

"You really shouldn't be with me," he said.

"Why not?"

"You just shouldn't."

"You'll have to come up with something better than that."

He tossed the piece of bread in his hand back in the cloth, tying the corners together. She watched his jaw clench and unclench, knowing he was searching for the right words to explain his situation. It was *adorable*.

"I'm wanted," he said. "I'm being chased."

"By whom?" Skylark played along.

"I'm an outcast. It's dangerous for you to even be here."

"You must be a terrible person," she said.

He caught her sarcasm and gave her a look. It sent a charge racing through her. "Whatever you've done, it can't be that bad . . . can it?"

"I assure you it is." He stood to go, tucking the blanket beneath his arm again. "I'd rather be alone," he said, but his words lacked conviction.

She got up and stood in front of him. "I don't care what it is you've done—honestly. I'm alone out here. I have no one. Whatever's troubling you, I forgive you."

He looked at her with such visible gratitude she nearly threw her arms around his neck.

"Please," she said. "Let me stay with you—just for a little while."

"No. You could get killed."

"I'll die if you leave me here. Do you think I can survive out here alone?"

He waffled. "I just don't want to be responsible . . . I can't carry the burden of another life. I've made some bad decisions, and people have been hurt as a result."

Skylark gazed deeply into his eyes. "My life is my own. I'm not afraid of you."

"You have no idea what you're saying."

"Then why don't you explain it to me."

He balked. She could tell he was about to tip his hand.

"I killed someone."

His admission thrilled her. The pain in her shoulder flared deliciously as the arrow's dark energy went deeper still. "Under what circumstances?"

He ran his hand through his hair. "Does it matter?"

"I think it does."

"I belonged to a group. We . . . worked together . . . for a new reality . . ." He stopped to judge her reaction.

"A world without sin," she said, her tongue finding the words so easily.

His eyes widened. "Yes."

The pain rippled through her body and she could feel her eyes grow even darker. When she spoke next, it was with two voices. "But sin found you. And now your hands are dirty, and your heart is heavy with guilt."

Poe lowered his head. "Yes."

"It's an old story. As old as the time before time. You're not responsible for this."

"I spilled blood," he confessed.

"You were justified in your actions."

"Is there ever justification for murder?"

She placed her hand on his head. "This earth was born in doubt and pain. It is the way of all things."

"But the Light . . ."

"The Light is the parent of the Dark. One cannot truly understand anything without knowing what opposes it." She brushed his cheek with her fingers. "Do you regret your decision?"

"To kill?"

"Yes."

The muscles jumped in his jaw. "No."

"Then free yourself." She lifted his chin with the gentlest motion. "It is a fanciful dream of mankind to live in peace. Peace exists only in the mind as the blade drives through the heart."

"I killed someone to save another."

"Then the best man won. The exchange was more than fair."

He frowned.

"Would you rather she'd died?" she asked.

"It's a sin to murder—it destroys all we've worked for."

"It's a greater sin to give your life so freely."

"I didn't want to do it."

"You had to. What good is resistance if one simply surrenders when pressed?" She took his hand and a wave of ecstasy rolled through her. "Do you want to die?"

"No."

She moved closer. She could see eternity in his eyes. She wanted to stay like this forever. But the breeze picked up and the spell was broken.

"We have to go," he said. "It isn't safe to stay here any longer."

Skylark shadowed him through the woods. "Can I at least know what we're running from?"

He pushed through the underbrush, holding branches so they wouldn't whip back in her face. "Company men."

"I've heard of them."

He stopped dead. "What? How?"

"Stories," she smoothly lied. "When I was a child. We thought they were only fairy tales to scare small children into behaving."

"Well, they're very real."

"And you killed one."

He nodded.

"How can it be wrong to defend yourself?"

He didn't answer. They walked to a stone outcropping at the edge of the forest. He crisscrossed through the boulders, Skylark following closely.

"This is a good place to rest," he said.

They sat together, backs against the rock. She let her vision travel far through the woods to where a meadow swayed around a small house that peeked out as bright as a polished bone from a hill. And beyond that, she could hear a waterfall. The pain in her wound flared, and she could sense Poe's thoughts as his consciousness shifted. She had successfully planted a seed in his mind. Kill one man, kill them all. He was ready to hunt the hunter. She shivered with pleasure, and the Ephemeral shivered with her.

"I can help you," she said.

He stared at his feet.

She reached over and touched his hand, lightly, and only at the fingertips. "I believe in your cause."

He smiled to himself. "I don't even know your name."

Leaning in, their lips almost touching, she could feel the invisible tendrils between them taking hold. "I'm Skylark."

"I'm Poe," he said, his name an opiate to her soul. He closed his eyes. He looked so tired.

"Rest," she said. "Sleep. I will keep watch."

He lay back, his head on the blanket roll. She took the opportunity to inspect her wound. It was dark and alive, an ugly mouth.

Its black ink had bled right through her armour. Pain gripped her shoulder. She could hear his voice so clearly now. Such loving whispers. Offering her the world. An image of Sebastian bobbed up in her mind and she was struck momentarily by another kind of pain, though fleeting. The bond between her and the mouse was fading. The whispers soothed, caressed. *All is exactly as it should be . . . exactly . . . as it should be . . .* Skylark curled around Poe, absorbing the warmth of his body, feeling his lifeblood coursing as she pressed into his dreams once again.

22

VENGEANCE

Skylark kept watch from her perch on the rock above Poe. She felt agile, powerful. Ready to fight.

"Can you feel them?" she said. "They're close."

He placed his hand over the mark on his arm. "Yes."

Hopping down from the rock, she landed beside him, smooth as a panther, and grinned. "The hunt is on."

Skylark lit out through the woods, Poe at her side, weaving between trees to the meadow she'd seen before. She dropped, crouching. Poe crouched beside her.

"My skin twitches," she said. "They are closer still." She searched the landscape, pointing to a spot in the field where the grass waved along a ragged hem of sky. "There!"

Poe squinted against the sun. "I can't see anything."

"Wait . . . there . . . see it?"

Cloud shadows scudded over the grass. The Company men emerged from the forest like ships from a fog, steaming toward the skull house where the Dreamers slept. Skylark stepped from the trees and swung the Ephemeral from her shoulder. In a motion as fluid as a river she drew an arrow and fired. It soared over the field, blackening as it whistled through the air. The

Company man's body rose with the impact and fell, the arrow piercing his chest clean through to the other side. The pain in her shoulder arced. She clasped her wound, eyes rolling back.

"Do you feel that?" she said. "That's the burn of victory."

Skylark dashed down the slope, shooting as she ran, Poe running wildly after her.

The door to the skull house was flung open and the Dreamers poured out. They fled to the woods, the Company men unleashing their dogs for the attack. Skylark laughed at the challenge, drew four arrows and shot in quick succession, one after the other, until all the dogs lay dead, filaments of ice blanketing their fur. She fired again, slicing a Company man clean in half. Trotting over to the body, she took the man's knife, its blade curved and gleaming, and put it in Poe's hands.

"Do you like it?"

"It feels alive."

"Use it," she said. "Save your people. Write your name in blood."

There was a scream and a Dreamer fell. Poe rushed the closest Company man, blade raised. The man faced him, an expressionless killer. Poe struck and they rolled to the ground. There was a sickening slash and Poe careened back, his arm bleeding. Skylark aimed at the man. But then Poe had the advantage. She lowered her bow and watched with satisfaction as his blade leapt back and forth in the sun. The man's arms flailed like the arms of a marionette and fell to his sides, unstrung. Poe reeled to his feet, his hands dripping red. Skylark took him in, every particle in her being humming.

"Today, you saved your brethren," she said. "You have secured your place in history."

He stood before her, chest heaving, the slash on his arm seeping blood into his shirt. He nodded at the Ephemeral. "Your bow . . . I've never seen anything like it. It's—"

"Special," she said, finishing his sentence. "It was a gift." She slung it over her shoulder. The bow wrapped itself around her and cloaked itself.

She smiled at him. How wondrous he was to her—as wondrous and mythical as the bow on her back. Her soul swelled with desire as she followed the trail of the Dreamers through the blood-stained grass, collecting her arrows from the corpses of her victims. Over the bodies of the vanquished Company men, shadows appeared and took form. The Nightshades had come to collect the bounty.

The surviving Dreamers cowered in the dank basement of an abandoned farmhouse. It was sheer luck they'd found it. They spoke in hushed voices.

Vengeance.

Murder.

Retribution.

The hand of God.

Caddy said nothing. She was sure she'd seen Poe in the meadow. Had he gone completely crazy? She feared the worst. Dozens of Company men had been killed. The Dreamers were terrified.

Someone shushed the room silent. Wooden footsteps tapped on the floor above. Who was coming?

April held on to Caddy. The basement door pushed open, the beam of a flashlight probing down the stairs.

"It's Red and Hex," someone said, and the Dreamers exhaled with relief. Except Caddy. Were they here because of Poe?

The Dreamers gathered around them like timid children. Caddy and April hung back. Hex stood at the base of the stairs, the glare of the flashlight reflected in her glasses. She was gunning for blood, Caddy could tell. Hex waited before she spoke, raising the tension in the room like a hammer above a window pane. Just get it over with, Caddy bitterly thought.

"There have been developments," Hex began. "Talk from the outside. The war between the nations has escalated."

Horrified murmurs rose from the group. April grabbed Caddy's hand. Caddy held her breath, counting heartbeats.

"There is more," Hex said, drawing the hammer artfully back. "There is talk of a bomb."

A cry of dread shattered the room. April doubled over as though stabbed, her body convulsing with sobs. Caddy held her close, comforting her. Was this another one of Hex's ploys? she wondered. Another device to smash the group's resolve to pieces? Hex called for quiet, April's muffled weeping penetrating the silence.

"It's what we feared most," Hex said. "But we can not let anything get in the way of the Dream. We knew this time would come. It was foretold. We knew we would face challenges. Now, more than ever, as we walk the razor's edge, we must remain united, determined, hopeful, strong." She removed her glasses and looked at Caddy. "Dream well, my children."

23

BLACK RAIN

Poe and Skylark moved through the woods. Between the trees and beneath the undergrowth, she caught glimpses of shadows moving. The shadows formed mouths and eyes, then entire faces.

"We're being watched."

Poe turned on his heels. "Company men?"

"Plant spirits. I met one before. Can you see them?" She didn't need to ask. She knew he couldn't. "They're curious," she said. "They are at the mercy of human activity."

"What do they want?"

"The same thing we want. Only they are powerless to acquire it. They must depend on us to fulfill their deepest desire, to bring peace to the world."

He stopped cold and looked at her. "What are you?" he asked.

"I am what I am," she said. This only confounded him. "Let me make this easier for you." Rearranging her particles, Skylark morphed into Meg, matching her features exactly, except for her soft grey eyes. Those she could not reproduce. She laughed at the look of disbelief on his face.

"H-how can this be?" he said.

"I am no ghost, I assure you." She touched the makeshift bandage on his arm where the Company man's blade had slashed him. "Does it hurt?"

"Meg," he whispered. "I don't understand . . ."

Skylark sidled closer. She could feel his breath on her lips. "Poe. I will never leave you again."

They fell together, mouths and hair and hands, kissing in the forest beneath the eyes of the plant spirits. The Ephemeral swirled on her back. Skylark wanted to consume him, to drink him in. For eons she'd held his memory in her soul.

There was a bright flash. Francis and Kenji appeared. Kenji strode over to Poe and touched him on the shoulder. Poe sank to the ground, unconscious. Skylark dropped protectively over him. "Leave us alone!"

"Skylark, honey, you need to come with us," Francis said. He went to take her hand. She blasted into the air, landing on top of a stone outcropping.

Francis and Kenji jumped behind her.

"Come back with us, Skylark," Francis said.

"Why should I?"

"The Speaker has poisoned your blood. You're not yourself."

"I've never felt better."

"What you're doing is wrong and you know it," Kenji said.

She sneered. Who was he to tell her anything? "Does Francis know your little secret, Kenji?"

He responded by firing a beam of light at her. Skylark easily avoided it, laughing mockingly. He would have to try harder than that if he wanted to catch her.

Francis barked at him. "Put your guns away!"

Skylark wagged her finger at Kenji. "Shame, shame, double shame, now we know your girlfriend's name."

"What's she talking about?" the cowboy asked.

Skylark looked at her nails. "Do you want to know where Kenji goes when you can't find him, Francis? He's got a girl in Japan. She's so pretty, he just can't let her go."

Kenji charged. She jumped, landing on Mount Fuji, Francis and Kenji streaking in her wake.

"Get away from me," she warned.

Francis stared at her shoulder. Skylark covered her wound with her hand. The black ink was bleeding through her shirt.

"You need help, honey," Francis said. "You're not well. Come back with us so we can get you fixed up."

How tiresome, she thought. Why didn't he give it a rest? "Save your breath, old man."

"You can't stay with him," Kenji said. "You know you can't."

"And you can't go around killing people either," Francis added.

She threw her head back, defiant. "I can do whatever I want."

Francis stepped toward her. "No, Skylark. There are terrible consequences to your actions."

"Ha!" she jeered. "That's not my problem. Free will and all that, remember, Fran?"

"That doesn't really apply here, darling."

"Doesn't it? Did it apply when you turned me into this?" Skylark raised her bound arm. "I had no say in any of this. I didn't ask for it. You took me away from the one thing I wanted in the world." She prepared to jump, and a magnetic force jolted through her body. The Speaker's words poured into her mouth. When she spoke again, it was in his demonic voice.

"Who are you to stand in the way of love?"

Francis and Kenji recoiled.

"It's him," Francis said. "He's taken possession of her."

Kenji fired a scorching volley. Skylark skipped over it, the bolts ricocheting off the mountain in a shower of dirt and rocks.

"Too late, too late, will be the cry," she taunted.

"Let her go," Francis ordered the demon. "She isn't yours to play with."

"Ah, Francis, ever the bleeding heart. Your paternal dust leaves my mouth dry, old man."

"Then have a sip of this," Kenji said, blazing another shot.

Skylark's hands flew to the Ephemeral and she fired, deflecting the beam to the top of the mountain. The peak exploded, snow and ice hailing down. Francis and Kenji jumped, and with a violent spasm, the Speaker left her body. She was alone on the mountain. Closing her eyes, Skylark traced Francis and Kenji's energetic trajectory with her mind. She tuned in. She could see and hear them perfectly. They were in Timon's office, taking an earful. Over the city, black clouds as thick as birds' nests had gathered.

"There's talk of war on earth," Timon said, his pipe held against his teeth. "Guides are reporting an all-time low in human morale. It seems hope is a rare commodity these days. The Council is very concerned. They're discussing the possibility of an intervention. Never before has such a thing been considered." He drew on his pipe, sucked air, plucked it from his mouth and scowled at the cold bowl. "And then there's you."

Francis squirmed in his chair like a schoolchild. He cleared his throat. "The Speaker is getting bold."

"He's been emboldened," Timon clipped back. He sighed, fumbling a match from the box next to the smoked glass ashtray by his chair and striking it. Holding the flame to the bowl, he puffed vigorously, shook the match out and dropped it into the ashtray. "We truly have no recourse. We can only hope the humans will figure this one out for themselves. Free will, and all that."

"Yeah, we've been hearing a lot of that lately," Kenji said.

"What?" Timon fixed an irritated eye on him.

Kenji muttered something incomprehensible in reply. Francis fidgeted in his seat.

"The problem is, there's no tracking the guy anymore," he said. "He shows up where and when he wants. He's more powerful than ever."

Timon nodded through his pipe smoke. "And growing more powerful by the minute. I'm afraid our hand has been tipped. The grey souls are no longer forthcoming. They're aware of their advantage. The first death was a shock—they were caught off guard. They've recovered nicely. Apparently, they're choosing obliteration over interment now. They're dying in droves, thanks to Skylark. Over two dozen in a single encounter. I shudder to think of her with the Elusive Ephemeral in her hands. With the mouse gone, she's without a moral compass." He contemplated the darkening sky. "I'm counting on you to figure this one out," he said to the clouds. "I don't care how. Be creative. Do whatever it takes. I don't even want to hear what you have in mind. But if you fail . . ." He puffed plumes of smoke toward the window.

Francis stood. Kenji pulled himself up from his seat. Timon didn't turn to see them off.

In the street, the temperature dipped. Dark drops as thick as oil plucked a tentative rhythm on the ground. Viscous starbursts the size of quarters stained buildings and cobbles. The sky broke open and the rain fell in a seamless curtain, the rivers and fountains of the city running black with it.

Skylark sharpened her focus, tracking Francis and Kenji to their headquarters. Francis was pacing back and forth. Kenji was leaning against the window ledge, brooding. He wiped a black smear of rain from his sleeve, rubbing it between his fingertips.

"I'm not gonna ask why," Francis started in. "Or who or how. Just fix this mess with the woman, PDQ, and that will be the end of it."

Kenji said nothing.

"I mean it, Kenji. I want this to end. Whatever human has you messed up, just cut it off—now—and nothing more will be said. But if I find out you're still mooning over some woman, I'm going straight to Timon." He continued to pace for the longest time, the black rain pounding on the window.

Kenji finally spoke. "I have an idea."

Francis turned to him like a dog following a tennis ball. "Lay it on me."

"We can protect the grey men."

"What?" Francis tipped back on his heels. "They're not the ones that need protecting."

Kenji faced him. "Think about it. All of this started with the human that kid Skylark is so hung up on—he drew first blood."

"No," Francis said. "You can't blame the boy for this. It's my fault. If I'd taken you instead of Skylark, none of this would have happened. I exposed her to the Speaker. For all we know, that was his plan all along—to get us to bring her somewhere so he could get his hooks into her." He pushed his hat to the back of his head. "Have you ever wondered why he didn't take her soul and put it in a little glass vial for his collection when he had the chance? He let her come here and transform into some kind of super-frequency. He wanted her to evolve. Somehow he knew what she was and we didn't. He wanted to take her at just the right moment and make her his own. And I walked right into it. I handed her to him with one of the most powerful weapons in the universe on her back. Now she's out there with the Ephemeral, picking grey men off like fish in a barrel. The Speaker's stronger than ever with her at his side. I'm the one to blame. It started because of me."

"It started because of them," Kenji said. "If it hadn't been for the first grey murder, we would never have had the intelligence to know where the Speaker was going to be. That kid killed the grey guy to protect his girl. Our guys picked the grey soul up and brought him here. We knocked him around for information and used it to meet the Speaker face to face. When he turned that arrow on Skylark and filled her with his poison, *he* changed the balance. I think he was just as surprised as we were that it had the effect it did. Now he's running with it. The grey men know he has the advantage, so they're choosing to obliterate their souls rather than risk giving up any more valuable information. They want to die. This has created an unprecedented rift in the Light that's allowing more Dark in than ever. That, you could never have predicted. Ergo, it wasn't your fault."

Francis clapped at Kenji's brilliant attempt at lawyering.

"Make a joke of it, old man. I'm dead serious," Kenji said. "For once I'm not blaming you for our problems." He stared at his blackened fingers, wiping them clean on piece of paper from Francis's desk.

Francis straightened his Stetson. "Are you feeling okay?"

"Why?"

"Because you're being all cozy with me. Makes me nervous."

Kenji shrugged. "It's the truth."

"If you say so."

"Why are you being all crusty about it?"

"I'm always crusty," Francis said.

Kenji wadded a piece of paper from the desk and tossed it at him. "If you say so."

They scowled at each other until Kenji withdrew and sat on the edge of the desk, serious again. "So . . . what if we stop the killing? Maybe we can keep things in a holding pattern while we figure out what to do next. Maybe something will happen to shift the balance back in our favour . . ."

"Like what? A miracle?"

"Yeah. Why not?"

"We'll be fighting against Skylark," Francis said.

"Not fighting—resisting. More Gandhi, less Attila the Hun."

"What if he shows up?"

"We'll distract him."

"And then?"

"We wait for an opening, the same as he did."

"What about the kid . . . ?" Francis asked. "The one she's interested in?"

"We'll deal with him later, once this blows over."

Francis looked out the window at the black rain. "This isn't like before. We're in some very hot soup."

"I know," Kenji said. "All we can do is try."

Francis flopped into a chair. "Hell, what else have we got? Let's give it a shot. But the minute we've got this in control, we're taking care of your little problem . . ."

The connection faded and Skylark's eyes fluttered open. A small part of her missed Francis and Kenji. But they intended to take Poe away from her—and the Ephemeral. She couldn't let that happen. She jumped to where Poe lay on the ground. Cradling his head in her lap, she woke him with a kiss.

Inside the farmhouse, the group laboured to dream. Caddy saw the Light and moved toward it. It pulsed, throbbed. She broadcast her intention, imagining the green sprouts of life reaching upward. The Dark advanced, shrivelling stalks and blackening sky faster than she could possibly create. Caddy fell back, exhausted, and landed in the Emptiness again, her fingers trailing ashes. Faces closed in around her, hungry, moaning, cold. The wind clawed at her with icy hands, stealing the voice from her mouth. *The end is coming*, it said.

24

SECRETS

"The Light is leaving us," Caddy whispered over the sound of the rain. The storm had come from nowhere and had been hammering the farmhouse for hours. The temperature had dropped along with rain. It made the house frigid.

"I know," April said. "You're doing better than the rest of us. Most can't find the Light at all . . . I can't find it."

They were lying on the cold floor, facing each other, speaking in low voices over a candle to avoid waking the others. The flame flickered in April's eyes. They were deep and warm, and fringed with dark lashes, like Poe's. It made Caddy's heart ache to look at them. She missed him so much.

"Tell me about your visions," April said.

Caddy had wondered when April would get to this. It was a simple enough question. Except she worried the others blamed her for bringing the Darkness in. No one had said anything directly, yet. She could tell by the way they looked at her that they suspected something. She'd lied when they asked her where she went during the dreaming. She didn't want to give them reason to turn against her. To be honest, even she had her doubts. Maybe she *was* responsible. Could she trust April to keep her secrets? Or had Hex and the others put her up to this? Either way, she had to tell the truth. Sooner or later someone would figure it out.

"I call it the Emptiness," she said. "It's a place without life. Completely frozen. Not even the Light can live there." She closed her eyes. She could see the mouths pushing through the ether. "There are souls, trapped for all eternity. They cry for help. They pray the Light will save them."

"Will it?" April asked.

"I don't know." Caddy opened her eyes.

April stared back at her, terrified. "Why does the Emptiness keep taking you?"

Caddy sighed. "I think it's a warning of some kind. It's like the Emptiness is one possible outcome if we can't stop the Darkness."

"I'm scared, Caddy."

She took April's hand and squeezed it. "Me too."

"Do you think there'll be a war?"

"Maybe. It looks that way."

"Hex said there's a bomb . . ."

"Let's hope it's not true."

April fiddled with the edge of her blanket, formulating a question she was seemingly reluctant to ask. "Is Poe to blame for the Darkness?"

"What? Why would you say that?"

April checked to be sure no one was listening. "I've heard rumours . . . they think Poe is killing them."

"The Company men?"

"Yes."

So it wasn't her visions the others suspected. This was a relief. Still, Caddy was sure she'd be hanged by association. She'd stood in front of everyone and defended Poe. She didn't regret it—not for a minute. She was sure now it was Poe she'd seen in the meadow. If she'd seen him, chances are someone else had too. With the number of Company men killed, someone must be helping him. But who?

"Even if he was involved, he was only trying to protect us. He couldn't possibly have killed them all."

April planted her chin on top of her stacked hands. "They say it's affecting the Light."

"They don't know for sure," Caddy said. "They're grasping at straws. The Darkness is growing everywhere. Whoever's responsible for protecting us, I'm okay with it. How can we dream if we're all dead?"

"They said the killings are good for us, but not for the greater good. The Company men want us to kill them. It gives them the advantage. It makes it difficult for us to reach the Light."

"Do you blame Poe for that?" Caddy asked.

April shook her head. "No. I don't want to die."

"Me neither."

Tears filled April's eyes. "We're all going to die one way or another."

"Maybe from starvation," Caddy joked, trying to change the mood. She rolled onto her side and pulled down the waistband of her jeans, exposing her hip bone. "These pants used to be tight." She made a face.

April forced a smile. She lifted her shirt. "I have too many ribs. I wish I had some ice cream."

"Don't say ice cream . . . or ribs."

"Ribs, ribs, ribs," April whispered.

"You're mean."

"I know."

Caddy covered her mouth to stifle a laugh. "I want a shower."

"With soap."

"Hot water."

"Shampoo."

"A razor."

"A toothbrush."

Someone stirred. They froze, eyes locked. It was a false alarm.

"I've heard other rumours too," April said.

"About what?"

"Hex ... mostly."

"Hex?"

"They don't trust her."

"Who?"

"Some of the Dreamers."

"Really? Why?"

April shrugged. "I don't know. If I'd asked, they would have known I was eavesdropping." She raised her eyebrows.

"Right. Do *you* trust her?"

April thought about this for a minute. "I don't know."

Was she just being careful? Caddy wanted to tell her exactly what she thought of Hex but decided to be cautious. "I'm not sure if I trust her either. There's something wrong with her."

"What do you mean?"

"Well ... how is it that the Company men always know where we are? And why is Hex never here when they come?"

"For security reasons," April said. "We can't risk losing her."

"That's what they tell us. She could just be protecting herself. Maybe she's not as dedicated to the cause as they'd like us to believe."

"Yeah ... but ... what about ... ?" April pointed to her eye.

"We have no way of knowing if that story is true."

"Why would she make it up?"

"To win us over," Caddy said. "To convince us she's sincere."

"Why do that? Why pretend?"

"Because maybe she isn't who she says she is. Maybe she's really on the side of the Dark."

April looked at her in alarm and Caddy knew she'd gone too far. She couldn't stop now. "What kind of person kidnaps people and forces them to join their cause?"

"She didn't kidnap me," April said. "I was called, like everyone else here."

"Oh."

April's disclosure drew them apart like rafters on an undertow. They floated in silence for a while, until Caddy threw a rope across the divide. She didn't want to lose April's confidence.

"I wish this rain would stop," she said. "I'm so cold."

April sighed. "Me too."

"Can I tell you something?" Caddy asked.

"Sure, anything."

"I miss Poe."

"Like . . . really miss him?"

"Yeah."

April rested her head in the nook of her elbow. She closed her eyes and stayed that way for so long, Caddy thought she'd fallen asleep.

"I think he's beautiful," she said at last, turning away from the light.

Caddy watched the candle gutter and die. She lay in the dark, unable to sleep, and was the first to hear the van coming down the road.

"April, wake up." Caddy shook her shoulder. "The van's coming. We have to wake the others."

The Dreamers mobilized in an instant. Blankets were rolled. Food was gathered. There was no time to eat. They would eat on the way. They stood in the downpour, the cube van tearing along the road, its lights dimmed by the rain. It was 7 a.m. and the sky was heavy as wet concrete, blocking out the sun.

Behind the van, another set of lights came into view. And another from the opposite direction.

"Company men!" someone shouted.

Caddy and April ran into the field. The van careened up the lane, wobbled and flipped. A pickup tore past the upended van, a trailer fishtailing behind it. At the house, the truck skidded to a stop, the trailer gate fell open, and a cavalry of Company men burst out, their horses frothing. They barreled down on the Dreamers, hooves thundering, mud spraying, nets billowing. Caddy heard a whiffling sound, and a net ballooned and dropped. It hit April, taking her down in a jumble of feet and hands. The rider spurred his horse on, cinching the net with a rope and dragging her through the mud.

"April!" Caddy screamed.

There was the slice and woof as another net was thrown. It fell over Caddy, heavy as chainmaille. She hit the ground, the air popping from her lungs. The Company man reined his horse around, galloped back and jumped over her. He pulled the horse in, its legs buckling under its hindquarters, and dismounted, clean as a switchblade. Caddy fought the net, kicking and tearing. The man stood over her, a predator savouring its prey. Without a word, he reached down, grabbed her by the throat and raised his knife. Caddy shielded herself with her arms, waiting for the blow. A spray of warm blood splashed over her. She drew back her hands in shock then realized it wasn't her blood—it was his. The Company man loosened his grip and toppled to his knees.

Caddy looked up to see Poe, his face a death mask of blood and muck running in the rain, his eyes glazed with the heat of delirium. He didn't acknowledge her, but ran for the woods, leaving her to wrestle herself from the net.

"Poe!" she shouted. He didn't respond, so she began searching for April, scouring the field.

The Company men had gathered in a group on the edge of the woods, their horses rearing and stamping along an invisible boundary. The men cropped and whipped, the horses refusing to advance. What was holding them back? Caddy wondered.

Twenty feet from the men, a body lay in a heap beneath a net. Caddy took a chance, hunching low as she moved. Edging nearer, she saw that it was April, cocooned and unmoving on the ground. Was she dead? The body of a Company man sizzled next to her, severed in half and scorched as if by fire. Caddy gagged at the smell. She yanked on the net, pulling her friend free. April groaned.

"Get up," Caddy said. "You have to get up." She hauled April to her feet, dazed and shivering, and together they limped toward the trees.

In the field, Skylark squared off with Francis while Kenji held a beam of light around the Company men. The men looked dumbfounded, unable to see the force that held them. They beat their frightened horses, trying to force them to move.

"You can't keep killing people, Skylark," Francis called out to her. "You're creating a rift in the Light and the Dark's getting in."

Skylark glared at him. She didn't have time for this. She needed to find Poe. "Get out of my way, old man."

Francis planted his cowboy boots in the mud. "I can't do that."

She drew her bow. "Then I'll make you."

"Give it your best shot," he challenged her.

Skylark growled and fired. The old man was quicker than she thought, deflecting the arrow with a bolt of light. It cracked in the other direction, hissing like a bottle rocket through the rain. Francis flew at her, landing inches from her face before she jumped.

Returning to the mountain, Skylark planned her next move. She focused her mind and could see Francis and Kenji still in the meadow, holding the men and their horses at bay. Where was Poe? Her vision swooped to the edge of the woods. Poe was sprawled on the ground among the trees, her arrow lodged in his side. "No!" How could she have done this to him? She prepared to jump, to go to him, but the voice took control of her again. Her master was calling.

25

FUGITIVES

Caddy and April made it to the woods, taking cover behind a bush. They huddled in the downpour, watching for horses. A thin moan filtered through the rain.

"Did you hear that?" Caddy asked.

April hung her head, hands clasped around her knees. There were raw marks on her arms where the net had cut her skin.

Caddy strained to listen. "There it is again."

"It's just the rain playing tricks on you," April said.

"I think someone's hurt. I have to see who it is."

April started to cry. "Please don't. Don't leave me here alone."

"I won't go far," Caddy promised. "I just want to take a look."

"What if it's a trap? What if it's one of them?"

"What if it's one of the others?" Caddy said. "I have to be sure. You'll be okay if you stay hidden and keep quiet."

April withdrew, making herself smaller. Caddy held her breath, trying to find the sound again. Had she imagined it? No, there it was, between the sheets of rain. Someone was in trouble. Heart pounding, she crept between the trees. What if it *was* a trap? The forest closed in around her. The rain pushed the hair into her eyes. After fifty feet or so she stopped to get her bearings.

Everything was the same desolate colour of grey. Except for a red high-top sneaker sticking out from the gnarled mass of an uprooted tree.

"Poe."

Caddy crawled through the mud to where he lay. She saw the arrow and her stomach tightened. It had pierced his side from the back. The arrowhead was protruding just above the pelvic bone. It looked blackened, burned, and was covered in strange blue filaments. She touched it, snatching her hand back in shock. It was colder than ice. Poe's eyes were glassy and his clothes were drenched in blood. It ran, slick and red from his wound, staining the puddles around him. His breaths were shallow, erratic. He would have to be moved somewhere safe and dry or he would die. She would need April. She couldn't possibly do it herself.

"Hold on, Poe," she said. "I'm going to get help."

The rumbling groan of a horse snorting against the rain stopped Caddy where she stood. Her eyes trapped on Poe's sneakered feet. She had to hide them. She reached to pull Poe's legs in but drew back when the horse and rider spirited into view from between the trees. Poe moaned and the Company man's face snapped in their direction. Caddy held her hand over Poe's mouth to quiet him. "I'm sorry," she whispered in his ear.

The man and horse wove slowly toward them, stopping not ten feet from where they hid. Caddy held her breath. The horse stamped and blew. It pawed the ground, champing on the bit and tossing its head at the scent of blood. The man's eyes skimmed over them, hunting, and for a quick second she was sure they'd been seen. A high whistle penetrated the rain, and the man turned his horse and disappeared into the forest again.

Caddy exhaled, though there was little to be relieved about. Poe was bleeding worse than before. There was no time to waste.

"I'll come back with April," she told him. "Hold on." If April was still there. The men could have gotten to her already.

But April was sitting exactly where Caddy had left her.

"I found Poe," Caddy said.

April lifted her head. "Where?"

"We have to help him. He's in bad shape." Caddy put her hand on April's arm. "The Company men are out there. Keep your eyes open."

April started to panic. "Maybe we should wait until it's safe . . ."

"There's no time. We have to go now."

April walked on Caddy's heels, matching her footsteps as they scouted back through the woods. When they reached Poe, April took one look at him and fell apart.

"Oh, no . . ." She covered her face with her hands.

"Help me lift him," Caddy said.

April choked and sobbed. "He's dead . . . he's dead . . ."

"Pull yourself together," Caddy told her. "He's not dead. But he will be if we don't do something, now."

April looked blindly around. "We need to find the others . . ."

"The others can't help us. It's just you and me. Understand?"

April continued to cry.

Caddy shook her. "Do you understand?"

April nodded, simpering.

"Good. Now, help me get him to his feet."

Poe cried out in pain as they took his arms, hoisting him clumsily to his knees. He lost consciousness, his body going limp.

"He's too heavy," April said. "We're killing him."

"We need to find a better spot for him." Caddy pointed to a large spruce tree. "Over there."

Gasping from the effort, hands wet and slipping, they dragged Poe through the mud, his head lolling, his feet twisting unnaturally over the ground. At the spruce, they hunched below its boughs, knees buried in the bed of brown needles beneath its branches, and tugged Poe by inches under the shelter of the tree.

Caddy held her ear to his mouth.

"Is he dead?" April asked.

"He's still breathing."

"What do we do now?"

"You stay with Poe. I'm going to search for shelter. We found one farmhouse, maybe we can find another."

April looked like she was going to cry again. "I don't want to stay here. I want to come with you."

"No. I can move faster alone. And someone has to stay with Poe."

"I'm hungry," April said.

"Me too." Caddy squeezed her hand. "Stay hidden. And don't come out unless you're absolutely certain it's safe."

Caddy had no idea where to go, only that she would move in a direction and hope for the best. She was counting on the rain to conceal her movements, though it would make it difficult for her to find her way back. She would rather have stayed under the spruce tree with Poe, but she couldn't rely on April for anything.

The forest floor dipped and rose. The mud sucked at her sneakers. After several miles Caddy stopped beside a boulder and pushed the strands of wet hair from her eyes. She was certain she saw movement. The trees seemed to breathe around her. She scanned the woods and a man's face popped out of the rain. Caddy shouted, stumbling back, her feet sliding over the ground. The man was on her in seconds. He grabbed her arm and spun her around, grunting when her closed fist caught him in the chest. It was Red.

"Come with me," he said.

"We need help," Caddy blurted out. "Poe's been hurt. He's back a couple miles through the woods. April's with him."

"We have them," Red said. "Come with me."

Caddy pulled away from him. "I won't go without them."

"They're waiting for you."

"Where?"

"Somewhere safe."

Caddy refused to move. How did she know he was telling the truth?

"We found them under the spruce tree," he said, giving her just enough information to change her mind. "That boy doesn't look so good. If you want to waste time out here in the rain, be my guest." He walked away.

Caddy chased after him, struggling to keep up. Red moved as sure as a fox through the woods, his steps quick and light for such a big man. And he saw things she didn't. Several times he made her hide until it was safe to continue. They went on like this, trekking to the base of a huge escarpment. Hugging the rock, they laced in and out of the pine trees to a stone outcropping the shape of a shark's tooth.

"In here," he said.

Caddy hesitated. Had she made the right decision in following him? What was the point of questioning her choice now? She squeezed through the opening in the rock. There was no light. She trailed Red closely. After twenty feet or so, they came upon a slender fracture in the rock. They pushed through the gap, faces turned, hands feeling the stone. It was so restricting Caddy was afraid she'd get stuck again.

"How did you get Poe through here?" she asked.

"We took him another way."

"There's another way?"

"There are many."

"Why didn't you take us all together?"

"Better to go separate ways in case someone follows."

The passage abruptly opened into a deep cavern. Red lit a match and held it to a length of waxed rope. The cave walls jumped into the foreground, glittering with diamonds.

"Mineral deposits," he said, when he saw the look on her face.

The rope torch threw moving shadows as they walked, the dark swelling and receding around them. Where the cave tapered, Red stopped and doused the light. He took her by the arm and pulled her in front.

"Go down here."

"Where?"

"In the hole."

Caddy couldn't see a thing. She squatted, the blood thumping in her ears, her hands shaking as she felt around for the edge of the opening. Please, don't let the bad feeling come, she prayed. Red nudged her to move. Caddy stuck her feet down the hole. They swung free.

"There's no bottom," she said.

He nudged her again. "Go."

Caddy pushed off, sliding down a kind of chute, her back scraping against the rough surface the entire way. At the bottom, she fell, bashing her hands and knees against the rock. She groaned softly. A small chink of light perforated the dark. She was in a corridor. It was cold and damp. Water dripped a slow rhythm against the stone. She winced as she stood, and with hardly enough time to jump out of the way as Red came plowing down behind her. He landed easily on his feet, fumbled a set of brass skeleton keys from his pocket and jerked his head for her to follow.

At the end of the corridor was a small door. It looked ancient, with heavy, hand-forged hinges, and metal straps holding the wood together. It had a series of locks—seven in total—and Red set to work opening them. Some were turned, only to be relocked as others were opened. Caddy tried to memorize the pattern but it was too complex, and Red's hands were a blur, they moved so quickly.

At last, when all the locks were released, Red pulled the door open. It complained loudly, creaking like the hull of an old ship.

"Go," he said.

Caddy stepped into a dimly lit hallway. Red closed the door, securing the locks in another flurry of keys and turns. When he was finished, he stashed the keys back in his pocket and escorted her along the hall to an empty room.

"Stay here."

"No," Caddy said. She hadn't come all this way to sit alone in a room. "You said I could see Poe."

He towered over her. "You will stay here."

"Take me to Poe," she demanded.

Skylark found the Speaker on his throne. Behind him, in rows on shelves that stretched out and back upon themselves in endless reflection, tinkled millions of tiny coloured glass vials. She approached, soundless as a prowling lion. In his hand, the Speaker held a vial. The mist inside was violet. Skylark felt a remote twinge at the sight of it. She knew the vial contained the soul of the mouse she called Sebastian, her connection to him now a cold memory.

She knelt before her master, bowing in submission. "I am yours to command, Father."

The Speaker placed his hand on her head, his voice spellbinding. "My child . . . you are the fulfillment of a long-held dream."

Skylark looked into his frozen eyes. She could see only him—she wanted to please only him. Still, deep inside her, there was doubt. "Must there be destruction, Father?"

The Speaker rolled Sebastian's soul vial between his fingers. "It is the way of all things. There can be no beginning without an end."

She lowered her face though she could not hide the worry that plagued her. The Speaker understood.

"You are concerned for him—the one you call Poe."

"Yes, Father. I feel him close to me, closer than ever before."

"As do I, child. His mind is one with ours."

"What is to become of him?"

He stroked her hair and she purred at his caress. "He shall be yours if that is what you desire."

"Forever?"

"For all eternity."

Skylark kissed his hand, overwhelmed with gratitude.

"The forces are gathering," he said. "We are stronger than ever before. Soon you will see the power of the Dark, my love."

"The Light has power too, Father. I have seen the legions. They are strong and many. Even now they prepare for war."

"The earth is weak, child. The humans will destroy one another. It will advance our cause."

"Will Poe join us?"

"When the Dark has devoured the Light, he will be yours."

His words ignited her soul, his promise the most precious of gifts. She wanted to repay him in kind. "I know a secret, Father, about the one they call Kenji."

His eyes burned into hers. "Speak, child, and let it be known."

26

TRUST AND TREACHERY

Poe was on a cot in a small room, delirious with fever, the arrow embedded in his side. Next to the cot was a large, sober-faced woman in a white kerchief and a long blue cotton skirt. She was mixing something in a stone bowl. April stood in one corner of the room, bundled in a red wool blanket. She saw Caddy and ran to her, throwing her arms around her neck.

"It's so awful," she sniffed. "They're afraid to pull the arrow out in case something bad happens. They've never seen anything like it before."

Caddy walked across the room and sat beside Poe, laying her hand gently on his forehead. "He's burning up." She eased the bloodied fabric of his shirt to one side of the wound. The skin was black and necrotic. The icy filaments from the arrow had spread across his abdomen. "We have to remove it."

The sober-faced woman turned to Red, and some unspoken exchange took place.

"Everybody leave," she abruptly said.

"I'm staying," Caddy told her.

"The procedure could kill him."

"He'll die if we don't do it."

The woman conceded. "The shaft can't be broken—we've tried." She set the stone mixing bowl next to some rough-woven cloth bandages and a brown stoppered bottle on a small wooden table by the bed. Beside this was a pitcher of water, a roll of gauze, a drinking glass, a plain silver teaspoon and some bread. "I don't know what the arrow is made of. Nothing I've ever seen. We'll have to pull the whole thing through, fletching and all. It won't be kind."

"We have no choice," Caddy said.

The woman gathered her skirt and leaned over Poe. "Help me shift him."

Poe moaned as they moved him closer to the edge of the bed. Caddy clasped his hand. The woman wrapped the tip of the arrow in a length of cloth. She secured her footing, nodded at Caddy, and pulled. Poe shouted and fell unconscious. The arrow resisted, clinging to his flesh before giving way. The fletching drew through, bloodied and wet as a hatchling. As soon as it was free the arrow disintegrated to a fine dust. The woman stepped back, mystified, staring at her hands as though she'd seen a ghost. Poe groaned and the woman quickly collected herself, reaching for the stone bowl. Inside was a thick, yellowish-green gruel.

"What is it?" Caddy asked.

"A poultice. Comfrey leaves, scalded milk, and garlic." The woman stirred the bowl with a whittled willow branch, clucking and muttering under her breath.

Caddy inspected Poe's wound. It looked worse. "Will the poultice work?"

"It'll pull the poison out, I hope." The woman spread a thick layer of the gruel on a piece of bread and covered it with a square of cloth. Pressing it over the wound, she secured it with strips of gauze. "Now, we pray," she said, drawing a frayed quilt over Poe.

"What about infection?" Caddy asked.

The woman handed her the brown stoppered bottle from the table. "Give him a teaspoon of this tincture in a small bit of water every four hours. There's water and a glass on the table." She retrieved the stone bowl and left the room.

Caddy measured out the tincture and poured it in the glass with some water. Supporting Poe's head with one hand, she held the glass to his lips. He sipped the fluid weakly, mumbling through his delirium. Caddy was sure more than once she heard him call for Meg.

"Rest now," she said, easing his head onto the pillow.

Red appeared, standing in the doorway. "Come with me."

"No," Caddy refused. "I won't leave him."

"There are things you must know. People you must meet."

"I won't go."

Red left and came back with the sober-faced woman. She fixed her small dark eyes on Caddy. "I'll watch him like he was my own," she said.

Caddy was outnumbered. She took the time to smooth the hair on Poe's forehead before following Red from the room. They walked down the hall. It was lit by candles in tin sconces along the walls. They reached an arched wooden door, not as old as the one with many locks, but close. Red opened it. Caddy stopped dead on the threshold to the room. Her hand flew to her safe stone. Hex was there, sitting half-seen in the shadows in a worn, overstuffed chair.

"Come closer," she said.

Caddy turned to Red for an explanation. Was she the next to be punished? He nodded at her to comply. She took a tentative step. Hex leaned into the candlelight and Caddy stared at her in confusion. It wasn't her after all. It was a woman who looked just like her. Was this some kind of trick? The woman was missing her left eye—just like Hex—though she didn't hide the barren socket behind a pair of dark glasses. She motioned toward a low wooden stool.

"Please, sit."

Caddy perched on the stool, stupefied. Now that she was closer, she could see that the woman's face was beautiful, like Hex's, though older. She spoke with a Russian accent too, but less pronounced. Her eye, the one remaining, was blue as a robin's egg. Around her neck she wore a burnished gold pendant of a tree in a circle. It glimmered in the candlelight.

"I . . . I don't understand," Caddy said.

"We're happy you're here. We had hoped for this." The woman's voice was soothing. Sincere. There was honesty in it. Still, Caddy remained guarded.

"You're perplexed," the woman said. "It's not your fault. I have a lot of explaining to do." She settled back in her chair. "We call ourselves Weavers of Light. We are the true Dreamers."

Caddy shot Red a questioning look.

The woman understood. "You're wise to be cautious. There are wheels within wheels. It makes one circumspect. I can only show you what we are. I can't convince you to stay, though I hope you will. You have an exceptional ability. We'd be blessed to have you join us."

"I don't like being held prisoner," Caddy said.

"There are no prisoners here. You're free to go. I only ask one thing . . . that you stay long enough to meet us before you make your decision."

Her show of kindness filled Caddy with contempt. Here was another person telling her she had choices when clearly she didn't. "Why should I trust you? How do I know you're not the imposter?"

"I can only hope your heart will lead you to the truth," the woman said.

"The truth? I've been drugged, starved, hunted like a dog. I've seen people killed. My father may be dead. I don't know what the truth is anymore."

The woman listened sympathetically. "I'm sorry for your pain. We tried to reach you earlier. But there were . . . complications. The Dreamers got to you first. It made things difficult. We had to take a chance, wait for the right moment. We couldn't risk exposure."

Caddy had heard enough. She was so tired, so wrung out. She rested her elbows on her knees, covering her face with her hands. "I don't understand any of this."

"It's purposefully complex," the woman said. "Hex and the Company have created an elaborate ruse, a skillful trap. They took what they knew of our society and replicated it to catch as many Dreamers as they can. Without the Dreamers, there is no dream. Without the dream, the Emptiness is certain."

Caddy met her gaze at the mention of the Emptiness. "So, what you're saying is that Hex is a liar and a murderer . . ."

"Quite simply, yes."

Caddy pointed at Red. "Then what's he doing here?"

"Red is a Cheyenne elder, a deep operative. Among his people, he is known as Tatananayaho—he who sees far into the distance. He works both sides to our advantage. He's very good at what he does. We would have never gotten as far as we have without him."

"Why did he bring me to Hex?" Caddy asked.

"The Company men had already seen you. He needed to maintain Hex's trust. If he'd brought you to me right away, we would have all been endangered."

"And Hex's eye?"

"Another deception."

Caddy wasn't buying it.

"Think of what's at stake," the woman said. "It's essential that the trap be as detailed and convincing as possible. Hex is willing to do anything for what she believes."

"What about the mark?"

"It's a way to trace you."

"Why not just kill us all?" Caddy said. "Why go to the trouble of such an intricate deceit?"

"Drastic action would tip their hand, and those with the vision would go elsewhere. Hex plays a subtle game of trust and treachery. The Company men give her credibility. Few things cloak true intention like fear and an emotional cause."

"What about the other Dreamers? They're innocent. How can we just sit here, knowing what's happening? Why don't you try to help them?"

"We can't take the chance."

"Yet you went to such lengths to find me."

"Yes," she said without hesitation. "We are all equal ... but you are exceptionally talented. Each Weaver brings a unique perspective, a singular thread to the tapestry. Your ability is very strong, very deep, binding the many threads together so we can see the greater picture, so we can move in the right direction."

"I've done nothing."

"It's not what you've done," the woman said, her blue eye catching the light. "It's what you will do."

Her words exhausted Caddy. She didn't want the responsibility of anyone's hope. "You don't even know me. How can you possibly say this?"

"And Hex ..." the woman countered. "How could she possibly have known this about you?"

Caddy thought about this. And then it clicked. "My father."

The woman smiled. "Forgive me, but you remind me so much of him. You have his fire. It's a privilege and an honour to meet you."

"I'm not my father," Caddy said, but she could feel her resolve breaking. "Hex told me he may be dead—that he wasn't strong enough to handle the truth."

"Another lie," the woman said. "Your father is more than capable of handling the truth. In fact, it was his relentless pursuit of the truth that put his life in jeopardy. He knew something the Company didn't want him to know. He took something he shouldn't have. Something that will expose the Company's lies. Because of this, because of his visions and his rare ability to dream, the Company wants him dead. He ran to keep you safe, to lure the Company men away. Unfortunately, you went looking for him. Hex took you to get to him. I'm sure she suspects now that you're the bigger prize."

Caddy hung her head, her heart in turmoil. If she could only go back to what was, to the way things were before. As if to mock her, the mark on her arm started to throb. She pulled back her sleeve. The tattoo looked infected. How could she have been so stupid? To allow Hex to brand her—she wanted to gouge it from her skin.

"You couldn't have known," the woman said.

Caddy felt the blood rush to her face. She should have fought harder. "Can it be removed?"

"Not without causing you harm. Its power is limited here, if that's any solace. It's strongest when you gather in a group."

"They told us it would join us, make it easier to dream together."

"Yes . . . and easier to track and kill. It wasn't always that way. The mark used to be sacred, a carefully guarded secret, known only to the Weavers. Its purpose has since been hijacked. We no longer use the mark for this reason."

Caddy yanked her sleeve to her wrist. They sat in silence, Caddy sniffing back the tears. After a while, the woman made an offer.

"Come and meet us. If you decide to stay, we can talk some more."

Caddy wiped her eyes. "I don't even know your name."

"I'm Zephyr," the woman said. "And you're Cadence."

Zephyr stood, and Caddy followed her and Red along the hall to a heavy wooden door. Beside it was a room, filled with firewood, and a splitting axe buried in the side of a thick stump. Red shouldered the door open.

"The Gathering Space," Zephyr said.

Caddy was met by laughter and people sitting in a big circle on the floor, engaged in conversation. There must have been fifty or sixty of them. They looked healthy and well-rested. A fire crackled in a sunken, stone-lined pit in the middle of the room, and a man with a large kettle made his way around the circle, pouring tea into raised cups. There was an open kitchen to one side and a table with food—soup and bread and small cakes. And bowls of fresh berries. Caddy could hardly believe her eyes.

"You must be hungry," Zephyr said. "Go and eat. You can shower later."

Caddy moved toward the circle and a hand shot into the air.

It was April, sitting with the Weavers as though she'd always been there. She waved Caddy over. "Food!" she said, making room for Caddy to sit beside her. "Real, delicious, hot food."

Caddy spoke in a low voice. "Do you know what's going on here?"

April nodded.

"Do you believe what they told you?"

"About Hex?"

"Yes."

April grew thoughtful. "I didn't want to . . . but what alternative do we have?"

"I feel like I'm going crazy," Caddy said.

"These people seem nice."

She was so innocent and trusting. Caddy envied it.

April placed a bowl of soup and a heel of bread into Caddy's hands. "Take it. It's my third bowl. I'm just eating for greed now." She held up some raspberries and pushed one into Caddy's mouth. It tasted sweet and sour and alive. "Have the rest," she said, tumbling the berries into Caddy's cupped palm.

Caddy savoured each one then sniffed the soup.

"It's lentil," April said, handing her a spoon. "It's good. And you can have all you want—no limits."

Caddy ate like a hungry dog, dribbling soup down her chin, licking her fingers. When she was close to bursting, she slowed, allowing herself to look around the room. The ceiling was vaulted with huge beams that connected at a central hub in a giant wheel. To one side of the hub was a copper flue, hanging from the ceiling over the fire. The smoke drifted languidly up. There were no windows, but plenty of light from many small portals on the walls circling the room. And the air was fresh—not at all damp or stuffy.

"Are we underground?" she asked.

A young man sitting next to her answered, "We are." He was copper-eyed with a disarmingly open smile and long wheat-coloured hair that hung in thick braids down his back. His gold beard was neat and closely cropped.

Caddy wiped her mouth with her hand, glancing down at her crumb-covered rag of a shirt. She was a mess.

"We're below a large escarpment," the man said.

"The Everwilds," April chimed in.

The man smiled at her. "Yes."

April rested her hand on his shoulder. "This is Dillon. He helped rescue me and Poe."

There was something between the two already. Caddy could see that. She was happy for April.

"Nice to meet you," Dillon said. "April has told me all about you."

"Oh." Caddy laughed self-consciously. "I hope you're not disappointed."

"Not at all."

"The air is really fresh in here," she said, changing the subject. "How is that possible?"

Dillon pointed to several louvred openings in the ceiling and walls. "Conduits. The air circulates from the outside in."

"What about the lights?"

"Solar powered."

"Makes sense. How deep are we?"

"Hundreds of feet," April jumped in. "Safe from bombs and war. And there's a waterfall on the other side of the escarpment. They use it to generate power."

Dillon smiled. "Anything else you'd like to know?"

"Yeah. Where does the smoke go and how do you conceal it?"

He turned to April. "She's good."

"I told you," April said.

Caddy felt embarrassed. She was being so practical. Not everyone was in survival mode. Would it hurt her to relax a little? "My dad is into this kind of stuff. He'd love to see this place."

"It's pretty cool," Dillon agreed. "We filter the smoke to avoid detection. The heat gets circulated where it's needed and the exhaust is released near the swamp where no one will see it."

It was brilliant. "And there are showers, I hear."

"And soap," April said. "They use rainwater where they can. The rest comes from the river."

Caddy dredged the last bit of soup from her bowl. "Some of the building is quite primitive . . ."

"The corridors were the first structures built, a very long time ago," Dillon explained. "This part of the complex is much newer."

"How long ago?"

Dillon pulled on his beard. "Originally? The 1200s, or thereabouts."

Caddy lowered her spoon. Surely he was mistaken.

"The Weavers are a very old organization. Would you like more soup?"

"No, thank you." Caddy set her bowl on the floor and brushed the crumbs from her shirt.

"Do you sleep in here?" It was a stupid question. She realized it as soon as it came out of her mouth.

"We have separate dorms for men and women. They're very comfortable. Are you sure you've had enough to eat?"

She leaned back on her hands. "That's the most I've eaten in weeks. Maybe even years. I think I overdid it."

"There's always room for cake, right?" Dillon rose and grabbed three small cakes from the table, one for each of them. "It's best if you eat them like this." He shoved the whole cake in his mouth, chewed it twice, and swallowed.

April did the same. Caddy stuffed the cake in her mouth, choked, chewed, and laughed, the sound of her own laughter a surprise in her ears.

"It's really good," she said, spraying crumbs everywhere. She slapped her hand over her mouth.

"Ready for another one?" Dillon asked.

She shook her head. The laughter subsided and she was suddenly saddened by the thought of Poe lying in agony while they made merry over cakes and soup. She excused herself, much to April's disappointment, and left the room.

Down the hall, Caddy opened Poe's door to discover him alone and dripping with sweat. She moistened a piece of cloth with water from the pitcher and held it against his forehead. He was burning up. His eyes were haunted, unfocused.

"I can hear him," he whispered.

It was the fever talking, Caddy thought, making him hallucinate. "Hear what?"

"The voice . . . it's speaking to me . . ."

Caddy dabbed his forehead with the cloth. "Try not to upset yourself. We're safe now."

His eyes fluttered and his mouth gaped. "He knows I'm here. He knows we're here."

"Shh . . . try to sleep . . ."

His face contorted with anguish. He clawed his arm, tearing at the mark.

She took his hand and held it. "It's okay . . . no one can find you."

"Meg," he said, and fell quiet, his head listing to one side.

The sober-faced woman came into the room. Caddy stopped her with a finger to her lips. The woman retreated, pulling the door closed. Refreshing the cloth with more water from the pitcher, Caddy continued to dab the sweat from Poe's face. She wouldn't leave him alone again.

Skylark and the Speaker stood in the teahouse, watching. Kenji's woman was the rarest of flowers. She danced in a shower of rose petals, her gold fan snapping and fluttering against her red silk kimono. The Speaker licked his lips with predatory delight.

Francis and Kenji appeared across the faintly lit room. Skylark tuned her mind to their frequency. The cowboy give a low whistle.

"A geisha," he said at the sight of the girl. "She's a beauty." He was about to elaborate but stopped when he saw the look on Kenji's face. His heart was obviously breaking. Francis gripped his shoulder as an offer of support.

"I can't do it," Kenji said.

"You have to, old friend. It's for her as much as you."

"I can't say the words . . ."

"It's easy—*I release you*. Give it a try."

Kenji's lips trembled. He'd taken a breath, poised to speak, when Francis locked eyes on Skylark.

"He sees us," she warned the Speaker.

The demon launched across the room, cutting the geisha down with a slash of his hand. She dropped, an exquisite bird shot from the sky, her kimono a pool of red silk around her on the floor. The crowd cried out in horror. Kenji hollered as he dove, firing a beam of light. The Speaker scooped up the geisha's soul and was gone before he could reach him. Skylark lingered to witness

Kenji's pain. He fell to his knees and gathered his lover's lifeless body in his arms.

"No, no, no . . ." he moaned.

The sky over the teahouse began to thicken.

"I know how hard this is but we have to go," Francis said. He looked out the tearoom window. "We're creating ripples."

Kenji sobbed. "My love . . . my life."

"If you'd said the words, this wouldn't have happened."

With a sound like splintering wood, the sky began to crack.

"Pull yourself together," Francis ordered. "We need to go."

Kenji howled in despair.

It was a moving sight. At least, it would have been had Skylark felt the slightest bit of sympathy for his suffering. But Kenji's loss was her gain. Besides, he was the one who'd told her to leave her love behind. And now look at him, bawling like a child. She would sacrifice a thousand geishas for the chance to be with Poe. She strolled in front of him.

"It hurts, doesn't it?"

A shot blasted from the cowboy's hands. Skylark jumped, quick as lightning, leaving them behind.

27

SEEDS

Caddy woke to an empty room. Poe was gone. She leapt to her feet and ran for the door, bumping into the sober-faced woman on her way in.

"Where is he?" Caddy demanded.

The woman looked puzzled. "I was just coming in to change his poultice."

Caddy shoved past her and raced down the hall. At the room with the firewood, she found him, the axe in his hand. She stepped toward him and he raised it threateningly. His eyes were unrecognizable, wild.

"Stay away from me, Cadence."

She stood dead still. What was he thinking of doing? "Poe . . . you should be in bed."

"This is all my fault," he said.

She held up her hands, attempting to reason with him. "What is?"

"All of it."

"I don't understand . . . how can you be responsible for any of this?"

He brandished the axe. "I can't escape him. He's in my head. He won't stop talking."

"Who?"

"*Him.*" Poe gave a sob and fell to one knee, stretching his arm across the splitting log. "He's coming for me—for all of us. I have to stop him."

"Please, Poe, you're sick. It's the fever—it's making you hear things."

"It's him, I'm telling you!" he shouted. "I have to stop him or everyone will die!" He swung the axe.

A scream split the room. The sober woman came rushing in, tearing her apron from her waist, and wrapping it around Poe's arm to stop the bleeding. There were more screams as others arrived. Someone picked Caddy up and carried her from the room before she realized that she was the one yelling.

"Hush, now," a man said, putting her to bed.

She fought to get up. He restrained her, pressing a green glass bottle to her lips.

"Drink this," he said. "It will make you feel better."

The liquid was bitter and earthy. Caddy thrashed wildly, the man holding her down until the medicine took effect.

She came to, hours later, Zephyr sitting beside the bed.

"Where's Poe?" Caddy immediately asked.

"He's fine," Zephyr assured her.

Caddy moved to get up but her legs were wobbly. "I have to see him."

"He needs to rest. And so do you. You've had quite a shock."

"I don't want to rest. I want to see him." She needed to know that he was okay. She didn't want to take Zephyr's word for it.

"He's been sedated."

"His arm . . ." Caddy said.

Zephyr shook her head. "We had to take it. The cut was clean. It should heal well."

"Oh, poor Poe . . ." Caddy broke down, clutching her safe stone. "He thought he was protecting us."

"He may have been."

"Do you believe that?"

"The mark is powerful."

"I have the mark, too. You told me its power is weak here. He heard voices. I hear nothing."

"Yes," Zephyr agreed. "There was something else at play, here. The arrow that hit him ... it may have enhanced the mark's power. Do you know where it came from?"

Caddy didn't know. Maybe Poe did. She would keep her thoughts to herself, though. Who could say if Zephyr could truly be trusted? Or any of these people? She'd been fooled before. As had Poe. And he'd lost his arm as a result.

"Do you know what's going on out there?" Zephyr asked.

"In the world?" Caddy sniffed.

"Yes."

Surely this woman had operatives gathering intelligence. What could Caddy tell her that she didn't already know? "There are rumours of a bomb. I don't know much more than that."

"We believe these rumours are accurate," Zephyr said. She stood. "I have something I'd like to show you—something I think you'll find very interesting."

Caddy allowed Zephyr to help her from the bed. They walked along the corridor, Caddy disoriented, unstable, supporting herself with one hand against the wall in case her legs decided to give out. She kept her eyes lowered, avoiding the concerned looks from the Dreamers as they passed on their way to the Gathering Room for supper. She felt exposed, transparent, like they could see right through her.

Zephyr guided her to a room. Its door was carved with the image of a tree in a circle, the same as her pendant. She pressed the latch on the handle and opened it. The room was huge, with wall-to-wall cabinets made of cherry wood that stretched from floor to ceiling. Each cabinet had hundreds of little drawers with brass plates, carefully inscribed.

"What is this place?"

Zephyr ran her hand lovingly along the drawers. "The sum total of our work."

Caddy looked at the writing on one of the brass plates. "It's Latin—these are plant names." She traced the shape of the letters with her finger. "What's inside?"

Zephyr opened a drawer and pulled out a muslin sack the size of a spice bag. "We've been collecting and storing them for a very long time." Loosening the drawstring, she poured the contents into her hand. It was seeds. Golden seeds.

"Wheat," Caddy said.

Zephyr nodded. "Grown and gathered from grain found near Turkey. It dates back to the Neolithic era, nearly 8,500 years ago."

"These are the original seeds?" Caddy marvelled.

"We grew small crops from the original seeds and collected them. We grow all the seeds in our bank to keep them viable."

Caddy opened another drawer. And another and another. Each one held an identical muslin bag. "What's it all for?"

"The future." Zephyr poured the wheat seeds back in their bag and returned it to its drawer. "The collapsing economy, the threat of war—these are just distractions from the real danger. The Company has been hard at work, infiltrating governments and corporations, advancing their interests through the propagation of genetically modified seeds, among other things."

"Why? What can they possibly achieve?"

"Control," Zephyr said. "Control the food source, control the people."

"I don't understand."

"The Company has been genetically modifying seeds for decades—to combat famine, to feed the growing population, to enhance production in areas with depleted soil. But the seeds they create are sterile. They can't reproduce beyond one cycle. They're no longer life-sustaining. At first we thought that was their plan—to control the economy by limiting how much could be grown and by whom. Now we know the whole truth. Greed is only one part of the scheme, one the government willingly supported. Even they don't know the extent of the deception. The seeds are genetically encoded to prevent us from dreaming. There are a select few who are immune to the dream suppressant. Something in their DNA allows them to dream despite this genetic assault. The ability may be passed along in generations to come, who knows. It will take years before we can say. But we may have run out of time. With the world focused on war, the Dark is advancing faster than we can push it back. The seeds hold the key to the Light and the future of the world. We must preserve them at all costs so the people can dream again. Your father knew this, and that's why they wanted him dead."

"He knew about the modified seeds?"

"He helped create them."

Caddy's knees buckled and she collapsed against the wall, her hands shaking. Zephyr must be mistaken. Her father hated the Company and all it stood for. He would never help them for any reason, let alone design seeds to undermine the very thing he held most sacred. "Why would he do that?"

"Please, don't misunderstand me," Zephyr said. "Your father's intention was good. He tried to control the process by ensuring the genetic encoding of the seeds was pure. At one time he believed he was helping to feed the world. When he learned of the Company's true purpose for the seed program, he planned to stop them. He stole valuable information—information he intended to use against them."

Caddy's mind whirled. If what Zephyr said was true, it would explain why her father might be sitting in a hotel with a gun to his head.

"Come," Zephyr said. "You're feeling weak. I'll show you to the showers. You can clean up then get some food."

"Wait." Caddy grabbed Zephyr's arm. "Tell me the truth . . . do you know where my father is?"

A sadness veiled Zephyr's blue eye. "No."

"Please . . ." Caddy said. "I saw him in a vision. He tried to shoot himself. Maybe he succeeded, I don't know. If you have information about where he's hiding, you have to tell me."

Zephyr shook her head. "We don't know any more than you. We lost contact with him weeks ago. We hope he is still alive. Please, no more for now. Get yourself cleaned up. It'll make you feel better."

The showers were as well designed as the rest of the building, with stone tiles on the floor and walls, and neat cedar shelves stacked with towels. There were at least ten stalls, open, like a locker room. Zephyr handed her a robe. "There's shampoo and soap in the stalls. I can take your clothes and have them washed."

Caddy refused the offer. It was a feeble protest but she was tired of people telling her what to do. And she suspected Zephyr knew more about her father than she was letting on. It wasn't fair for Zephyr to keep things from her, to administer information like doses of medicine.

"I want to see Poe."

"You can see him tomorrow, when you've both had a chance to rest," Zephyr said. "Come to the Gathering Room when you're done. There's food."

Caddy waited for Zephyr to leave, then stripped out of her dirty clothes, leaving them in a heap on the floor. Hands fumbling, she turned the taps in the shower. The water was cold at first, then scalding hot. She adjusted the temperature and stood in the spray, arms hanging at her sides, hoping it would stop the bad feeling from coming. The shaking in her hands only got worse. She convulsed, the smell of burnt toast filling her nostrils as she crouched so as not to fall, water streaming over her back. The bad feeling hit, dropping her into the eye of the gale. Ash stung her face. The lost souls shrieked around her. They grabbed at her hands and her hair, more terrifying and urgent than ever before. Something black and evil was coming. Something darker and colder than death. Caddy covered her ears and yelled.

The sound of her own cries jolted her into the present, shivering on the shower room floor. She blinked the water from her eyes. Alone. She was mercifully alone. Rising to her hands and knees, she stayed there, unsteady as a newborn calf, until she was able to stand, and even then only by propping herself up in the corner of the stall. When her breathing slowed she righted herself and began methodically washing her hair, the smell of the shampoo green and fresh as rosemary, the suds swirling over her feet into the drain. She wouldn't go to the Gathering Room when she was done, she decided. She would go see Poe.

28

THE VISITOR

Caddy's dirty clothes smelled of sweat and dirt against her clean skin. She wrinkled her nose, walking as casually as possible so as not to draw attention to herself. She didn't want to talk to anyone, especially April or Dillon. They would want to hang around and try to make her feel better. Poe was the only one she wanted to see.

She found his room easily enough and discovered that he was not alone. There was a girl sitting by the bed, her back to the door. She was holding Poe's hand and whispering something in his ear. She glanced over her shoulder when Caddy walked into the room.

"Oh!" Caddy exclaimed. The girl was exquisitely beautiful with long shiny black hair and eyes the most impossible shade of violet. She seemed to burn like a fire. And she looked so familiar.

The girl ignored her, continuing to hold Poe's hand while he slept. What was left of his arm was swaddled in a white bandage to the shoulder. The rest was missing from the elbow down. His skin was pale and his eyes were shadowed and sunken. Seeing him so fragile and wounded made Caddy want to cry. She held her safe stone.

"I just wanted to see him," she said.

The girl bristled, straightening her back. Her voice was sharp as a razor. "What have you done to him?"

Caddy stiffened. "I . . . he . . . it was a mistake."

"A mistake?" The girl's words dripped with incrimination. "How does someone lose an arm by mistake?"

"He heard voices," Caddy said, not at all sure why she felt compelled to explain anything to this girl. "He tried to stop them."

"By cutting off his own arm?"

"Yes."

"Is this how you repay him?"

Repay him? "Who are you?"

The girl rose, her violet eyes darkening. "I'm the one who loves him."

Caddy caught her breath. Now she remembered where she had seen her. It was the girl from her vision! She was much more imposing in person. Otherworldly and commanding. Caddy hadn't even recognized her.

A clatter of dishes outside the room caught Caddy's attention. April and Dillon were there, carrying a tray with soup and bread.

Caddy pressed a finger to her lips. "He's asleep."

"How could anyone sleep with all this noise?"

To Caddy's amazement Poe was awake and sitting on the edge of the bed. His eyes glittered with life and the colour had returned to his face. How could this be? Caddy looked for the girl. She was gone.

"There was a girl here a second ago," she said. "Did you see her leave?"

Dillon shook his head. "I saw no one."

"She was right here," Caddy insisted. "I spoke to her."

"You must be hungry," April said.

"Don't patronize me. She was sitting by the bed when I came in, holding Poe's hand."

Dillon and April exchanged worried glances.

"Well, she's not here now." April placed the tray on Poe's lap. There was an awkward moment as he tried to manage the soup spoon and the chunk of bread with one hand.

Caddy rushed to help him.

"No." He pulled away from her.

She stepped back, stung. "Well, I'm glad to see you're feeling better. Isn't this miraculous?" she said to April and Dillon. "When I walked in two minutes ago, I thought he was dying."

"Caddy," April admonished her.

"It's true," she insisted. "There was a girl here—she did something to him."

"No one did anything to anyone," Dillon said.

"Why don't you believe me?" Caddy shouted.

"We're going to dream tonight," April said in a controlled voice, changing the subject. "Will you be joining us?"

Caddy didn't care if she ever dreamed again. "No, I don't think so."

April looked disappointed, but she recovered immediately and smiled. "Okay, well, let us know if you need anything—either of you. We're happy to help."

"Dream well," Caddy said, the words leaving a bitter taste in her mouth.

As soon as they'd left the room, Poe cornered her, his eyes fierce. "I want to go back for the others."

"What?"

"We can't leave them at the mercy of the Company men. It's as good as murder."

"You're not well," Caddy said.

"I feel fine."

"Your arm . . ."

"I'm better for it. With the mark gone, I can move undetected."

This was madness. He must still be delirious. Caddy couldn't possibly agree to his idea. "Even if you are feeling strong, how will you find them? They could be anywhere."

"I have a feeling they're close by."

"A feeling?"

He glared at her with frightening intensity. "Don't underestimate me, Cadence."

"You can't blame me for being worried, Poe. One minute you're on your deathbed, and the next you're planning a rescue mission halfway across the woods. How is that possible?"

His face darkened. "What are you getting at?"

Caddy sat on the edge of the bed. "She did something to you."

"Who?"

"That girl."

"What girl?"

"The one who was here when I came in. She told me she loved you."

He laughed, the derision in his voice cutting her to the bone. She swallowed her hurt and took a different tack.

"I'm sorry . . . you have every right to help the Dreamers . . ."

"I can't leave them out there," he said. "They should be here."

"Do you know about Hex?" Caddy asked.

"Yes. I know everything."

"How?"

He clenched his jaw. "Why are you trying to stop me, Cadence? I have to help the Dreamers before it's too late."

"Then I want to come with you."

"No. You'll slow me down. And the mark will make you vulnerable."

Caddy wasn't going to be put off so easily. "You need me to find the way back through the forest." It was a lie. She didn't know how to get back. Red had taken her through the caves. She was so turned around there was no way she could possibly find her way out. Poe didn't know that though. "When do we leave?"

"Tonight."

Caddy and Poe waited for the Weavers to gather for the dream. Poe took his knife, struggling to secure it to his belt. Caddy pulled her bag over her shoulder and offered to help him. He refused. He had to learn to do it himself, he said. When he'd managed to secure it, he hid the knife beneath his shirt, in case they met someone on the way out. They would walk apart until they cleared the compound, he decided, so as not to arouse suspicion.

Caddy stuck her head out of the room. The hallway was empty. She wasn't sure which way to go so she went the only way she knew, to the left, toward the Gathering Space. She changed her mind immediately and went right. She passed the showers and Poe began to follow, keeping his distance.

At the end of the corridor the hall broke left and right. The place was a rabbit warren of passages. Caddy decided to go left. The hall constricted and broke left and right again. To the left, the hall seemed to double back on itself. To the right, it narrowed even further to a low, arched door. She checked over her shoulder. Poe was waiting at the end of the hall. She went right, stooping as the ceiling closed in on her. Reaching the door, she saw that it was heavily bolted. She tested the latch. It wouldn't budge. Using the heel of her hand, she pressed with all her strength. The bolt was fixed. Poe would have to help. She waved him forward. He ducked into the shadows and crept along the hallway, his head nearly touching the ceiling by the time he reached the door.

"It won't open," Caddy said.

He tested the bolt. It wouldn't move it. Taking his knife from his belt, he tapped the butt end on the lever. After several quick hits he was able to pry it into position, then hammer the bolt loose.

It gave, and the door popped open. The air was musty and smelled of stale water and earth. The passage was little more than a rugged tunnel carved from the rock, claustrophobic and pitch black.

"I have this . . ." Poe fumbled his knife back onto his belt and pulled an old Zippo lighter from his pocket. He worked it open with his thumb and lit it. The flame reflected off the rocks and tree roots, freeing the shadows from the stone. They danced erratically against the wall.

Caddy peered into the tunnel. She definitely hadn't come this way with Red. "It looks as though no one's ever used it."

"It's probably some kind of emergency exit," Poe said. "They must not expect people to come in this way with the door bolted from the inside."

"How will we lock it behind us?"

"We won't."

"We can't just leave it open."

"We'll hide the entrance from the outside. That way no one will find it."

Caddy had her doubts, but she didn't want to argue with him. She followed him into the tunnel, pulling the door closed behind her.

It was a challenging passage. The rocks were sharp and the tunnel went deeper before it began to rise. The air was suffocating and thin. She could barely catch her breath. Poe didn't complain, but she could see his disadvantage was making things difficult. The roots caught on his bandage, causing him to curse under his breath.

After a hard stretch, the passage took a turn upward. They could see another door, bolted from the inside at the top of makeshift stairs chipped from the stone.

Caddy held the Zippo while Poe worked the bolt, water drops ticking out the seconds through the seam in the door onto the stairs. This one gave easier, the weight of the door assisting the bolt in the mechanism. The whole thing was grown over, a mass of soil and roots fusing it shut. Bracing his back, legs straining, teeth clenched, Poe heaved the door open, soil and rain showering down. He struggled through the opening and reached back to help her up. Holding his hand, Caddy climbed out, her feet scrabbling, the rain beating around them.

Poe closed the door and fit the green wig of grass over it, pressing the roots and earth in place so that it was impossible to see the entrance.

"How will we find it again?" Caddy asked.

"Here." Poe held up a square chunk of limestone. "Remember it. It'll be our marker." He placed it near the door. "Which way?"

They walked along the base of the escarpment. It seemed like a good direction to go. So what if they didn't find the others? Caddy thought. The best thing they could do would be to keep walking until they were as far away from everyone as possible. They could find a place together and just live, the two of them. Grow things. Forget the Company and Hex and the war. She occupied her mind for miles with this silly fantasy.

Poe stopped and leaned against a maple tree, breaking her reverie.

"Do you need to rest?" she asked.

He shook his head, grasping his arm. Blood was seeping through the bandage with the rain.

"We could take cover under the trees for a while . . . get out of the wet. . . ."

"No!" he shouted.

His anger scared her. How long before he realized she didn't know where she was going? She was thinking of telling him the truth when she recognized the spruce tree, the one they'd used to hide him.

"There," she said. "There's an upturned stump not far from here. If we find that, we're close to the edge of the field."

A sudden movement in the woods sent them both to the ground. They stared through the rain. She saw it first: someone slipping from the shadows into a clump of cedars. And another.

"Company men?" he whispered.

"Dreamers. Why are they still here?"

"Waiting for communication."

"Shouldn't Hex have contacted them by now?"

"Maybe they're in trouble. We have to talk to them."

"No," Caddy said. "Let's watch for a while to be sure it's safe."

THE DARK RISES

Skylark sat at the Speaker's feet. With his right hand, he stroked her hair. In his left, he held two soul vials. The violet one was Sebastian's. The other one, the one with the green mist, held the soul of Kenji's woman. The Speaker rolled the vials mechanically between his fingers.

"Did you see your precious boy?"

Skylark's spirit leapt. "Yes, Father. He is everything to me."

The demon turned his ice-chip eyes on her. "Did you do as I bid?"

"Yes, Father. I gave him the strength and desire to seek out the Dreamers. He will lead the men to their quarry."

The Speaker growled deep in his throat. "Good. Now rise, child, and take your place beside me as the battle begins."

Skylark looked to the horizon. In the distance, the Warriors and their lions filed in rows without end. Behind their ranks, the Nightshades hovered, their ravens calling for the souls of the damned. The Speaker yawned, his mouth stretching open. With a deafening shriek the Dark issued forth, coiling upward in a black column against the bloated sky. Serpents slithered from his sleeves. Vermin crawled across his feet. Sizzling globs of black ooze dropped from the column, spawning towering golems. Teeth flashing, arms and legs pumping, they lurched single-mindedly toward the Light. Skylark shuddered to see it. The horror. But she could think only of Poe. Everything she did, she did for him.

The column of darkness grew, twisting as it poured from the Speaker's mouth. Rearing up, it met the legions and exploded in a shower of flames and black rain. The golems tore through the ranks. Skylark averted her eyes as Warriors and their totems blew apart, forever lost, the tinkling of their captured souls rising with the cacophony of pain. The Nightshades circled, swallowing the Dark ones as they fell, the demonic column advancing without mercy.

Caddy and Poe watched for movement in the cedars. The Dreamers were holed up like hounded rabbits in the trees. No one had come in or out for some time, and there was no sign of Company men.

"We should make a move," Poe said. "I'll go first."

Caddy vetoed that. "They don't trust you. You're an outcast in their minds. They don't understand why you killed the Company men. I'll bring them to you and we can explain everything once we take them to safety."

Caddy slipped into the cedars. The Dreamers huddled in a ragged group on the ground. There were only seven—three women and four men. They barely acknowledged Caddy, they were so beaten.

"Is this all of you?" Caddy asked.

One of the women nodded.

"Where are the others?"

The woman shook her head.

"We found sanctuary," Caddy said. "There's food, warmth, real beds. It's safe from war and bombs and Company men. I can take you there. But we have to go now."

A man spoke. It was the angry one Caddy had argued with before. "We must wait for Hex. She'll take us to the next dreaming place."

"There's no time. The Company men will come."

"The world is at war," the man said. "It's more important than ever that we hold the vision."

Poe appeared through the trees. "If you don't come, you'll die out here."

The man sneered at the sight of him. His voice was caustic. "Leave us. If we're to die, we'll do so on our own terms."

"Your own terms are based on a lie," Poe said. "Hex is working against you. The mark will condemn you to death and everything you care about will be lost."

"He's right." The woman spoke. "We should go with him. What good is it to die in the rain?"

"Shut up," the man ordered. He pointed at Poe. "You brought this upon us. Your hatred will condemn us all."

"We came to help you," Poe said. "You'll die for nothing—all of you."

The man spat on the ground with loathing. "Then let us die."

They'd wasted their time. Caddy knew there was nothing she could say to persuade them. "We should go," she said to Poe.

They'd cleared the spruce trees when they heard the screams. The Company men had routed the Dreamers. Caddy ran, the rain stinging her face. Poe was somewhere behind her. She looked back and the sky split open with a fiery blast. The earth shook, and the wind rushed in, the trees bending like grass. Caddy was blown face down to the ground. She covered her head, shouting into the blur of branches, mud, and rain.

When the wind finally stopped, Caddy knew the city was gone, and perhaps her father with it. Her shining song played in a loop over the whine of white noise in her head. Something was pulling her arm. It was Poe, trying to get her to stand. She teetered to her feet, fell, and staggered up again.

Poe's face was savage. "They're here," he yelled, his voice small and far away in her ears.

"The bomb," Caddy said, her own voice a muted garble of sound, as if she were speaking under water. "I think it hit the city . . ."

He grabbed her hand and dragged her stumbling through the woods, her feet catching on broken tree limbs and clumps of earth. The forest was torn apart. He kept pulling her forward, yelling at her to go faster, but her feet wouldn't listen.

At the limestone rock, Poe dropped to his knees and clawed at the grass with his hand. Caddy saw torches leaping through the rain. "Hurry," she said.

Poe found the door and yanked it open. He pushed the Zippo into her hand and fed her by one arm down the hole. She slipped on the wet rocks, hitting the ground at the bottom of the stairs. Poe started yelling and she cried out as the Company men swarmed him. The door smacked shut. Over the noise in her head she thought she heard Poe say, "Run!"

Caddy crashed through the tunnel, the Zippo's flame wobbling frantically as she ran. She cleared the door, the Company men behind her. Fighting with the bolt, she managed to secure the lock, but only just. There was a crash of splintering wood and the door broke away from its hinges. Caddy ran down the corridor, shouting. The Weavers poured out to meet her, panicking when they saw the Company men with their knives and fire.

In the crush of bodies, Caddy slipped into the seed room. She stayed there, cowering in a corner, screams and cries filling the corridor. From the chaos, Hex emerged slithering into the room, her blue eye dancing with delight over her luck.

"Well, well, well . . ." she hissed and raised her knife, its silver blade stained red with Weavers' blood.

Caddy braced for the strike. The hit never came. Zephyr had jumped between them.

"Get away from her!"

Hex struck with the speed of a cobra, slashing Zephyr across the chest before she was able to knock the knife from Hex's hand. The viper attacked again, this time tearing the medallion from Zephyr's neck. Caddy rushed her and was heel-punched in the chest and sent crashing against the wall. Hex and Zephyr fought, blow for blow, hitting the floor in a tangle of arms and legs. Hex grabbed Zephyr's hair, yanked her head back and drove her thumb into Zephyr's sky-blue eye. Caddy flung herself on Hex and was thrown to the ground. Red burst into the room. He grabbed the knife and lunged, pushing the blade beneath the curve of Hex's jawbone. She writhed to the floor, blood throbbing from her neck and lips.

Zephyr lay in a pool of blood, gasping blindly. She lifted her hand, the medallion clenched in her fist.

"Take it, Caddy," she said. "Live."

Her face slackened and the light slipped away from her.

Tears spilled down Caddy's cheeks as she untwined the bloody medallion from Zephyr's fingers. She had saved her life. Caddy would never forget her for that. But there was no time to mourn. Red was lifting Caddy to her feet and pushing her toward the door.

"Go!" he said.

The corridor was a maelstrom of smoke and fire. Bodies of Weavers and Company men covered the floor. Caddy stumbled over the dead, choking for air. Through the confusion, someone called her name. It was April and Dillon, beckoning to her from the end of the hall.

"Come on!"

Dillon had found a set of stairs. He yelled over the noise.

"It takes us to the cliff. Where's Poe?"

"Outside," Caddy said. "We have to find him."

"We'll look when we reach the top. We have to go."

April pulled back. "It's too dark."

Caddy grabbed Poe's Zippo from her bag and sparked the flint. "It's all I've got."

"It's good enough," Dillon said.

They pounded up the stairs, Dillon leading the way. At the top was a tunnel, carved through the cliff. The sound of dampened thunder rumbled all around them.

"It's the waterfall," Dillon said.

They worked their way to the end of the tunnel, where more stairs waited. The steps were dangerously narrow.

"We'll have to go single file." Dillon nodded at Caddy. "You go first. I'll go behind in case someone comes."

They climbed, April holding the hem of Caddy's shirt, the thundering growing louder as they went. The stairs switched directions several times. When they reached the top, a stone barricade blocked the way.

"We're trapped!" Caddy yelled above the noise.

Dillon ran his hands over the stone. "There's supposed to be a door here." He sat down and began to push with his feet.

Caddy and April did the same, kicking and pushing until the stone gave way, scraping by inches along the ground. Dillon kicked harder.

"Keep going!" he shouted, forcing open a gap big enough to squeeze through, one at a time. Cold air rushed in. The waterfall roared.

"There's something you should know," Caddy shouted. "The city—it's gone. And Zephyr." She held up the medallion.

"We can't stay here," Dillon shouted back. "We have to find a place to hide."

April pointed down the stairs. Torchlight swam in the darkness below. "Someone's coming!"

They struggled through the opening onto a thin ledge, the falls a moving wall of sound in front of them. In the distance, the city burned orange against the sky. Caddy stuffed Zephyr's medallion into her pocket and looked over the edge of the cliff. The water plunged into a black abyss.

"I guess it's a one-way kind of thing," Dillon said.

April started to cry. "I can't do it."

"Yes, you can," Dillon said. He forced her to look at him. "Aim for the centre of the spill. Cover your head with your arms and take a deep breath before you jump."

Caddy closed the Zippo, extinguishing the flame. "You have to do it," she told April. "I'm not going without you."

April crumpled to her knees. "I can't!" she sobbed.

The torchlight swelled in the tunnel.

"They're here!" Dillon shouted.

Caddy pulled April to her feet. "Hold your breath," she yelled, and took her over the edge.

They hit feet first, April wrenching away from Caddy, the power of the water driving them down. Caddy jackknifed, her arms brushing stone, the water wringing her body like a rag and throwing her back to the surface. She breached, sucking air, and just in time to see Dillon enter the water. The river was fast. It grabbed Caddy's legs, pulling her under. She fought the current, arms flailing, feet kicking toward a calm pool at the river's edge. She floated there, scouring the banks for April. In the gloom of the rain, she saw her, clinging to a rock in a small eddy, her face pinched with pain.

"My arm," April moaned, as Caddy swam up. "I think it's broken."

THE DARKEST HOUR

The black column roiled from the Speaker's mouth. It bulged, and a winged beast the size of a skyscraper was born. Flapping its wings, the creature shrieked, soaring over the armies and scattering Warriors with its barbed tail. There was a powder keg flash against the sky, and Francis, Kenji and Timon dropped in, narrowly missing the creature's claws. Timon and Kenji reverted to their etheric forms and opened with heavy artillery. Francis jumped straight for her.

"Skylark! Come back to the Light!"

Skylark fired. "Never!"

The cowboy dodged the arrow and was nearly singed by Kenji's light blast. "It's not too late!" he shouted.

"Old fool," Skylark cursed. She fired again, the arrow winging the cowboy's arm and flipping him end over end. He hit the ground, his Stetson rolling in the rain. Skylark laughed with delight as he reached for the hat, shooting it from his hand and searing a hole clean through the top.

"Dang blast it!" Francis swore. He grabbed the hat, smacked it on his knee, and planted it, still smoking, on his head. He jumped, landing right beside her.

She rocketed into the air. "Get away from me, Francis."

The cowboy drafted in her wake. He just wouldn't give up. "There's nothing for you here," he called after her.

"Leave me alone!" she shot over her shoulder, flying higher.

"I'm not giving up."

"I won't come back."

He accelerated, closing the distance between them. "The Speaker is using you. Once this is over, he'll toss you aside."

"He's my father."

"He's a demon!"

Skylark corkscrewed upward. "Everything I want is here."

"The boy?"

"Yes."

"How do you know he isn't already dead?"

Now he'd gone too far. Skylark pulled back and faced him. "Liar!" she accused, and let fly with a scorching volley of arrows. One hit his left thigh, spinning him around and dropping him like a brick.

Francis hit the ground with a grunt, reverting instantly to his etheric form. Timon and Kenji swooped in with a suppressing blast. Skylark deflected it with a well-aimed shot, bowling them over.

Francis squirmed, the arrow buried in his leg. Skylark landed next to him, sneering as she raised her foot and slowly pressed the arrow deeper with her heel. She watched the cowboy wriggle, relishing his pain. He looked so helpless.

"The boy's dead," Francis sputtered, filaments of ice spreading across his leg.

"You lie."

"Ask the Speaker yourself."

"My father would never betray me."

"He doesn't care about you—or the boy. He has what he wants. He doesn't need either of you anymore."

Skylark eased back on the arrow. What if he was telling the truth? She would find out for herself. She blasted into the air, leaving Francis suffering on the ground.

"Tell me he lives, Father." She confronted the Speaker.

The demon cranked his head around, disconnecting from the black column, a sulphurous green cloud spewing from his mouth. His eyes were glaciers, and his skin was crystallized with frost. "You dare to question me?"

Skylark hovered over him. "The boy is mine!" she shouted.

"He is yours as sworn," the monster growled. "Forever!" He hurled a blue vial into the tempest.

"No!" Skylark shrieked as she plunged, the vial whiffling beyond her grasp into the whirling column. Poe was gone!

With a deafening crack, her soul light fractured, the pain of loss and betrayal shattering the bonds that held her captive to the Dark. She flew at the demon, bow drawn. "Die!" she screamed.

The Speaker roared, and a ball of dark energy flew from his mouth, knocking her from the air. Skylark fell, reverting as she dropped, her robe flapping wildly around her.

Kenji soared to her defence, light beams searing from his hands. The Speaker deflected the shots back at him, sending Kenji hurtling through the air. Timon jumped between them with a protective field of light. The demon answered with a torrent of black flames and ice.

Skylark lay on the ground, clutching the Ephemeral, the Speaker's dark poison draining in an oily pool around her. A stream of shaming images washed over her—Sebastian, Kenji's woman, Francis, Poe. She was responsible for so much misery. Francis groaned beside her, the arrow protruding from his thigh, the icy filaments nearly covering his entire body. The light in his blue eyes was growing dim. He shivered uncontrollably. She crawled over to him.

"Forgive me, Fran."

With the last of her strength, Skylark gripped the arrow and pulled. The arrowhead ripped through Francis's etheric form. He coughed, black ooze spraying from his lips. Skylark held her hand over his wound. Her light was weak, faltering. She barely had enough to save herself. Her soul was guttering out by the time Kenji soared down to help her, placing his hand over hers. Their eyes met, and she silently begged for his forgiveness as their energies merged, the war raging around them.

Caddy led the way through the rain, the burning glow of the city an incendiary sunset behind them. April leaned against Dillon for support. She whimpered as she walked, wearing a makeshift sling from a strip of Dillon's shirt. It was amazing she was on her feet at all, Caddy thought. The break was bad. It was swollen and blue, the same way hers was when she'd broken it as a child. It would have to be tended soon or she would lose it. April stumbled, her face a portrait of anguish.

"We need to stop," Dillon said.

"It's not safe. We've only just cleared the falls."

"Then go without us." He helped April to the ground, resting her back against a tree.

There was no way Caddy was going to leave them. "We need to put a splint on that arm." She searched for suitable branches, collecting willow whips to secure them, thanking her father for the wisdom he'd given her as she tested the strength of the branches against her knee.

April's arm was on a funny angle. She cried out and fainted as they attempted to set it. When Caddy was finished, the splint looked convincing enough. If nothing else, it made her feel better.

"She needs to sleep," Dillon said.

Caddy agreed. "We all do."

"I'll keep watch."

"No, I will. You stay with April."

It would have been impossible for her to sleep anyway. Caddy positioned herself beneath a nearby hemlock. The tree afforded shelter of sorts, breaking the ceaseless drive of rain. She stuck out her tongue, catching several drops from a branch, then cupped her hands and held them up until they were full. Sipping the water, she realized how hungry she was. And tired. It can only get worse, she thought. She opened her bag and carefully checked the contents. The muslin pouches of seeds had miraculously survived the waterfall. There were five in total. She wished she'd been able to take more. Though she couldn't identify the ones she had except for the ancient wheat that Zephyr had shown her. The others—she hoped they would be as useful.

Caddy fastened her bag shut and reached for her fluorite necklace. It was gone. It must have broken free when she jumped into the water. She wondered if her stone was at the bottom of the river, then remembered Zephyr's medallion. It glistened as she pulled it from her pocket. Tracing the lines of the tree with her finger, Caddy vowed to continue Zephyr's work—if she was given the chance—and the work of all the Dreamers. She sealed the promise by securing the medallion around her neck and tucking it under her shirt against her skin. She rested the back of her head on the tree trunk, allowing her eyes to close, despite the rain and the threat of the Company men in the shadows. In her mind, Caddy could see the fire from the city leaping in the sky. She thought about her father and Poe. Were they all right? The smell of burnt toast came on without warning and before she could think to resist, the bad feeling swept over her.

Caddy stood shivering in the Emptiness, her feet buried in ash, the barren grey landscape stretching endlessly in every direction. It was colder than ever. Frigid. But for the first time, there was no wind. There were no voices. It was hauntingly quiet as if the fate of the lost souls hung in the balance, waiting for something to tip the scales in either direction. But what . . . ?

The Speaker and his golems razed a swath through the Warriors. Skylark and Kenji focused their energy on Francis's wound. Timon touched down, beaten and bruised, and added his energy to theirs. The light flowed in and around the four friends, strengthening and healing them. The ice crystals retreated from Francis's form, but not fast enough.

"The Dark is advancing too quickly," Timon said. "We must return to battle or the Light will be defeated for certain."

Skylark blinked back the tears. "We can't leave Francis. He'll be killed."

The old cowboy coughed. He screwed up his face and cracked an eye open. "Now, honey, don't count me out just yet," he rasped.

"Fran!" Skylark threw her arms around him.

"Let me give you a hand, old man," Kenji said. He shouldered Francis to a standing position, propping him up with one arm.

With great effort, Francis morphed into his human form and surveyed the destruction.

"I'm afraid we're not doing very well," Timon said.

"We have to get back in there." Francis attempted to stand on his own, Skylark flying to his aid when he nearly fell again. The black stain where her arrow had punctured his thigh was seeping through his jeans.

Kenji helped him upright. "You're not going anywhere, old man."

Skylark clenched her fists, wracked with guilt. "This is all my fault," she said. With a missile blast she shot into the air, streaking across the sky toward the black column.

Timon cruised up beside her. "Let's work together. Aim for the Speaker."

They charged, Timon driving forward with a wall of light while Skylark released a battery of arrows. One penetrated the dark energy, hitting the Speaker in the face. There was an electric snap, and the buzz of current spiking as the beast broke from the column. He convulsed, growing in size, a whirlwind of lesser demons orbiting around him. Skylark swept in like a fighter jet, arrows raining from her bow. The demon bellowed with rage.

"Get back!" Timon shouted, cannons firing. The Speaker screeched and struck, hitting Timon in the chest and punching the light from his body. Timon rolled and flipped, plummeting lifeless from the sky.

Skylark attacked, firing arrow after arrow. With every shot, the Speaker swelled and grew. He sliced the air with his giant arms, Skylark dodging the blows, until all at once he connected. She fell, her body paralyzed from the impact, the Ephemeral tumbling away from her as she hit the ground, blasts of light exploding in her head. Arm outstretched, she strained to reach the bow, the monster towering over her. Silver lay just outside her grasp, wounded and beaten, scrolling helplessly through its colours. This is how I will die, Skylark thought, fingers inches from my weapon. "Come on, girl," she pleaded, trying to raise the bow. "Get up, Silver . . . please, get up."

The Ephemeral retreated inside its cloud of mist. The demon hissed as it drew back its fist and swung.

Skylark abandoned the bow, cupping her hands above her chest, teeth clenched. "Eat this," she snarled. A supernova detonated from her palms, burning through the air and smashing the demon in the mouth. The beast howled, collapsing in on itself in a cyclone of rain and black ooze that sucked the Dark in. Skylark shielded her eyes, the cyclone circling tighter and tighter, the wind roaring, dark entities wailing. With a dying shriek, the cyclone vanished, leaving a heavy black scorch on the ground.

Skylark struggled to her hands and knees. Retrieving the Ephemeral from its mist, she drew it tenderly over her battered shoulders. The bow curled around her, purring against her back. "It's okay now," she said. "Everything's okay."

Labouring to her feet, Skylark looked across the field, every light molecule in her body sinking when she saw the devastation. Before her, stretching to the horizon and far beyond, was a blackened wasteland of mangled bodies and shattered swords. Lions lay next to their Warriors, their charred remains burning. Nightshades swept through the desolation, searching for dark souls that may have been left behind.

Skylark limped through the carnage, holding the Ephemeral close. When she found Timon she fell to her knees and cradled his body in her arms. Francis and Kenji straggled over, looking broken and grim. Francis pulled his hat from his head, his jaw clenching with emotion. Kenji removed his glasses, his face sober, resolute.

"He saved my life," Skylark sniffed.

Francis turned away, overcome. He kicked the scorched spot where the Speaker had stood and three small glass vials rolled from the ashes.

The sun teased Caddy awake, shining through the branches of the hemlock. The rain had stopped. She'd slept through the night. Where were April and Dillon? She called for them.

"Over here," a voice answered.

They were beside a stand of birch trees. April was nursing her broken arm, looking drawn and pale. Dillon was hunched over something. He rose, stepping somberly to one side so Caddy could see, though she already knew.

Poe was bruised beyond recognition, and his clothes were bloody and torn. Caddy knelt next to him, unable to summon the tears she needed to cry. She pried the knife from his fingers and buried it in a hole she dug in the ground with a stick. Gathering stones, she set them carefully around him. Dillon joined her, and even April gathered as many as she could manage with her broken arm.

After Poe was covered, Caddy pulled the small sack of wheat seeds from her bag and sprinkled some over his grave, saying nothing. No one spoke. There were no words adequate to the task. They held the silence while Caddy returned the remaining wheat seeds to her bag and tied it closed.

"What do we do now?" April asked.

They expected her to make a decision. Caddy pressed her hand over the gold medallion around her neck. She could feel the warmth of it, the life. She hoped she could be half as brave as Zephyr. "We keep moving," she said.

"What about food and water?" Dillon asked.

"We collect them where and when we can."

"And then?"

Caddy squinted at the sunlight dancing off the leaves. "We search for survivors, for others like us. We keep the Light and plant seeds, to make the earth whole again, to build a place to call home."

INTO THE LIGHT

B eneath the diminished light of a once brilliant sky, the bodies of the dead stretched out, row on row. There was no fanfare. There were no ribbons or heraldry. Throughout the city, the repair work was halted as the ceremony began. Skylark stood with the multitudes on the practice field to send off the fallen. Joining voices, the crowd struck a note. The sound rose, gathering in intensity, the bodies vibrating with the frequency, ascending with the sound.

"Be brave," Skylark whispered as Timon's body shimmered and was gone. "What will happen to his Light?" she asked Francis.

The cowboy rolled the brim of his Stetson through his fingers. "It'll wait along with the rest of the souls who were taken."

"Wait where?"

"Between the Frequencies."

It was her worst fear. She'd hoped for something better. "What if we can't get it back?"

"We will," Francis promised.

If only she could feel so sure. Her wound started to ache. She rubbed her shoulder to alleviate the pain. "It isn't over, is it, Fran?"

He put his hat on. "Not by a long shot. We may have won the battle, but I expect we're nowhere near winning the war."

Skylark looked at the glass vials in her hand. Poe's was blue. The other, the one that held Sebastian's soul, was the most beautiful shade of violet. Kenji had a similar vial, only his was the richest shade of green. He nodded at her, indicating that it was time.

"They'll regenerate once they rejoin the Light?" she asked.

"Yes," Kenji said. "Their energy will reconfigure itself."

"We won't recognize them anymore."

"Their imprint may not be the same. But their souls will have been saved."

"Let's get this done," Francis said. "No sense keeping them from the Light any longer than we have to."

Kenji raised the geisha's vial.

"Wait," Skylark stopped him. "What was her name?"

Kenji removed his glasses, his blue eyes ringed with grief. "Sakura," he said. "Her name is Sakura."

"Sakura," Skylark repeated.

"It means cherry blossom." Kenji broke the vial, Sakura's green mist twirling into the air. "I release you," he said, letting her go at last.

Skylark held Poe's soul vial to her chest. She would never see him again. But he was free. Her lips trembled as she spoke. "I release you." With a quick breath in, she snapped the glass. Poe's blue mist swirled before her in a little tornado and vanished.

Kenji placed his hand on her shoulder. Francis looked at her expectantly.

"There's one more thing you need to do," he said.

Skylark stared at the purple mist inside Sebastian's vial. She wasn't ready to give him up. Not yet. Not here on this barren field with the multitudes of nameless soldiers.

"You can't keep him forever," Francis said.

She sniffed. "I know. I'll do it . . . It just needs to be right." She looked into his blue eyes. "How did you lose your totem, Fran?"

The cowboy lowered his gaze, his beard quivering. "The Speaker got him."

"Oh." At least she'd got Sebbie back. As much as it hurt to let him go, she knew she was the lucky one.

"Promise me you'll do it," Francis said. "It isn't fair to keep a soul trapped, no matter how much it hurts to say goodbye."

"I will," she promised.

After the ceremony, Skylark wandered through the city streets, a heartsick spirit. Everywhere, beings were mending and cleaning and planting. It seemed an insurmountable task to rebuild things. She stopped at the spot where the little garden had been, hoping to release Sebastian there. It was as black and devastated as the rest of the city. She wanted green, somewhere familiar. And then it came to her.

Skylark touched down in the field by the maple tree, the one where she'd lost Sebastian before. There was a gentle breeze and the birds were singing. Sitting on the rock beneath the tree, she raised the vial. The sunlight winked against the glass. "Goodbye, dear friend," she said, releasing the mouse's soul. Sebastian's violet mist whirled with the breeze. It climbed, mingling with a flock of tree swallows winging overhead. A young male swooped down and landed on Skylark's hand, its blue wings catching the light. It cocked its head, studying her with mischievous eyes.

"I expect you'll have a harder time losing me now," it said.

CADDY'S SONG

There is a light that shines in the night,
There is a light.
And though you are far from home,
And though you are all alone,
There is a light, there is a light, there is a light.
Come to me in honesty,
Honesty.
And though the road is long,
And though you don't feel strong,
There is a light, there is a light, there is a light.